The Awakening

Praise for The Gifting (Book 1)

"Set in a not-too-distant future that feels frighteningly like home, this novel immerses readers within the heart of Tess's fear from the very first chapter. This is not, however, a novel of horror. Guaranteed to leave you breathless, *The Gifting* is an eerie merging of Gothic-like dystopian mystery and YA romance within a pulse-pounding supernatural thriller. Expect to lose sleep over this book! A must-read addition to any YA reader's collection, this one's a keeper!"

~Serena Chase, *USA Today*'s Happy Ever After blog, author of *The Ryn*

"Chilling from start to finish! K. E. Ganshert delivers an exciting young adult fantasy that's just as fun as it is riveting. THE GIFTING will keep you turning pages in an effort to unlock the mystery of this unsettled world."

~Addison Moore, New York Times Bestselling Author

"K.E. Ganshert brings a fresh new voice to the dystopian romance scene for young adults. Ganshert will wow her audience with captivating prose, a well-paced plot, and just the perfect amount of swoon!"

~Heather Sunseri, author of the Mindspeak series

THE AWAKENING

BY K.E. GANSHERT

Edited by: Lora Doncea
Cover Design by: Okay Creations
Interior Design and Formatting by: BBeBooks

Copyright © 2015 K.E. Ganshert
Print Edition

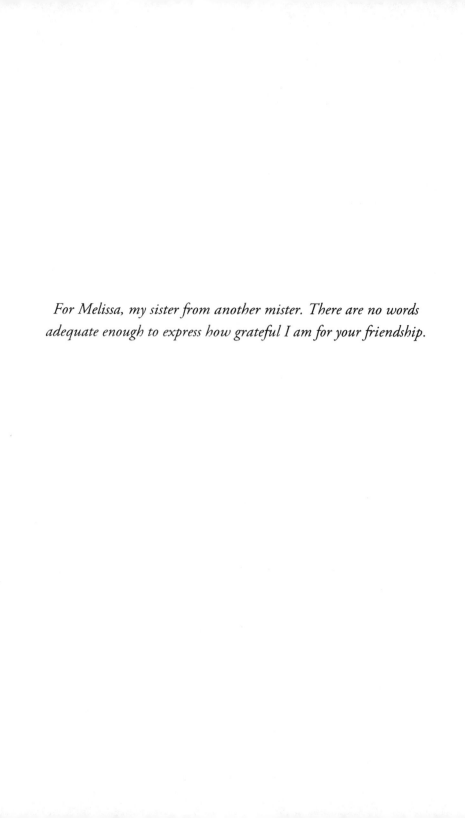

For Melissa, my sister from another mister. There are no words adequate enough to express how grateful I am for your friendship.

CHAPTER ONE

DEAD MAN HANGING

Darkness has never been a friendly thing. Not to me. But now, huddled behind a dumpster in the alleyway behind Dr. Roth's apartment building, I burrow into its protective arms, pulling it around myself until I'm wrapped up as tightly as a swaddled infant.

Perhaps we should make a run for it. Sprint as far away from here as possible. But fear paralyzes me. I'm pretty sure it has the same effect on Luka, too, because we crouch there—me and him, this boy who has come to mean so much—holding our breath as if the police might hear the sound of breathing five stories up.

Raindrops begin falling from the sky—fat, cold globs of moisture that plop against the dumpster's top and soak into the cotton of my sweatshirt. Luka wraps his arm around my hunched form and pulls me so closely to him I am unsure where he ends and I begin. It's not enough. I want more. I want the things he makes me feel to carry me off into oblivion, some place where this reality we're facing now no longer exists.

The clank of footsteps on the fire escape forces us to duck further back. A beam of light slices through the darkness, searching. My heart hammers against my chest. I'm sure Luka can hear it, maybe even feel it. They are looking for me, those people upstairs. They want to take me away and lock me up in Shady Wood with my grandmother, where I will never see my

1

family or Luka again. I don't breathe until the light finally goes away and the footsteps retreat.

The police are not coming down here, at least not right now. Dr. Roth is a smart guy. Surely he will find a way to throw them off our scent. Even so, we stay where we are, as still as statues, afraid to blink, afraid to think, until my legs cramp and the chill in the air turns my fingers numb. Northern California in January is not an ideal time for a night spent outdoors. For the first time since moving to Thornsdale in September, I find myself wishing for the balmy Florida heat I'd taken for granted back in Jude. But as cold as it might be out here, what other choice do we have?

We can't go home. I'm sure mine is under surveillance and Luka's isn't safe. His father would hand me over the second we arrived. The two of us can't be seen at all. I'm sure by now, my escape from the Edward Brooks Facility has been splashed on the news, along with my face. Nowhere is safe. Which means we will have to wait out the night behind this dumpster. Dr. Roth gave us specific directions to come back in the morning. He promised to explain everything.

The raindrops thin out into a misty drizzle. Luka loosens his grip around my waist and we stare at one another through the dark. He straightens his legs, as if his muscles are cramped too. I want to tell him to stop moving, but I'm doing the same thing.

"Are you okay?" he whispers so softly I have to strain to hear.

It's a silly question. Of course I'm not. He knows it. I know it. Over the course of six days, my brother almost died, we broke into a high-security psyche ward and discovered rows upon rows of patients in medically-induced comas, my deranged grandmother said I was "the key", I was dragged out of school against my will by government officials, locked up and drugged in the Edward Brooks Facility, then rescued by Luka Williams and my psychiatrist, who turns out, isn't who he claimed to be. All I can manage is an almost-silent, "I can't feel my fingers."

Luka takes my hands between his own and rubs until they are slightly warmer than frozen.

"Do you think they're still up there?" I whisper.

"I don't know."

A shudder takes hold of my body and convulses through my limbs. Even in the thick of night, I can see the concern pooling in his green eyes. "I have so many questions."

"Me too," he says.

"What do you think he meant about there being 'more of us'?"

"I'm more concerned about the part where we're all in danger."

A shudder ripples through my arms.

Luka sits against the brick wall of the apartment building. He pulls me beside him and wraps his arms around me. "Is this all right?"

I nod against his chest, too frightened and cold to be self-conscious.

"It's going to be okay, Tess." My body rises and falls with his breath. "We'll get answers from Dr. Roth tomorrow. You can go to sleep. I won't let anything happen to you."

Despite the chilly nighttime air outside and the cold fear inside, something about his nearness warms me. I am not alone. Luka is here—brave, handsome, confident Luka. I can almost believe it's true—that he has the power to keep me safe.

That I might really be able to go to sleep.

I curl up against him and wrestle my fear into submission. I don't let myself think about my family or how much I miss my mom. I don't let myself think about what my life will be now. I take deep, even breaths. I borrow Luka's warmth. And I force all my attention onto one thing.

I'm not suffering from psychosis. Neither is Luka.

Dr. Roth gave us a name. We are The Gifting.

Movement awakens me. It's a twitch at first. Then something bigger, like a jolt. My eyelids flutter open. I am wrapped up with Luka, tangled into a knot on the hard cement. We are face to face, our bodies pressed together. Only his eyes are closed. His face twitches. Then his eyes fly open. Before he can make a sound, I cup my hand over his mouth, trapping the noise inside.

His nostrils flare.

"Shhh, Luka. You were having a nightmare." Something I know all too well. My nightmares are what put us in this position. He stares down at me with pupils so large, his irises are nothing but the thinnest ring of green. Slowly, his breathing regulates. His pupils shrink.

I remove my hand.

And without the slightest warning, his fingers twine into my hair, he pulls my face close, and his lips crush mine. A quick burst of intense passion before he pulls away and hugs me to his chest, where his heart crashes against my ear. The whole thing happened so fast, I barely had time to register it, let alone kiss him back. Three times now he has kissed me and three times now, they have come as complete surprises. He springs them on me when I least suspect, like in a crowded locker bay at school or on the dirty ground behind a dumpster. Perhaps this is a good thing. His method leaves no time for agonizing over how awful I must be at it.

He untangles himself from my arms and sits up, propping his elbows on his knees, digging his fingers into his hair, staring at some arbitrary spot on the ground. A white-throated sparrow lands on one of the fire escapes and lets out a wavering whistle.

"Do you want to talk about it?"

He avoids eye contact.

I should probably push him, but honestly? I'm afraid of his answer. Luka has had dreams about me long before we first met in September. In every one, I'm in danger. In one of his dreams, I actually died. I'd rather not know if it happened again. I sit up beside him. The faint glow of early morning filters into the alleyway, softening everything around us—the dumpster, the trash cans, the brick walls. The night has given way to dusk. And I am desperate for answers. "Do you think it's safe to go up now?"

"He said the morning. He never said how early." Luka stands and pulls me up with him.

His grip tightens around my hand as we tiptoe toward the fire escape and climb the metal stairs on silent feet.

One flight.

Two flights.

Three.

Four.

We stop before landing on the fifth. Luka holds up his finger, his meaning clear. I am to wait here while he pokes his head inside the open window. We have a wordless argument with hand gestures. I don't want to stand by while he puts himself in jeopardy, not when I've already put him in enough. But he refuses to let me go first. So Luka wins and I wait. When the coast is clear, he waves me over. He climbs through the window first, then helps me inside Dr. Roth's apartment.

It's too quiet. Too still.

Goose bumps march up my arms. My palms turn cold and clammy. What if this is a trap? What if Dr. Roth was arrested and the minute we open our mouths, the police will descend and the two burly men who dragged me out of Thornsdale High School will drag me away again. Only this time Dr. Roth and Luka won't be around to break me out.

Luka pulls me forward, toward the bedrooms. I want to dig my heels into the carpet. Fear claws about inside my chest, scrapping and scratching for an exit. I have no idea why I don't want to see whatever it is we are about to see. Until we round the corner and find him—the man with all the answers.

Hanging from a noose at the end of the hallway.

CHAPTER TWO

CLOSE CALL

Footsteps sound outside Dr. Roth's apartment door. Luka clamps his hand over my mouth to muffle my scream and wraps his arm around my waist. There's a knock. Something like a squeak issues from the back of my throat. Luka tightens his grip around my waist and half-drags, half-carries me up the hallway, toward the still, hanging body, and into a room. The same one I woke up in not more than twelve hours ago.

Another knock at the door. "Rise and shine, Dr. Roth. It's the police."

The room looks untouched and unruffled. Nobody would suspect somebody had slept in the bed recently. In fact, it looks as if the guest room is perfunctory and really, the doctor hasn't had a guest in years. Luka pulls me toward the bed and the two of us hide underneath. I cup my hand over my mouth to mask the sound of my breathing.

"All right, I'm coming in," the voice says. There's a pause, then a loud bang. I jump. Luka tucks me closer. Another bang, followed by a thud, as if the door has swung open and crashed into the wall. "You awake in here?"

Footsteps draw nearer, then stop. Whoever it is clucks his tongue. "Well now, Doc, why'd you go and do a thing like this?"

Luka cups his hand over mine, whether to provide an extra sound barrier or as a gesture of comfort, I'm not sure. The frayed hemp of his bracelet bites into my skin. With eyes buggy and unblinking, I stare at the police officer's shoes in the hallway. He pivots and walks out of eyeshot.

"Hey-a Manny, it's Jake. Patch me through to the Chief, would ya?" Officer Jake is on his phone, calling the chief of police, which happens to be Leela's uncle. How long before this place is swarming with cops? The floor creaks. It doesn't seem possible, but my eyes grow wider. "Yeah-a, Bill? Looks like the doc offed himself ... No, he's hanging right here in front of me. Apparently, the threat of losing his license did a number on him."

I picture Dr. Roth's limp body hanging from the noose, his neck bent at a weird angle. I'm not sure I will ever be able to scrub that memory from my mind. He's dead. The man with all the answers is dead.

More floor creaking. Officer Jake's shoes come back into view. "Suicide's a pretty safe bet, but the medical examiner will need to verify."

Another pause, longer this time.

My mind buzzes in the silence. It doesn't make sense. Dr. Roth would not have hung himself. He was waiting for us to return. He told us to come back. He called himself "a believer". He said he had been gathering evidence.

"So now what? I can't exactly question a dead man ... No, there's no sign of the girl, but I'll look around. See if there's any evidence that she's been here."

I swallow another squeak and press back into Luka. His grip tightens.

"A national alert, huh? I don't understand why she's so important. Have to imagine a teenager can't be much of a threat ... Right, I understand ... I have a jump drive. I can copy all the files and bring it into the station. Hold on a tick." His shoes shuffle past the doorframe. Beneath this bed, with my hand cupped over my mouth and Luka's cupped over my hand, sound seems to be magnified. A chair groans. Computer keys clack. He's accessing Dr. Roth's computer files.

Luka nudges me, then points toward the nightstand. A crate holding two thick manila folders sits on the ground, as if Dr. Roth had been preparing for our visit.

More computer clacking. "Bill, there's nothing here. His computer's wiped clean."

A memory floats to the surface. It all feels like a lifetime ago, back when my biggest problems came in my sleeping hours and Dr. Roth was nobody but a psychiatrist at the Edward Brooks Facility. I had questioned his archaic record keeping.

"Pen and paper doesn't crash. It's not nearly as accessible, either."

A flood of gratitude toward the man washes over me. He knew all along that something like this could happen. That digital files were not safe or indestructible. He was protecting me from the very beginning. But as soon as the relief comes, so does the panic. Because all Officer Jake has to do is walk into this room and he'll see the files that are not more than five feet from our heads. Not only will he come into possession of extremely confidential information, he'll see us as soon as he bends down to get it.

"Either he erased them or somebody else did … Yeah-a, I'll look around … is the medical examiner on his way?" Something snaps shut, like a laptop. "Ten-four. I'll be waiting here. See ya at the station."

A chair squeaks, followed by a stretch of silence.

I feel immobilized, paralyzed. Even my thoughts are frozen. I wonder if Luka feels the same way, because he does not move behind me.

"Tut, tut, Dr. Roth. Just what were you hiding?"

My heart thuds so loud I'm terrified Officer Jake will hear it. I can cup my hand over my mouth to silence my breathing, but there's nothing to silence my heart.

"You don't mind if I use your bathroom, do you? I didn't think you would."

The man is having a conversation with a dead body. A psychiatrist, to boot. If I weren't having a silent panic attack, if Luka and I weren't in such horrible danger, if our only ally wasn't the one hanging out in that hallway, the situation would be laughable.

"Now, you stay there. Don't move. I'll be out in five and we'll see if I can't find where you hide your secrets."

Officer Jake's shoes appear in the doorframe again.

Please don't see the crate ... please don't see the crate ...

His shoes keep going, followed by a soft click of a door latch and a tuneless whistled melody from the bathroom beside us.

Luka goes from statue-still to a flurry of silent motion. He releases my waist and my mouth, then quickly and silently shimmies out from under the bed. I want to pull him back under, because—is he nuts? We can't be seen. If we're seen, we're dead. I will be locked up in Shady Wood and he will be put into prison and our keys will be thrown away. There will be no escaping this time.

"Luka," I hiss.

But he pulls me out alongside him, grabs the two manila folders, takes my hand and leads me out into the hallway. A strip of light shines beneath the bathroom door, the man's whistling muffled by the droning of a fan. Without hesitating, Luka pulls me toward the window. We climb out. I hold my breath while Luka shuts it as quietly as possible and we tear off down the steps.

Away, away, away ... as fast as we can.

Not until the entire length of the alleyway is between us and Officer Jake do I dare talk. I huddle against the brick façade of a building, my words escaping in huffs and puffs. I'm not used to sprinting. "We need ... to get ... out of here." And by here, I mean Thornsdale. In five minutes that apartment is going to be crawling with police, which means we need to put as much distance between us and this place as possible. Much easier said than done when all we have is our feet and our backpacks, and now, these two folders containing who knows what.

Luka swings his backpack off his shoulders, unzips the zipper, and pulls out two baseball caps and a pair of sunglasses. "Hide your hair in there and put these on." He pulls his hat over his hair and stuffs the folders inside his bag.

I do as he says, stuffing my hair up in the hat and putting on the glasses. I try not to think about Officer Jake's words about me and a national alert. I can't process that right now. Or Dr. Roth's death. All I can think about right now is making it to safety. Wherever that is.

"All we have to do is make it across this street. Walk normally. Do you see that alley over there?" Luka points to the other side of the street, toward an alleyway between an insurance building and liquor store.

I nod.

"I'm pretty sure it will lead us to some more. Once we're out of Thornsdale, we can find a motel and figure out what to do next."

"What if somebody recognizes us?"

"They won't. Not if we stick to the alleyways." He grabs my hand. "And not if we hurry."

"Luka," goose bumps march across my skin, "that wasn't a suicide."

"I know." He squeezes my hand and we step into the hazy sunlight.

CHAPTER THREE

FUGITIVES

Following a labyrinth of alleyways and side streets, some tighter than others, we walk until the morning haze turns into afternoon storm clouds. We run across stray cats and the occasional homeless person, but neither gives us any hassle. Questions and what-ifs spin through my mind, each one worse than the one before, but I do not voice them. Luka and I journey in silence.

I am hungry and cold and filthy and then it starts to rain, so I'm wet too. If only this was the worst of it, I could deal. But it's not. I'm not sure if I'm extra thirsty from the heavy doses of drugs that were pumped into my system or what, but the thirst is unbearable. Luka packed two water bottles, one for each of us, and he insisted on letting me have half of his. I find myself tipping my face up into the drizzle and letting the moisture fall over my tongue. Had he known we'd be on the run like fugitives, he would have packed provisions. But he didn't. He had thought we could stay at Dr. Roth's, where we'd not only get answers, but food and water too, and *then* be on our way— well rested and properly fed. We did not expect to be tossed into the night mere hours after my escape.

The drizzle turns into a heavy rain. In a matter of seconds, Luka and I are soaked through and my entire body has gone numb. We come to the end of another alley. He peeks out to survey our surroundings. "It's a motel."

My teeth chatter. "Wh-where?"

"Over there."

Sure enough, there it is—a flashing neon sign that reads Motel California. If the owner used the name as a play on the popular oldie, Hotel California, hoping the cleverness would entice guests, it didn't work. The place looks rundown and abandoned. The O and the T on the sign don't work, so from afar it looks like M e l California. To my eyes though, it might as well be paradise. "Do you think it's s-s-safe?"

"As safe as we're going to get. You need food and water. And we need a place to rest for the night."

"S-s-sounds good."

"You stay here." He looks around and spots a couple tin garbage cans. "Hide behind these. I'll go get us a room."

I don't want him to leave me. I don't want to separate. I'm convinced if we do, we won't find our way back to each other again. But I know Luka's plan is best. I can't walk into the front office of that motel. Not if the police are out looking for me. So I do what Luka says. I squat behind the garbage cans and watch as he jogs across the street, dodging puddles, and disappears inside.

Come back to me, Luka ... don't get caught ... don't leave me here ...

The longer he is gone, the more horrendous the what-ifs become in my mind. I imagine Luka being cuffed and dragged to some place far away. I imagine him being tortured for the location of my whereabouts. I imagine sitting out here, forever and ever and ever, never to see him again—all alone without anywhere to turn. What did Officer Jake mean by a national report? Surely he's wrong. They only broadcast people nationally when they are sociopathic murderers or highly dangerous criminals. I'm just a girl who misses her mom and her warm bed and her best friend.

Leela.

I imagine her now, at school. Does she regret the way things ended between us? Does she miss me at all? Or is she glad I'm gone? A ball of heat gathers in my throat. I swallow it down and pin my gaze on the front doors of Motel California.

C'mon, Luka. Where are you?

As if sensing my desperation, the door opens. He steps out into the rain, looks over his shoulder, then hurries across the street and pulls me out from my hiding place. "It worked." He holds up two plastic cards. "I got us a room."

We climb the cement steps and hurry beneath the awning to the fourth door, the aqua paint peeling and chipped. Luka swipes the key card. The light flashes green and the lock clicks. He opens the door and motions for me to go first.

Inside, it's dark and dank and smells like mothballs. Luka turns on the light. It flickers once, twice, then casts a yellowish-orange hue over the room, revealing dull, worn carpet, a rickety armoire with a boxed-set television that looks like an ancient relic, and a full-sized bed.

Just one.

The door closes behind us and shuts out the rain. I stand there, unsure what to do next while Luka shrugs off his backpack and walks over to the heater and air conditioning unit. He hits a button and the unit rattles and clanks to life.

He holds his hands in front of the vents. "It should warm up in here soon."

A weight I didn't know I was carrying slides off my back.

We are inside, where it is dry and soon-to-be warm. Far away from the police or anybody else who might recognize me.

"I saw a vending machine outside." Luka squeezes my shoulder as he passes, then leaves again. Only this time our separation doesn't cause me anxiety. He's just slipping outside to find us something to eat. The thought has my stomach growling.

I slip off my waterlogged sneakers and close myself inside the bathroom. I turn on the faucet, bend over the sink, and drink gulps of lukewarm water from my cupped palm until the bite of thirst loses its sharpness. When I unzip my bag, I find neatly folded clothes and a bag of toiletries. I imagine my mom, carefully considering what I might need, tucking each item into the cosmetic bag. Did she wonder if she'd ever see me again? Did she cry? The same hot ball of emotion that came when I thought about Leela in the alleyway swells again.

Forcing it down, I slide open the shower curtain. A warm bath sounds heavenly, but one look at the mold growing on the grout between the tiles, the soap scum, the rust staining the tub, and I'm not touching any of it. I peel off my soaked clothes, ring them out over the bathtub drain, and hang them on one of the hooks on the back of the door. I turn on the water. The pipes hiss and groan before releasing a steady stream. Cold at first, but then almost scalding hot.

I grab my toiletries, step beneath the spitting stream, and let it soak my hair and my skin. I shampoo and condition, work the body wash into a lather and get to work shaving my legs. I'm not sure how long I stand beneath the shower with my eyes closed. I just know it's long enough for the entire bathroom to morph into a dense steam cloud. I don't move until my gurgling stomach convinces me its time. Reluctantly, I shut off the water, and when I do, I hear Luka shuffling around in our room.

I towel off as quickly as possible, dress in a pair of heart-dotted pajama bottoms and an oversized t-shirt with a monkey face on the front (thanks Mom), and step into our room. Luka is right. The musty smell remains, but the room is warm. He stops digging through his bag and turns around. He's removed his rain-soaked sweatshirt and stands there with a t-shirt that clings to his body. My attention flickers to the muscles of his chest, the well-defined lines of his flat abdomen, and the air turns thin.

His smile doesn't help. It's a slow, crooked kind of smile. The same one that made all the girls at Thornsdale googly-eyed. And he's aiming it directly at me. "Cute pjs."

I look down at my bare toes—the same pale blue as my chipped nail polish. My cheeks are entirely too prone to flushing.

"Do you feel better?" he asks.

"A little more human."

He motions to the bed where an assortment of vending machine food sits in a pile. Chips and Hostess pies, animal crackers and Pop-tarts and candy bars. And on the nightstand, a bottle of chocolate milk. For me.

My cheeks flush hotter. "Did you buy everything in the machine?"

"I thought about it." He grabs his backpack off the one-and-only chair tucked into the corner of the room. "I'm going to get cleaned up."

He's probably long past eager for a shower himself, only I stood comatose in the tub for who knows how long. How thoughtful of me. "Did you eat yet?"

"I'll join you as soon as I'm also feeling … a little more human." His hand brushes my arm when he walks past. "Go ahead and dig in."

After the way we huddled together for warmth the night before, you'd think I'd be more accustomed to his touch. But I'm not sure Luka's touch is one I'll ever get used to.

He shuts himself inside the bathroom where the pipes make the same groan-squeak they made for me. Tucking my damp hair behind my ears, I shuffle over to the window and peek through the blinds—nothing but a sheet of rain. It's good we found this place when we did. I climb onto the bed and sit cross-legged in the center, twisting open my chocolate milk and taking a long, delicious drink before searching through the feast. I pick up the remote near my knee and point it at the television. The power button doesn't work. I give the remote a few whacks against my palm and try again. The TV comes to life, but the screen is mostly fuzz. I flip through the channels and settle on the one with the most clarity. A local news station broadcasting a seven-day forecast that looks abysmal.

I'm halfway through a bag of Cheetos when Luka comes out of the bathroom towel-drying his thick, dark hair. He's wearing a comfy pair of sweatpants and a familiar white t-shirt and the glasses I saw on his nightstand all those days ago, when he first told me about his recurring dream. He must wear contacts. And he must have taken said contacts out in the bathroom. I bite the inside of my cheek. No boy should be allowed to look that sexy in a pair of sweatpants and glasses. And yet Luka does. Of course he does. He wears those sweats and glasses so well it's distracting.

"That might have been the best shower I've ever taken." He tosses the towel off to the side, joins me on the bed, cracks open a can of Mountain Dew, and holds it up in the air. "To Motel California."

"To being out of the rain."

We tap our drinks together and I lick the cheese off my fingers when a static-filled name from the television grabs my attention. I freeze with the tip of my thumb in my mouth. On the screen, a female reporter stands in front of an all-too-familiar apartment complex.

"Forty-six-year old Charles Roth, a renowned doctor in the field of psychiatry, most recognized for compiling several important anthologies on the human brain, was found dead in his apartment early this morning."

Luka gets off the bed and twists the antenna until the picture is clearer.

"The medical examiner has declared the cause of death suicide. There was no note left, but it is believed that the threat of losing his license after helping a highly-deranged and dangerous mental patient escape from the very facility where he was employed prompted such a fateful decision."

My school picture from Jude fills the screen.

My mouth drops open.

"Seventeen-year-old Teresa Ekhart moved to Thornsdale with her family in September of last year. A reliable source tells us that her family moved in order to give Teresa the help she needed after she experienced a mental breakdown. Take a look at this."

The TV pans to Thornsdale High, where students mill about in the courtyard.

And there she is—Summer Burbanks—looking at the camera, beautiful and smug and hateful as ever. I want to jump through the screen and clutch my hands around her neck.

"Nobody really noticed her at first. She was the quiet new girl. Looking back, I can see the signs. She was always fidgeting or staring intently at nothing. But then things started to go downhill really fast after we came back from winter break. Out of nowhere, she attacked me in the locker bay. My boyfriend, Jared, had to pull her off me."

The screen pans back to the reporter. "Last week, Teresa was admitted full-time into the Edward Brooks Facility, a privately owned psychiatric center here in Thornsdale, where she was previously being treated by Dr. Roth. A team of doctors were working on getting her properly medicated so she could rejoin her classmates at school. According to a nurse there, she was not cooperative and had bursts of violence that required restraints."

"They're lying!" I may not be able to remember much about my two-day stint there, but I remember enough to know that they were pumping me full of so many drugs, I couldn't have been violent if I tried. That nurse kept telling me Luka wasn't real. That my grandmother was dead. She was lying to my face and now they are lying to the world.

"Before doctors could help the young girl, Dr. Roth broke her out of the facility. So far, his motivation for doing so is unclear."

I wait for them to mention Luka, because surely they have put two and two together by now. Surely reporters have dug into history and realize that Luka was once a patient at the Edward Brooks Facility, too. All of our classmates saw him fight to get to me when those two burly bodyguard men dragged me away.

"Teresa is currently at large and is considered highly dangerous. If you think you might now know of her whereabouts, there is a bounty for any successful tips or leads. Please call the Thornsdale Police station."

A number flashes on the screen.

"And now back to you, Jeff, for a look at sports."

I stare with mouth open, unable to think. I was just televised over the entire Thornsdale viewing area. I have a bounty on my head. They've labeled me as highly dangerous. But Luka, somehow, is still in the clear. He jabs the power button on the remote.

The television screen goes black.

Guilt digs in its claws. Despite my good intentions, I have done exactly what I promised myself I wouldn't do. I dragged Luka into this dark pit right alongside me. His father was right. He should have stayed away. My life will never be normal again. Never. But Luka? He still has a chance. It's not too late for him. "You need to go back."

"What?"

The words cause me physical pain, but I have to say them. "They aren't looking for you. There's not a bounty on your head. They must not know you're involved. You can still get out of this mess."

"I'm not going anywhere."

"Dr. Roth is dead. He's dead because he helped me." What if next time, Luka's the one hanging at the end of a rope? My head begins to shake of its own volition—back and forth, back and forth in a panicked, jerky fashion. "You should have left me in the Edward Brooks Facility."

"Tess, look at me." Luka steps forward and takes my face with firm hands, giving me no choice but to look at him. "They would have taken you to Shady Wood. I never would have seen you again. I wasn't going to let that happen."

"The entire town is looking for me. Maybe even the entire nation. I won't be able to get anywhere. I'm going to be caught."

"There's a Walgreens a couple blocks up the street. I have plenty of money. I can go there and buy hair dye and a phone. We'll figure out what to do."

"You're throwing everything away."

"Throwing *what* away? Don't you understand? *You* are everything."

As soon as the words hit, they quickly bounce away. Because they're too unbelievable to stick. I sink onto the edge of the bed, my vision growing blurrier by the second. Luka doesn't know what he's saying. He is committing suicide, and what's worse, I'm letting him do it. I should insist he return. I should demand it. But I'm too weak, and deep down, I don't want him to go. "We don't have IDs. We don't have a car. We can't call my family or yours. Their phones will be tapped. And if we're caught, you'll be locked away too. We'll both end up at Shady Wood."

"We won't be caught. Listen, Tess, I don't know why I wasn't on the news. I have a feeling it has to do with my father's connections. But it's a good thing. Nobody's looking for me. That gives us options." The confidence in his voice is so strong, so sure, I almost believe him. "I need you to trust me."

Trust Luka.

It's something I've never fully done before. There was always a smidgen of doubt. A pocket of fear and uncertainty holding me back. Sure, the man with the scar warned me against Luka in my dreams before I knew the man was no good, and there were other things that muddied the waters.

Deep down though, I know it was never about those warnings. Deep down, in my most honest parts, I just couldn't believe that a boy like him would go out of his way—risk everything— to protect a girl like me. Not without ulterior motives. Deep down, I believed that the man with the scar made sense. Turns out, the man with the scar is malevolent and unreliable. It's time to stop believing his lies. I look into Luka's eyes and for reasons I will probably never understand, I know that he will stand by his word, with or without my cooperation—he will not leave me. I give him a small nod. For now.

"You should eat something else."

The pile of food that looked so appetizing moments earlier no longer has any appeal. I know my body needs more than a bag of Cheetos, but my appetite has gone into hiding. He picks up an orange and peels it in the same way he did in the cafeteria. I'm mesmerized by the slow, even, unbroken way he removes the peel. When he finishes, he splits it apart and hands me half. I break off a slice and put it into my mouth. It's bitter and dry, but there are vitamins, so I force myself to chew.

"The first thing we need to do is look for some answers." Luka grabs the two thick manila folders from the nightstand and plops them on the bed.

CHAPTER FOUR

THREE CLUES

L uka takes one folder and I take the other. The more files I
scan, the more tangible my disappointment. I'm sure Luka
feels the same. We were counting on concrete answers to our
questions. What is The Gifting? Why are we in danger? Who
and where are the others? Maybe some clear-cut direction as far
as what to do next. All we find are a bunch of patient files.
People we don't know suffering from every sort of disorder
under the sun—bipolar, obsessive compulsive, narcissistic
personality, and on and on and on. With each file, my hope
dwindles. Dr. Roth must not have left these folders for us after
all.

"The only connection I can make," Luka says, picking up
another sheet, "is that the patients in my folder all live in the
Detroit area."

Mine too.

Of all the places I've lived, Michigan was never one of
them, but that doesn't mean I haven't heard plenty of things
about Detroit. The crime rate is off the chart. Drug cartel.
Prostitution. Overcrowding. Muggings. Drive-by shootings.
From all accounts, it's a war zone. I can't imagine Dr. Roth
there. "Do you think that's where he worked before Thornsdale?"

"That would be my guess."

We go through several more. The only sound in the room

is the shuffling of papers. Until abruptly, Luka stops and there's nothing but silence. With his thumbnail between his teeth and a divot between his brow, he focuses on one file. "Look at this," he finally says, handing me the sheet.

Client's name: Josiah Aaronson.

Age: 60

Diagnosis: Paranoid Schizophrenia

It's the first I've seen of it—the same diagnosis as my grandmother. My heart rate speeds up as I scan over his symptoms.

Prophetic dreams. Hallucinations. Unexplained flashes of brightness.

"Tess, look." Luka hands over a stack of papers stapled together, photocopied pages filled with a slanted, rough scrawl. It's Josiah's dream journal. None of the other patients had one. But my grandmother did. And so did I. As soon as I got honest with Dr. Roth and explained my symptoms, he had me start one. Luka points to the upper right corner on the first page. The letters TG are written in perfect, miniscule script. Even though it's only two letters, I recognize the handwriting as Dr. Roth's.

"TG," Luka says.

I look at him. "The Gifting."

We set Josiah Aaronson off to the side and look through the files with renewed fervor. From the two heavy stacks, we weed out three similar files. Each person was clinically diagnosed with paranoid schizophrenia. Each person kept a dream journal. And each journal has the same two letters written in the upper right corner on the front page. Two males. One female. Ranging in age from twelve all the way to Josiah, who was sixty. All three have symptoms that are not exactly the same, but similar enough to mine or Luka's that it can't be a coincidence. He shows me one of Josiah's papers and points to a name next to Roth's. *Primary physician: Doctor Carlyle.* "It's the same doctor who referred the other two."

"Do you think he's a believer?"

"Maybe." Luka gathers the other patient files. We look through them four times more, double, triple, quadruple checking. When we're positive we haven't skipped over something important, Luka stacks all the non-relevant diagnoses into one manila folder. It's incredibly fat. Then he puts the three relevant diagnoses, along with their correspond-ing dream journals, into the other. It's much too thin. I wish I could add my dream journal to the mix, or my grandmother's. But I gave mine to Dr. Roth, hoping to never see it again, and my grandmother's is buried in the bottom drawer of my desk in my bedroom.

Luka carefully slides both folders into his backpack. "You want anything else to eat?"

I shake my head.

He stuffs half the food into my backpack, half into his, then sets both bags onto the chair. The clock says midnight. It's time for bed and although we've been sitting on the same mattress for the entirety of the evening, sharing it now makes my stomach do some impressive acrobatics. This isn't our first time sleeping together. It's not even our second. Besides last night in the alleyway, there was another night a few days ago, when I had that horrible nightmare about crashing cars and Pete ended up in ICU and I didn't want to be alone. Tonight feels different though. We're in a motel room. My mother is not down the hallway. And we aren't in survival mode, at least not like we were last night.

Luka scratches the back of his head. "We should probably get some sleep."

I nod, feeling far from tired.

"I'll, uh, just sleep on the floor."

"You don't have to."

He stops mid-reach for a pillow.

"I mean, the bed is plenty big for the both of us, if you want to sleep in it. With me. Not *with* me, just beside me. It's not like we have to … you know." *Oh my goodness, Tess, stop talking right now.* "I just mean that we've already slept beside one another, so it's fine, if you wanted to sleep … on the mattress."

He smiles.

I look down at the comforter, entirely too embarrassed to maintain eye contact.

"Tess?"

"Hmm?"

"If me sleeping in the bed makes you uncomfortable …"

"It doesn't. Honestly." *Look at him, Tess. Stop acting like you're eleven.* I force my chin up, as if to prove I can handle this. "Really, I'm fine."

He studies me for a moment, as if assessing the validity of my words. It reminds me of the way he used to look at me when I first moved to Thornsdale and he was the completely-out-of-my-league, massively popular kid at my new school. Whatever he finds in my expression must convince him that I mean what I say, because he switches off the light and the mattress springs squeak as he lies down. He stays on his side. I stay on mine. It's entirely opposite from last night, when our bodies were tangled up in a knot. Yet somehow, I'm more aware of him—his breathing, the warmth radiating from his skin, the crisp clean smell of his shampoo. I swear I can even hear his heartbeat.

Is it me, or is the heater working exceptionally well in here?

"Luka?"

"Yeah?"

"I'm sorry for dragging you into this mess."

"Tess?"

I pull the covers up to my chest.

"Before you label me the martyr, you should know that breaking you out was as much for my well-being as it was for yours." The mattress lets out another squeak as Luka turns over on his side. "I didn't know the true meaning of insanity until those men dragged you out of school."

The confession turns the air in my lungs all light and fluttery. I bite my lip and blink up at the ceiling. What exactly am I supposed to say to that? There's nothing adequate, that's for sure. I want to ask him why. Why do I matter so much to him? It doesn't make any sense. Instead, I scratch the tip of my nose and turn my thoughts to less confusing topics. Like who killed Dr. Roth? Or maybe it's not *who*; maybe it's *what* killed him. The term *demon* sounds incredibly archaic, like it belongs to the time period of medical leeching and a flat earth. My father would be the first to scoff. Science has disproven God, and demons pretty much come with the God-territory. But how can I deny what's right in front of me?

The question that has been circling my thoughts ever since we crawled out of his apartment creeps its way to the tip of my tongue. "What's going to happen now?"

"We find a way to get to Detroit."

I pick at a loose thread on the sheet, wishing I could communicate with Leela. Maybe, if I could talk to her and tell her everything that has happened, maybe she would believe me. Maybe Leela could help.

CHAPTER FIVE

AN ALLY

I'm standing on a grassy knoll with noise all around me. Kids chasing kids in a game of tag, younger ones rolling down the hill. There's a field and players in uniform—one in blue and gold, the other in red and gray. Referees in black and white. Bleachers filled with spectators. The scoreboard at the end of the field displays a large red dragon.

I'm at a Thornsdale football game.

A tall, lanky kid walks toward the bleachers with two cups of hot chocolate in his hand. My brother! My legs take off, sprinting after him. "Pete!" I yell, my voice drowned out by the mixture of cheerleaders chanting and the crowd cheering and children giggling and referees whistling and coaches yelling. Closing the distance between us, I call his name again. My voice rises above the din, but his stride doesn't falter. "Pete," I say, grabbing his elbow.

But it's like he doesn't feel my grip on his arm. He doesn't even look at me. I wave my hand in front of his face. "Pete?"

He walks up the bleacher steps. Clank, clank, clank.

I stop and watch him go, baffled and hurt. How could he ignore me like that? I know Pete and I haven't been on the best terms lately, but things seemed to be getting back to normal in the hospital ...

Wait a minute.

Pete was really banged up the last time I saw him. They

moved him out of ICU, but he still had a long road to recovery ahead. He wouldn't be released so soon. And what am I doing out in public like this, at a Thornsdale football game? It's not even football season.

I scratch the small patch of eczema on the inside of my wrist and feel nothing. I'm dreaming. Which means at any second, something frightening will appear. A skeletal, white-eyed man will show up and attack these people and my classmates and this crowd. Only it won't *just* be a dream. I have no idea how it works. Dr. Roth didn't give us answers. All I know is that my dreams have a direct impact on real life. My brother is proof.

Pete stops a few steps ahead and hands one of the hot chocolates to somebody I can't see. When he sits down and pulls a blanket over his lap, the person I can't see comes into view.

"Leela!" Her name explodes from my mouth, equal parts joy and desperation and relief all encompassed in a two-syllable squeak.

Unlike Pete, she hears me. In fact, she looks at me as soon as her name escapes.

I run the short distance Pete walked, then stop suddenly in front of her. I have no idea what she will do. Leela and I might have been best friends once-upon-a-time, but that was before she found out I had been lying to her about my whereabouts after school every Monday. I told her I took piano lessons when I was really seeing Dr. Roth, my own personal shrink at the Edward Brooks Facility. I brace myself for the cold shoulder. Instead, she throws the blanket off her legs and wraps her arms around my neck.

She squeezes the air out of me, and when she lets go, her

brown eyes are warm and friendly and every bit as excited as I feel. Oh, how I've missed my friend. Her excitement quickly morphs into alarm. She grabs my elbows and yanks me down into a crouched position, as if this will hide me from the crowd. "Tess, what are you doing here? The police are looking for you. If anyone sees you, you'll be reported!"

"Leela, it's okay. Nobody is going to see me."

"What happened? Those guys—they came and took you and then you were gone. Your mother was in a panic. And now you're on the news. Tess, you can't be here." Her voice grows increasingly freaked. She looks around again and spots a patch of teachers beyond the student section. "Principal Jolly called the whole school together for this big meeting and told everyone that if any of us have any clue where you might be, we are required to report it. The police interrogated almost everyone."

As Leela panics, Pete sits under his half of the blanket with a blank look on his face, staring mindlessly off into the football field. I ache to talk to him. To ask how he's doing. How our parents are doing. But I understand now that this isn't Pete. This is a figment of Leela's dream. Leela's version of Pete doesn't see me. He can't interact with me. Only Leela can, because somehow, I have entered into Leela's dream. I have no idea how it works, but it has to be it.

A puzzle piece clicks into place. This is not the first time this has happened. I visited Summer Burbank's dream once, only at the time, I thought I was visiting Luka, because up until that point, I had only ever visited Luka. It all makes sense now. The Luka who was making out with Summer and completely ignoring me was never really Luka at all, but Summer's wishful thinking.

"Nobody else can see me but you. This is your dream."

"A dream?"

"Yes."

She lets go of my arm, her face transforming into a mask of skepticism. Her attention flicks to Pete. Disappointment floods the brown of her eyes. It's no secret she has had a crush on my brother since our first day at Thornsdale High School. Only she never got to meet the real Pete. She met the sullen, surly Pete, the one being controlled and influenced by a darkness he didn't know existed. Now, thankfully, he is safe. He is my brother again. Maybe Leela will get to meet that Pete soon. "You mean this isn't real?"

I don't want to dash her hopes, but we have so much to talk about. I need to convince her, and convince her quickly that this is a dream so we can move onto more important things. "If you don't believe me, pinch yourself."

"Huh?"

"Pinch your arm."

"Tess, I'm not going to—"

I reach out and pinch her arm for her. Hard. Instead of pulling away or yelping, she rubs her thumb over the spot. "I didn't feel anything."

"That's because we're dreaming."

She plops onto the bleacher looking bereft. Pete has disappeared altogether. "I knew this was too good to be real."

"Listen to me, Leela, this is a dream, but I'm not part of it."

"What do you mean?"

"I mean I'm really here. What I tell you now, you have to remember. And you have to believe that I'm not part of the dream. You have to believe that this is really *me* talking to you."

"This is weird."

"I don't know how much time we have." That's the thing about dreams. They are unstable. Leela can wake up at any moment, or her subconscious mind can drift somewhere else and maybe I won't be able to follow. Or worse, something bad could show up. A wave of cold fear stretches through my body. My muscles coil. Adrenaline pulses through my veins. If anything tries to attack my friend, I will be ready to fight. I sit beside her on the bleacher. "How's my brother?"

"From what I've heard, he's out of the hospital. I'm not sure when he's coming back to school, though." Leela shifts so she's facing me. "Tess, what's going on? The news reports are saying that you're dangerous."

"I'm not dangerous. I'm so sorry for not trusting you before with the truth. But I didn't even know what the truth was—honestly, I still don't." I grasp her hands. "Leela, I need your help. Luka and I both do."

Her eyes widen. "Luka's with you?"

"Yes." For now, at least.

"I wondered. There's been so much speculation. Luka hasn't been to school, but none of the teachers will talk about him whenever we ask where he is."

"Nothing is like you think it is."

"What do you mean?"

I search through my thoughts, trying to figure out a way to explain everything to Leela. How do you tell a person that everything we've learned our entire lives, everything our parents and the government and our schools have taught us, is wrong? "Our world is more than physical."

Her brow furrows. Leela and her family are supposedly Catholic, but even she admitted that the title was born from tradition more than anything. She called her parents closet atheists.

"I know this is going to sound crazy, but there is supernatural stuff all around us."

She looks around, as if she might see it for herself, the furrow in her brow deepening.

"Science is wrong. The government is wrong. There are real, legitimate evil forces in this world." I realize as I speak how crazy I sound, but onward I press. Because it's true. All too clearly I remember the man with the scar marking my brother with that strange symbol, preparing to claim him. If not for Luka and I being in the right place at the right time, he would have. And then what would have happened to Pete? "They're able to impact things—people and events. I see them. And somehow, so can Luka. That's why we have such a connection."

Leela stares at me with her mouth hanging open, her hands limp in mine. I can imagine what I look like—this wild-eyed, frenzied girl who busted out of a mental institute and is now spouting off things that sound certifiably insane. I wouldn't believe me if I were her. Except we are in a dream, so surely that has to bring some validity to my proclamations. Or maybe Leela will wake up and think she's the insane one.

"You need to believe this. You're not crazy. I'm not crazy. I'm not mentally deranged or a danger to society. Dr. Roth knew that all along. That's why he broke me out. He didn't commit suicide. He was murdered."

She blanches.

"I have to get out of here. I have to get to Detroit."

"Detroit! Tess, Detroit is awful. It's—it's ..." She twists up her face, as if searching for the proper description. "Well, if this evil stuff is real like you say it is, then Detroit is like hell. You can't go there. You'll be killed."

"We have to. Dr. Roth said there are others out there like us—people who can see the things we see. Luka and I think some of them live in Detroit. At least they did six years ago. We have to find them. In order to get there, we need fake IDs. Is there a way you can get a hold of my dad without the police catching on to you?" He's a man who stands toward the top of the ladder at Safe Guard Security Systems. Surely, with those types of connections, he can get Luka and me a fake ID. "Maybe you can contact him at his work. I can give you the number."

Leela slides her hands from mine and looks down into her lap.

"Is something wrong?"

"Your dad ... he's on some sort of probation with Safe Guard. They didn't fire him, but I don't think he's working right now." She bites her lip. "I guess they aren't letting him return to his job until you turn yourself in and get treatment."

My hope plummets. For my family. For me. What's going to happen to them if he gets fired at Safe Guard? What's going to happen to Luka and me if we can't figure out a way to get out of here?

Leela's eyes light up. "Bobbi!"

"Your cousin?"

"Her dad's the chief of police."

"You can't tell him, Leela, he'll come after us!"

"I know that, but there's a whole bunch of confiscated fake IDs at the station. Kids make them all the time. Bobbi and I used to look through them when we were younger. They're put into Evidence, which is this small locker in the basement. Her dad keeps the key in the top drawer of his desk. I can find a way to get them."

"How?"

"I'll go visit him first thing in the morning."

"Has he questioned you about me?" I have to imagine she was interrogated more than anyone else. It was no secret that we were close.

"Yes, but Bobbi told him we had a falling out. He told his officers to leave me alone. But Tess, they're tracking your parents, twenty-four seven."

Which means I can't see them. I can't contact them. I can't speak with them. Not until this is over. If it ever is. "You're positive nobody's following you?"

"Not that I know of."

So maybe our falling out was a good thing. A silver lining. There's a dragging sensation in my stomach, as if I'm about to wake up or go somewhere else. I grab onto Leela, wondering if I can bring her with me like I did with Luka. "I'm going to call you in the morning when we wake up."

She shakes her head slightly, as if grasping for clarity. "If you say so …"

"If I say so?"

"This is a dream. It's not real. You're not real."

"No, I'm real. This is me, in your dream." Desperation stains each one of my words. She's going to wake up and discredit all of this. I grapple for a solution. Something that won't negate the progress I've been making while we sleep. "A password."

"What?"

"We need a password. Something random. Something I wouldn't know. You tell it to me now and when I call you, I'll say it as proof that all of this was real."

I'm slipping ... slipping ... "Leela, a password!"

"Jelly donuts."

The crowd erupts into cheering. Everybody jumps to their feet, Leela too. Whooping and clapping, because Matt Chesterson scored the winning touchdown.

My eyes fly open. I'm awake in bed at Motel California. Shafts of light squeeze through the cracks in the blinds, turning a whole host of dust motes into floating sparkles. I sit upright. Did that really happen—me, visiting Leela in her dream, or was it some weird, hopeful dream of my own? The details begin to fade, like all dreams do. I squeeze my eyes shut and hold the details tight, running them through my head until they are committed to memory.

When I look around, I find that I'm in bed alone. I kick the sheets off my legs and quickly stand, then brace myself against the wall to ward off a sudden bout of dizziness. For one panicked moment, I think Luka left in the night. But both of our backpacks are on the chair, and there's a white note on the pillow. I pick it up.

Tess,

At Walgreens. Got an early start. Getting supplies. I didn't want to wake you up and I don't want you to worry. Hopefully I'll be back before you read this. But in case I'm not...

Yours,

Luka

I look at the clock. It's seven in the morning. What if Luka doesn't come back to me? I should want that. I should want him to come to his senses and leave; but I'm not ready to be on my own. Not yet. Before panic can have its way, the lock clicks and the door opens and Luka steps inside with two plastic bags in hand. I run to him and fling my arms around his neck, like Leela did with me in the dream. He drops the bags and wraps his arms around my waist, his hands splayed wide on the small of my back. "Good morning to you, too."

The sound of his voice in my ear has me remembering myself. I let go and take a step back, cursing the blast of heat in my cheeks. Seriously, enough with the blushing already. "Did you run into any trouble?"

"It's seven in the morning on a Saturday. The only person I saw was the checkout person at Walgreens and she was half asleep." He picks up one of the bags and dumps the contents onto the bed. Two bottles of orange juice. Some bananas. A box of donuts. A buzz cutter. A box of hair dye. And a phone—a cheap plastic mobile one that allows a person to pay for minutes as they go.

I pick it up. "I have to call Leela."

"Leela?"

"I visited her in my dream."

"What do you mean?"

"I mean I visited her like how I sometimes visit you. I told her everything and she believed me."

He looks skeptical. "I don't know if that's the smartest idea. To her, it was just a dream. What if she doesn't even remember it?"

"Leela won't report us."

"Are you sure about that?"

I nibble the inside of my bottom lip. Am I? "If she does, we'll ditch the phone and run. I mean, what's this for anyway? Who else *can* we call?"

"The Greyhound bus station, for one."

"And how will we get tickets without IDs? How will we even get there?" The closest Greyhound station is a forty-five minute drive to Eureka. I listened to Luka's skepticism once about Leela, when he didn't want me to tell her what was really going on. Maybe he was wrong. Maybe I should have told her everything from the beginning. Or maybe he was right. Maybe telling her everything would have ruined our friendship before it started. "Leela's our best option."

He stares down at the carpet, working a muscle in his jaw. I wait to see if he will extend the same trust I extended to him last night. Finally, he looks me in the eye and gives me a small, singular nod.

I dial Leela's number. Five rings, then voicemail. I hang up and try again. "C'mon, Leela, answer the phone."

This time, the second ring is followed by a groggy hello.

"Leela, it's Tess!"

My enthusiastic greeting is met with silence. I picture her sitting up in bed, rubbing her eyes, trying to bat away the web of confusion. "Tess?"

"Yes, Tess. Do you remember the dream?"

She says nothing.

My heart thuds much too fast. This has to work. "Do you remember *jelly donuts?*"

Luka quirks his eyebrow.

"Leela, please say you remember."

"I do."

"Do you believe this is real?"

There's an agonizing pause. I wish I could see her face. I wish I knew what she was thinking. I wish, I wish, I wish … until she says two glorious words. "I'm in."

She is resolute.
She is determined.
We have an ally.

CHAPTER SIX

PLANS & DISGUISES

After talking with Leela for who knows how long, we have a plan in place—most of which involves us sitting around the motel while Leela does all the dangerous work. We will call her at nine tonight to see if she was successful. If so, she will drive to Motel California. Luka and I will hide in the back of her car while she drives us to the nearest Greyhound station in Eureka. We will buy tickets and we will leave on the first bus out of town.

To Detroit.

In the meantime, Luka and I will disguise ourselves.

After eating two donuts and drinking all my orange juice, I examine the box of hair dye. Luka sits on the edge of the bed, pouring over the three files we picked from the large pile as though committing every symptom, every jotted letter to memory. I begin removing the items from the box of dye—two pairs of plastic gloves, two plastic hair caps, a packet of bleach primer, another packet of light brown dye, a small bottle of golden boost to give the brown a honeyed tint, two application bottles, and directions, which I unfold. I've never in my life colored my hair, not even professionally at a salon. It's always been the same shade as my mother's—a brown so dark it's occasionally mistaken for black.

I hold up a plastic glove. "I'm going to look horrible."

"Impossible." Luka shuts the manila folder. "Do you want

some help?"

"Do you know how to help?"

"It can't be that hard."

His words do not instill much confidence, but we read the directions together and he pulls on one pair of the plastic gloves. He pours the pouch of bleach into an application bottle and shakes it up. I put a towel over my t-shirt while Luka removes the backpacks from the chair and has me sit in front of the vanity. The first squirt is cold. So much so that I hunch up my shoulders and squeal.

"Sorry." I don't miss the laughter in his apology.

He continues, squeezing the cold goo all over my head, then slowly massaging it into the roots and out to the ends. My scalp tingles. I'm pretty sure it has less to do with the bleach and more to do with Luka's fingers. It takes him a while to finish. My hair, which grows like a weed, has grown out since I got it cut with my mom before my first day of school. It hangs well past my shoulders and my bangs are long enough to tuck behind my ears. Once my hair is properly soaked, he hands me the cap. "You're supposed to leave this on for twenty minutes."

Just what I need. A shower cap. When I put it on, the tingling turns to burning. "Is it supposed to sting?"

"According to L'Oreal, that's normal."

"Are you sure you don't have a sister?" As soon as the question is out, I want to yank it back in. My teasing smile falls away. Luka might have had a sister if his mother hadn't listened to the doctors after her first failed government-mandated pregnancy screening. They told her the fetus had an abnormality. Like the many women before her, she underwent a procedure that would fix the problem. Nothing too alarming about that. After all, pregnancy screenings have been part of life for years now. Fetal modification is as common as the flu shot. Not just here in America, but all over the world. It's the second part of the story that makes it alarming. I look down at my feet. "That was insensitive."

"Tess?"

I keep my attention fixed downward.

"I don't shatter easily."

This is a good thing. Lately, I've been feeling all too shatterable.

"Did you ever find out whether your mom passed her pregnancy screening when she was pregnant with you?"

"I could never figure out how to ask without arousing suspicion."

"Maybe she never had one. Lots of women were slipping under the radar back then."

My mind wanders to Luka's mom, failing her second screening but carrying the baby to term anyway, and for the first time, a fierce sense of admiration blossoms in my chest for the woman. All the worry she must have gone through during her second pregnancy, and then the confusion that must have occurred when she brought forth a healthy, beautiful baby boy. "Why do you think your mom failed your screening? Do you think the tests somehow picked up ... *the gifting?*"

"It's crossed my mind." He nods at the manila folders on the nightstand. "I was looking through the files hoping to find something about it. But the screenings weren't around when that older guy, Josiah, was born and it doesn't mention anything about them for the other two."

I shake my head. I'm so tired of having all these questions and no answers. Dr. Roth's death was frightening and horrible, yes, but it's also incredibly frustrating. He had our answers. He was going to tell us everything. But now he's dead and all we have to go on are three client records that are six years old. And these three records are leading us to Detroit, a gigantic, over-populated city we've never been to, in search of three people who might not even be there anymore. For all we know, they are in Shady Wood with my grandmother. The chances of finding them is an impossibility that I'm foolishly hanging my hopes on. Because without them, we will be at a gigantic dead end.

The stinging of my scalp intensifies. I attempt to scratch through the plastic cap. It offers little relief. I think about Leela at the station right now, either failing or succeeding in her mission, and an entire horde of butterflies unleashes in my stomach. I can't think about Leela. Distraction is key. I glance at Luka, who has taken a seat on the edge of the bed and fiddles with his frayed hemp bracelet. "You look deep in thought."

"I'm trying to figure out why we haven't seen anything lately."

He's right. Where have all the white-eyed men gone? And what about the guy with the scar? I've slept two nights in a row without evil infiltrating my dreams. The more I think about it, the less sense it makes. "You'd think if evil were after us, we'd be easy targets here."

"It's almost like …"

"What?"

"I don't know. It's almost like something's protecting us." Luka shakes his head and stares down at his palms. "It's driving me nuts, not knowing how I protected you."

"You mean with the force-field thing?" He's done it twice now. First in real life, when one of the white-eyed men lunged at me in the locker bay of our school, and again in a dream, while we were saving Pete. Both times, waves of light radiated from his palms and drove the darkness back. It was like a reaction, one he doesn't know how to reproduce.

"I was trying to figure it out for at least two hours the other night in the alley."

"Did you ever do it?"

"No, but it was exhausting work. I hadn't planned on falling asleep."

"You had a nightmare." I pick at a hangnail on my thumb. He wouldn't tell me about it yesterday, but maybe if I push now, with some distance between the memory of it, he'll open up a little. "What was it about?"

"Nothing." He's lying. It wasn't nothing. But he stands and holds up the now-empty hair dye box. "It's been twenty minutes."

Luka helps me rinse all the bleach from my head into the sink. I ring my hair out like a wet rag, then towel it dry. The sight of me in the mirror makes my eyes go a little buggy. "I look like an albino."

"A very cute one."

There it is again—one of those comments. They do funny things to my stomach.

"You sure you don't want to keep it this way?" he teases.

"You prefer blondes, huh?"

"I'm pretty sure that's more like white."

"I think we'll draw less attention to ourselves if I'm a brunette again." I fill the second application bottle with the brown dye, pour in the golden booster, shake it up, and hand it over to Luka, who has put on a new pair of gloves. Not many boys his age could pull off the look. Luka, however, pulls it off well—wearing the perfect amount of amusement and self-deprecation.

Our eyes meet in the mirror's reflection. One corner of his mouth curves up. "I have a thing for brunettes, by the way."

I bite the inside of my cheek to keep from smiling. Just how much would Summer and Jennalee mourn that statement? Once my hair is soaked in goo all over again, I don the second plastic cap and pick up the clippers from the vanity. "I'm assuming these aren't for me."

"Not unless you want a buzz cut." Luka is still standing behind me, and the vibration of his voice tickles my ear. It makes me think of the warning on most side view mirrors—*objects are closer than they appear.* "It's only a matter of time before I'm on the news too. Might as well disguise myself now. You ready to be the hair stylist?"

I've watched my mom give my dad haircuts with our clippers at home. This might be something I can actually do. "I think I can handle that."

I stand. Luka sits.

"Just an all-around buzz?"

"Sounds good."

It's not a very flattering hairstyle. The lack of hair has a way of exacerbating every flaw. Even Pete, loved and adored by the girls, got a buzz cut in seventh grade and his nose went from endearingly crooked to distractingly crooked.

Maybe this will be good. Maybe a buzz cut on Luka will even the playing field a little.

I set the clippers to the lowest setting, let out a shaky breath, and get to work. The second I run my fingers through his hair, my body grows warm and fluttery. Neither of us speak. By the time I'm done and everything is even and his scalp feels like prickly stubble and my feet are surrounded by tufts of thick, dark hair, the room is so charged I have to take a quick step back just to catch my breath.

He shakes off the towel and brushes hair from his neck. "How does it look?"

"Um ..."

"Uh-oh. It's that bad?" He stands from the chair, sets his hands on the vanity, and leans closer to his reflection. He puts on his pair of black-rimmed glasses. In his well-fitting dark denim jeans and his white undershirt, he looks ... incredibly sexy. There are no other words for it. The only thing the buzz cut has exacerbated is his perfection. He turns around and nods toward the clock. "Your twenty minutes is up."

I grab my backpack and close myself inside the bathroom. I shower down, lathering and rinsing my hair. I dry off and dress quickly in a pair of jeans and my orange Crush t-shirt. I wipe the fog off the mirror and stare at myself. The color is so much lighter than I'm used to. I don't look like me, and for the world I can't tell if that's a good thing or not.

"You gonna come out of there?" Luka calls.

No, actually, I'd rather not. But since I can't hide in here forever ... I take a deep breath and slowly step outside.

Luka wolf-whistles.

I blush.

"Ready for a cut?" he asks, wielding the scissors.

As much as I'd like to say *no, I've had enough change for one day, thank you very much*, the scissors are unavoidable. The more different I can look from the picture flashing about on TV, the better. I gather my hair into a long, wet ponytail at the nape of my neck and squeeze my eyes tight. Luka holds my hair in his palm and makes several slices right below the ponytail holder. When the slicing ceases, he holds up the ponytail no longer attached to my head. I take out the hair band and give my head a shake. The picture on the television screen showed a girl with long, dark hair. The girl in the mirror has chin length light brown hair. She is practically unrecognizable.

Luka tips his chin closer to my ear. "Mission accomplished."

CHAPTER SEVEN

GOODBYE

We eat bananas and beef jerky for lunch and spend the day pacing, speculating, studying the files, and fidgeting with the TV antenna. We've found a couple news stations, but the reception is so fuzzy we can barely make anything out.

One station airs a rerun of President Abigail Cormack's victory speech after she won the election in November. My dad had us all stay up late so we could watch it together as a family. It's a tradition—something we've done every four years—for as long as I can remember, a lot like Dad's morning newspaper read-aloud routine. The Ekhart children will be nothing if not informed. But November had been a dark period—the month Dr. Roth asked me to keep a dream journal in exchange for information about my grandmother. I'd been so consumed with the quick deterioration of my life that I hadn't paid much attention to anything our new president had to say.

Today, however, I find myself leaning closer to the screen, straining to hear the president's words through the static. Everything she says sounds good on the surface, but my current circumstances have prompted me to turn her face-value statements inside out, and what I find underneath does not bode well.

"In these increasingly turbulent times, with the threat of war looming and political unrest abroad, we need to set down our differences. We need to cast aside those things that burden us. Those things that hinder us. We need to step past party lines and rise up together—united as one country. For we will only be as strong as we are united, as powerful as our weakest links."

The crowd—democrats and republicans alike—rise up for a standing ovation.

She begins speaking about new initiatives and lofty plans and a fresh vision for our country. The audience is enthralled. They eat every promise from the palm of her hand. I vaguely remember my dad being impressed after it aired the first time, and he's very rarely impressed.

Luka jabs the power button on the remote and the television shuts off.

President Cormack's declarations must have rubbed him the wrong way, too. I stare at the black screen, chewing over her words. Is our president really concerned about weak links, or is she simply afraid of anyone who is different? It's that kind of philosophy that got me locked up at the Edward Brooks Facility. It's that kind of philosophy that birthed a place like Shady Wood. I recall the rooms filled with the living dead—rows upon rows of emaciated adults lying comatose in hospital beds, all in the name of rehabilitation. The image haunts me.

Luka peeks out through a crack in the vertical blinds, letting in a sunbeam. It's not a common thing in Northern California. I lift up my hand and place it in the thin stream of light. I'd give anything to be outside. When Luka lets go, the blind swings back and forth, chopping apart the sun, then extinguishing it altogether. He joins me on the bed, sitting on the edge near my feet. I've never seen Luka's wrist without his hemp bracelet. So when he slides it off and thumbs the three small stones woven in place, I'm a little more than attentive.

"Where did you get it?" I finally ask.

"My mom gave it to me when my visions first started."

"What are the stones?"

"Jade, onyx, and red jasper." He touches each one as he gives their name. "They're supposedly protective stones. Red jasper is known to protect against fears in the night. Jade guards against misfortune. And onyx ..." His green eyes meet mine. "Some people believe that the absence of light can be used to create invisibility."

I can only imagine what my dad would say to that. "Did she believe it would work?"

"I think she wanted me to feel safe."

I wait for him to slip the bracelet back on. Instead, he folds up the hem of my jeans and wraps it around my ankle. The feather light touch of his fingertips against my skin has my pulse skipping several beats. "Maybe you can borrow it for a while."

My body goes warm. I can't tell if it's an emotional reaction from Luka's sweet gesture, or if the bracelet really does have protective powers. I touch the stones, then fold down my jeans. The warmth remains.

We feast on dry cereal and raisins, talking about everything and nothing. Luka asks me questions—all kinds. About the places I've lived and the books I've read and the things that make me laugh. I'm positive I'm boring him, but he listens like he's riveted. Like the things I say are the most interesting things a person could hear.

I ask him questions, too. He tells me about the time his first and only pet—a Bernese Mountain dog named Jack—ran away. He tells me about his first trip to the ER, when he ended up with thirteen stitches on his right elbow after attempting a barspin on his buddy's BMX. He tells me about his favorite birthday to date—when he turned eight and his dad not only bought him a surfboard, but taught him how to use it. Luka rode his first wave on his fourth try and never looked back. The thrill was addicting. Listening to him talk about it makes me want to surf. He says someday he'll teach me. I've never been more eager for *someday*.

Later in the afternoon, Luka starts to doze. I let him. After the lack of sleep he's gotten over the past two days, he has to be exhausted. I lay on my stomach next to him, safely tucked away on my side of the mattress. When his breathing turns soft and rhythmic, I can't help myself. I stare, fascinated by the relaxed way his arm curls over his head. The long, dark eyelashes fanning his cheek. The straightness of his nose, the flatness of his abs, the thin strip of exposed flesh between the hem of his shirt and the waist of his jeans.

My heart thrums faster.

Luka stirs.

I look away. I will not have him waking up to me staring. How creepy can a girl get? I page through the dream journals, my mind rabbit-trailing in a thousand different directions—my parents, Pete, Leela, Luka, and where I'd be if he hadn't gone to Dr. Roth for help. I envision Dr. Roth swinging on the noose and then my grandmother, shackled inside a white box of a room, and suddenly, I am somewhere else. I'm still lying on the motel's bed, because I can feel my body against the mattress. But I must be somewhere else, too, because the bed is surrounded by a bright circle of sentinel-like creatures.

Each one radiates the same light that Luka threw out with his hands, only their entire bodies glow with it. Beyond the circle is the man who calls me Little Rabbit. The man who no longer has one scar, but two. The second one is angry and red, running the length of his once unmarked cheek. He's surrounded by an entire army of white-eyed men, and he's directing them like a puppeteer, flinging out his hands so they charge at me over and over and over again, gnashing their teeth as they attack. The bright light keeps them away.

But surely, it is only a matter of time before one of them breaks through.

"Tess." Someone shakes my shoulder. "Tess!"

My eyelids flutter. The light and the army disappear. I am lying in bed, surrounded by nothing but cheap motel décor. I sit up so fast my head spins. Somehow, the clock reads 8:55. I'm not sure how it's possible, since I'm positive I never fell asleep. I was never unaware of my body on that bed. Yet three whole hours passed like a snap.

"Are you okay?" Luka asks, his hand on my arm.

My heart beats wildly. "Yeah. I'm fine."

Luka's face fills with the same suspicion I felt when he shrugged off my question about his nightmare. He will want to know what happened, but how can I tell him when I have no idea what happened myself? Was that real, what I saw? I scoot off the bed and pick up the phone from the nightstand. "It's time to call Leela."

My heart doesn't settle down. Not when we call Leela and not when we prepare for her arrival. We make quick work of packing up our stuff, put all of our garbage in the two plastic bags from Walgreens, and check the place meticulously for any clues we might leave behind that would tip off the housecleaning staff that Motel California was unknowingly aiding and abetting a highly, deranged and dangerous, escaped mental patient. Luka stuffs the leftover food in our bags and waits by the window, staring out into the darkness.

My palms have turned clammy, my fingers cold. I wring them as I pace back and forth in the small room, hoping the red jasper stone on Luka's hemp bracelet works. Hoping it will protect us from all the things that go bump in the night. On *this* night in particular, when a whole lot of things could go bump.

Luka shifts the blind. "She's here."

Headlights do not cut through the parking lot. When we spoke with Leela on the phone, Luka told her to cut them before pulling in. He takes my hand, his grip steady and sure, and we step out into the chilly nighttime air. Our breath escapes in tiny, white puffs. Everything in me wants to sprint, but Luka sets a calm pace. A non-rushed, unsuspicious, maddening stroll. When we finally get to Leela's car and climb into the backseat, nobody speaks. I think we're all shocked that our plan worked. At least so far.

Luka breaks the silence first. "Nobody followed you?"

Leela shakes her head, her knuckles whitening as she grips the steering wheel at ten and two.

"Do you think anybody suspected anything?"

She shakes her head again.

I exhale my pent-up breath, then inhale deeply, hoping to still my nerves. Her car smells like sugar cookies. This is Leela's favorite smell. For Christmas, I bought her a small box of sugar cookie-scented car air fresheners. One dangles now from her rearview mirror. Our eyes meet in the reflection. There are a million things I want to say, a million apologies I want to make, but they all get stuck in my throat.

"Your hair," she says.

I touch it self-consciously. I forgot how different I must look.

"It looks amazing!"

My smile is uncontainable. So is Leela's. The wall between us crumbles. Despite everything—the immense danger we find ourselves in, all the unknowns before us—I am happy. I have my best friend back, even if only for a little while.

Luka pulls me down with him in the seat, to the height of small children. Between the dark and our hunched frames, nobody would suspect two teenagers in the back seat. "Make sure to go the speed limit. Not too fast or too slow."

Her hands tremble as she shifts the car into drive. Bits of gravel crunch beneath the tires. Every loud pop makes her flinch.

"Why don't you tell us how it went." Luka knows Leela better than I've given him credit for. If anything will set my jumpy friend at ease, talking is it.

She releases a shaky breath and dives in. "Great. Better than great, actually. I cut up an onion in my car before I went inside the station. You know, to make my eyes all watery. I've always been really sensitive with onions."

A fresh wave of affection swells inside my throat.

"By the time I stepped inside, tears were already streaming down my cheeks, and as soon as I sat down in my uncle's office, I burst into sobs. I'd say I deserve an Academy Award, but I was so nervous and worked up at that point that it wasn't really hard to break down. I was legitimately sobbing."

There is something so safe about hearing Leela's familiar chatter from the front seat, even if it's about something as crazy as this.

"I told him that I was afraid to tell the truth when the police first interrogated me, but I might know where you went. That's when I explained about your grandmother and how you were always talking about her and how scared I was that you were going to try and find her and that something bad would happen to you."

We were hoping this bit about my grandmother would serve two purposes—give Leela a reason for showing up at the station and throw the police off our scent. The story will be made extra believable if the authorities put two and two together and figure out that Luka and I broke into Shady Wood last week. The nurse we tied up and stuffed in the supply closet had to have reported the incident by now. "Do you think he believed you?"

"I think so. As soon as I said it, he thanked me for telling him the truth and then he left super fast to go report it. That's when I grabbed the key from the top drawer in his desk. I thought my heart would burst out of my chest. I had no idea how long he would be gone. When he came back, I apologized over and over again for being your friend." Leela shoots me a sheepish look in the rearview mirror. "And for not reporting the information sooner. I ended up crying all over again. By then, I was feeling a little sorry for him. My uncle's never been too comfortable with emotion and there was a lot of it coming out of me."

"Did you get the IDs?" Luka asks.

"I think there are a few that might work." Leela passes her purse back to us. "As soon as I left his office, I went downstairs to use the restroom. The coast was clear, so I opened up the evidence locker, grabbed all of them I could find, and ditched the key."

Luka pulls out a Swiss army knife from the front pocket of his bag. It has a miniature flashlight attachment he uses to study each of the IDs, searching for two that might pass as us, while I wonder over the fact that it worked. The plan was not an elaborate one. Or even a particularly smart one. But it was all we had, and somehow, we succeeded.

At least so far.

In the front seat, Leela fills us in on everything we've missed at Thornsdale—the police interrogations, the crack-down on the students, the wild rumors that are circulating about Luka's coinciding disappearance, and whatever she knows about our families. My dad has been suspended from his job and my home is under twenty-four-hour surveillance. Pete has not yet returned to school. She keeps peeking at the rearview mirror as she talks, as if unable to acclimate to our new appearances. I listen while studying each face on the IDs.

Fifteen minutes in, I think I've reached a decision. I hand the card to Luka.

He peers at the picture. Lily Evans is twenty-one, the youngest in the bunch. There's no way I can pull off anything older. I mean, I can barely pull off seventeen. Her eyes are slightly lighter than my navy blue. Her chin isn't as pointy, her nose is a little wider, and her honey-brown hair hangs past the frame of the photograph. This, I think, is a good thing. Perhaps whoever looks at the ID will attribute the difference in facial features to the change in hairstyle. She has the same fair skin and the same big eyes and we also happen to be the same height.

"What do you think?" I ask.

"I think I'll have to get used to calling you Lily." Luka

hands an ID to me.

Jacob Denton. Age twenty-five. It's an age that would make me nervous if I hadn't seen with my own eyes how well he pulled off being a doctor when we broke into Shady Wood last week. There's something about the way Luka carries himself—with authority, like his father. If any seventeen-year-old boy can pull off a man in his mid-twenties, it's this one sitting beside me. Plus, his buzz cut adds a maturity to his face that wasn't there before. He looks older somehow, more serious without the shaggy hair.

I study Jacob's picture. His face is thicker, his hair longer. Both of which are easily explained away by weight loss and a haircut. The essentials are there—green eyes, dark hair, and olive skin. Jacob's face, of course, does not measure up to Luka's, but perhaps people will think he's simply not photo-genic. "Jacob, huh?"

"I prefer Jake." He flashes me that crooked smile of his and takes back the ID when red and blue lights swirl in the back window. Luka clamps his hand over mine and pulls me all the way down to the floor. Everything in me seizes—my heart, my muscles, my lungs.

"Oh my gosh, what do I do?"

Luka tells Leela to pull over. Trying to out-race them will do nothing but confirm our guilt and get us all arrested. So Leela does. And the squad car races past us. None of us speak. Luka and I do not move. We crouch in the car on the shoulder of the dark highway, our hearts crashing into the silence. When the police car is long out of sight, Luka and I sit back on the seat and Leela pulls onto the road.

We don't say much after that. We're all too busy catching our breath. I wish Leela would resume her chattering, but I'm pretty sure the flashing lights gave her a miniature heart attack. My sense of urgency grows. We need as much space between us and Northern California as possible. And yet, with the urgency comes dread. Because what if this car ride is the last time I get to see my friend? What if I never see my family again? I'm used to moving around, but not without them.

By the time Leela pulls into a parking space in the parking lot of Eureka's Greyhound Bus station, my teeth chatter with nerves.

"Thank you, Leela," Luka says. He reaches up and gives her shoulder a squeeze, then takes his bag and steps out of the car to give us our privacy, but not before giving me a telling look. We have fifteen minutes to get tickets and catch the bus. We can't miss it, especially since the next one doesn't leave until later the next morning. Time is of the essence. Even so, he knows I need to say this goodbye.

Leela shifts around to look at me.

There are so many things I want to say. So many thank you's I want to give, ones that far exceed what Leela has done for us today. Before her, I didn't know what it was like to have a friend. She's the best one I could have ever asked for. With a lump in my throat, I lean forward between the two front seats and wrap my arms around her neck. "I should have told you everything from the beginning."

She squeezes back. "I understand why you didn't."

When we finally let go, her eyes are watery, only there's no onion in sight. "You'll be back, okay? Somehow, this will all get worked out and you'll come back."

Leela, the eternal optimist.

I want to believe her. So I cling to that hope with everything I've got, reach into the front pouch of my backpack, and pull out three letters. One for my mom. One for my dad. One for Pete. "These are for my family. Can you make sure they get them?"

"I will. I promise."

"I don't want you to get in trouble."

"I won't get caught. I'll wait until Pete comes back to school and find a way to slip them to him."

The thought makes me smile. Perhaps this is the silver lining. Maybe this fiasco will bring my best friend and my kid brother together. Maybe Leela will get to know the real Pete, the one unencumbered by darkness. The one who is not moody or taciturn or dark, but the one who is lighthearted and charming and the life of every party. How much more will she fall in love with that Pete? Somehow, with this possibility in mind, it doesn't feel so much like I'm losing Leela. It feels a little bit like she's becoming a part of our family. I wrap my arms around her neck again. "Best friends?"

"Always," she whispers.

After one final squeeze, I climb out of the car and close the door softly behind me. Luka grabs my hand, threading his fingers with mine, and leads me to the ticket booth. I don't look back.

CHAPTER EIGHT

RESURRECTED PILLS

I 'm twenty-one-year-old Lily Evans. He is twenty-five-year-old Jacob Denton. And if anybody asks, we're running away to New York to elope. I'm supposed to text into the phone Luka purchased from Walgreens and do my best impersonation of bored while he purchases our tickets. The key is hiding my face as much as possible without being obvious about it.

He asks for the tickets to New York City. They are twice as expensive, but we don't care. If anybody discovers we got onto a Greyhound bus, this will lead them to the east coast. But we will be in Detroit, one of the many stops along the way.

"Identification, please." The ticket lady is a beady-eyed woman who speaks in an impatient, annoyed voice. Like the customers who keep her employed are one giant inconvenience.

My stomach knots into a small, tight fist as I dig through my backpack in search of an ID that is right there. The feigned flightiness is all part of the plan. Luka thinks that looking unprepared will make us appear less suspicious. I pull it out after a couple seconds and hand it over with a breathless apology. I make brief eye contact with the lady, then quickly retreat to my phone, letting my short hair fall in front of my face.

Seconds upon seconds tick by.

I imagine her looking from the IDs—to us—the IDs—to us. The fist in my stomach clenches tighter. What if she's an avid news watcher? What if she's been on the lookout for Teresa Ekhart—a deranged and dangerous fugitive. What if, after all this work, we're caught before we even escape? I'm positive she's on to us. I'm sure she's pushing some sort of emergency protocol button beneath the counter and at any second we'll be surrounded by police wielding guns and shouting for us to put our hands up. And all I can do is stand there, typing fake texts into a cheap phone.

Finally, the woman speaks. "Cash or credit?"

Luka slips some bills from his wallet and slides them over the counter.

She hands him the tickets, the change, and our IDs.

Luka thanks her, then takes my hand and leads me toward the bus we will be boarding, casually swinging my arm back and forth. As if we don't have a care in the world.

The further we get from Eureka and Thornsdale, the more the fist in my stomach loosens. We do a fair amount of paranoid scanning, checking to see if any passengers are on to us. All of them are either sleeping or fiddling around on their iPads. I find myself relaxing into the seat. After such an onslaught of adrenaline, my eyes grow heavy. I rest my head against the cool window, ready to let sleep take me. But Luka gives me a gentle nudge.

A small, white pill sits in the center of his palm.

It looks all too familiar. "What's that?"

"I want you to take it."

I pull away from it as if it has venomous fangs. How could Luka ask this of me? How does he even have one? We flushed the entire bottle down the toilet, together, before we made our plans to break into Shady Wood. I look up into his face and notice the stress around his eyes. The deep knit of his brow.

"Dr. Roth has a theory," he says.

"About the medicine?"

"He thinks the pills mask your gifting."

Is this why Dr. Roth warned me against taking them back in November?

"He thought that was why you never had any dreams when you were on them. And why those white-eyed men never bothered you." Luka runs his hand over his short hair. "The meds close whatever window there is between the physical and the supernatural. They can't get to you and you can't get to them."

"Which is why Pete got into that car accident. It's why we decided I can't take them anymore." I don't understand. I thought we were on the same page.

"I don't want you to take them either. Not permanently. Not even long-term. But it's the only way I know how to protect you."

"Protect me from what?" I look around. "There's nothing here."

"I have this feeling I can't shake. And tonight, when I took that nap ..."

"What?"

He shakes his head, frustrated. Or maybe it's not frustration—maybe it's fear.

It makes me afraid too. "Luka, you have to tell me what you saw."

"The man we fought in your brother's hospital room is after you. He wants you locked up like your grandmother. And Tess, I don't know how to protect you. I can't figure out how to throw out that force field. I've tried and tried, but it's not working. Dr. Roth thought the pills would work as a type of camouflage. Before we broke you out of the Edward Brooks Facility, he gave me some in case we were in a bind, or needed help."

I look down at the pill in his hand.

"I think it will camouflage you. Just until we find these other people in Detroit."

I can't tell if this is a good idea. I'm confused and tired. Luka has gotten us this far. Leela and I never would have pulled off the escape plan without him. He's been the rock— strong and steady. And Dr. Roth gave Luka these pills, a man who proved to be trustworthy. That has to say something, especially since he didn't want me to go on them to begin with. Maybe they can serve a momentary purpose.

"I need to make sure you're safe." His eyes are ablaze. His voice, vehement. "Please."

I hesitate. With every second that ticks past, Luka looks more and more tortured. I don't want to see him in pain, so I pick up the pill and put it on my tongue. Pushing away the memory of the saccharinely sweet woman force-feeding me pills much the same as this one, I take a long drink from Luka's water bottle.

He lets out a relieved breath.

"What about you?" I ask.

"What do you mean?"

"Who's going to protect you?" Apparently, I'm too selfish to look out for his wellbeing. If I had a smidge of bravery, a hint of honor, I would have attempted to talk Luka out of coming with me to Detroit. Convinced him that he didn't have to get on this bus with me. That I would be fine without him.

"They aren't after me like they're after you. They never have been."

CHAPTER NINE

DEAD ENDS

Luka wakes me up when we arrive in San Francisco. We need to get off and transfer buses. I slept for five hours straight with zero dreams. Unlike the peace my dreamless slumber offered before, when I was a high school student grasping for normalcy, it offers no peace now. This time, I know what is happening. The joy and relief and wonder I felt the first time around is completely absent. How can I feel any of those things when I know that somebody may have died that I could have otherwise saved, all for the sake of *my* safety?

Luka grabs my backpack from the overhead compartment and discreetly scans the bus, checking to see if any of the passengers are looking at us. There are dark circles beneath his eyes.

"Did you get any sleep?" I ask.

"A little." His smile is strained. "Any dreams?"

I shake my head. Dr. Roth's theory is proving itself true. Luka places his hand on the small of my back and walks close behind me. We file outside with the rest of the passengers, stretch our legs, and board another bus. I long for the freedom of the woods that surround my home in Thornsdale, or the crisp briny air that rolled in from the ocean whenever I sat on the back deck reading or writing in my journal. Instead, we will be on another bus for the next three days. It feels like a prison sentence.

We ride down the coast of California, stopping for brief five-, ten-, twenty-minute stints in towns along the way. We transfer in Bakersfield and again in Las Vegas, where we ditch the thick, useless manila folder of Dr. Roth's former patients. I take another pill and sleep through a long stretch that lands us in Denver. We buy two winter coats, some extra clothes, and a rolling suitcase, which lightens the load considerably.

There seems to be a positive correlation between Luka's dark circles and the protective way he acts around me. The more pronounced they become, the more protective he becomes. When we stop in Ogallala, he's never more than two feet from my side. And yet, he no longer holds my hand. In fact, he has stopped touching me altogether. I don't know what to make of it. I encourage him to sleep, and he does a little. But it's fitful and sparse. Anytime I ask what's haunting him, he doesn't say. I can make my own educated guesses, though. I'm positive I'm dying in his dreams. And in them, Luka cannot save me. Whatever he sees when he sleeps, it has him with-drawing. Retreating into himself with haunted eyes, and I can't save him either. I'm not even sure I can reach him.

We have one final transfer in Chicago. By then my awe over the big cities has waned. We've seen at least seven or eight over the past few days and in that time, I've grown more accustomed to the masses of people, the cars and the horns and the smoggy air. On the final stretch to Detroit, Luka sits up straight with eyes wide open. I try giving back his mother's hemp bracelet. I think he needs it more than me. He insists I keep it on my ankle.

When we step off the bus for the last time, a wave of free-dom sweeps through my body. No more sitting in place while snow-covered countryside scrolls past the window. We are here.

We made it. I turn to smile at Luka, but his eyes are skittish. He looks back and forth, as if at any moment something might attack us. Thanks to the pills I have ingested, I cannot see or feel what he is seeing and feeling. But just because I can't see it or feel it, doesn't mean it isn't real. The sheer unease in his usually calm, confident demeanor turns my bones cold.

And places an ache in my chest. Because I know what I have to do.

It's late. We choose the first hotel we come to, practically across the street from the Greyhound station. Inside is a pair of double beds. Luka takes the one closest to the door. I take the other. I force myself to stay awake with an increasing sense of dread. Street lights and headlights filter through the cracked blinds of our hotel room window. I wait while Luka shifts and settles in the bed beside me. I wait until his breathing turns deep and rhythmic. I wait even longer.

I purposefully left my rolling suitcase packed and by the door with my winter coat draped over the handle. I slipped a roll of money into the front pocket as well as a note I jotted in the bathroom while brushing my teeth. All I have to do is slip out of bed, step into my shoes, and get out the door. I begin my escape with the speed of a snail. Every time the mattress springs let out a squeak, I hold my breath and stop moving.

Luka sleeps on.

I tiptoe across the room, my aching heart thudding heavy and thick in my throat. I place the note at the foot of the door and unclasp the hemp bracelet from my ankle. The soft latch of the door handle is barely more than a whisper. As soon as I'm out into the hallway, I hurry to the elevator and punch the button several times in a row. It doesn't come. Too impatient to wait for it, I jab my arms into the sleeves of my winter coat and take the stairs instead, my suitcase *clunk-clunk-clunking* behind me. Halfway down, my quick descent turns into a sprint. I don't know where I'm going. I just know that I need to get far away. I am a ticking bomb. It's only a matter of time before I detonate. I can't let Luka be with me when it happens. I can't ruin his life, not when he still has a future ahead of him. He needs to go back to Thornsdale, where he never had dark circles beneath his eyes. He needs to get back to his family and live his life.

Be brave, Tess. Be good. Do the right thing.

This is my chant as I run through the hotel lobby and burst out into the biting wind. Anxiety builds inside me, so much that it turns into terror. It has nothing to do with the supernatural and everything to do with my separation from Luka. The further away I get from him, the harder it is to breathe.

Be brave, Tess. Be good.

I turn down a side street, my breath escaping in quick white puffs around my face. Up ahead, a garbage can clatters against the cement. A figure steps out from behind an alley dumpster. The white puffs around my face disappear. I brace myself for a white-eyed demon, or the man with the scars.

Instead, a man with a scraggly beard and a tattered coat looks me up and down with greasy eyes. "Well, well, well, look what we have here."

I let go of my suitcase, fists clenching at my sides. I know how to defend myself. I've been trained in martial arts for years now.

But then a second figure steps out from the dumpster. Another man, with pointed shoulders and a twisted sneer. I take a cautious step backward. I may be quick. I may have experience. But I am small and physically weak.

The man with the sneer clucks his tongue and creeps closer. "No need to leave so fast, not when you just got here."

He steps toward me.

With terror clawing up my throat, I take a few more steps back, then turn around and sprint away. My suitcase clatters behind me. My short hair whips at my cheeks. I dash away faster than I've ever run—quick like a rabbit. I turn the corner, onto the busy street from which I came, and as I do I slam into something hard. Something warm.

Strong arms circle my waist. A familiar heart beats in my ear. I could stay here forever, in this spot, against this chest. But the arms let go. Luka wraps his fingers around my bicep and pulls me away from the side street. I look over my shoulder. The two men lurk in the shadow, unwilling to come out into the light. Luka drags me toward the hotel I attempted to escape. He doesn't let go until we stand beneath the awning.

Heat emanates from his body—wave after wave of white hot anger. The wind molds his undershirt to his chest, which heaves as though he just finished sprinting the four hundred. The light from the street casts gorgeously frightening shadows along his face. He holds up the letter I left him. "What is this?"

"A note."

He uncrumples it and begins to read. "*Dear Luka, please go back to Thornsdale before it's too late. I will be okay. I can find the others. You can still have a normal life. Don't waste it on me. Tess.*" When he finishes, his green eyes smolder. "Do you really think my life will be normal if I go back to California?"

"It will be more normal than this."

He grits his teeth.

"You're not sleeping. You're barely eating. Your dreams are getting worse. Something's torturing you here. Something was torturing you on the bus."

"You're right. The dreams are getting worse. But if you think going back to Thornsdale without you will make them better, then you don't know anything." He removes the hemp bracelet from his back pocket and wraps it around my wrist. "I'm not going back. I want to find these others as much as you. So please, do us both a favor and stop trying to save me."

The next morning, Luka's dark circles are worse. I want to help carry whatever burden he is carrying, but how can I when he insists I continue with the medicine? I suggest that I stop, but his *no* is so firm and unyielding, I put the pill in my mouth and swallow.

We take our continental breakfast back to our room and decide to look for Dr. Roth's three clients first. If those result in dead ends, then we will try finding Dr. Carlyle. No reason to drag him into it if the connection is a coincidence.

"Who do you want to start with?" I ask.

The three files sit in front of us on the bed. I expect Luka to pick up the one he's been poring over the most—a thirty-four-year-old male named Gabriel. Recurring dreams of a girl he'd never met, but whose safety meant everything. The symptoms are eerily similar to Luka's, only instead of the girl being me, this woman has light brown skin and dark brown eyes. At the time the records were taken, Gabriel lived in south Detroit.

Luka, however, doesn't pick up Gabriel's file. He picks up Josiah's—a man whose symptoms are much more similar to mine. At the time the records were taken, his wife, Dot, insisted that Josiah see a Dr. William Carlyle, who then referred him to Dr. Charles Roth. He would be sixty-seven now and lives, or lived, on the west side of Detroit.

I have no objections to finding him first, so thirty minutes later we are in a cab heading west with a driver who speaks a lot of Farsi and little English. We drive past tenement housing and masses of chaos—blaring music, wailing sirens, street vendors selling illegal contraband, even an angry protest outside a fetal modification clinic that breaks into violence. More than once, I see money exchanged for bags of white powder or various colored pills and abandoned churches with things like *where's your god now?* graffitied on stained-glass windows. Scantily-clad women show off cleavage and a whole lot of leg on street corners.

A street evangelist stands on a mountain of plowed snow that is more black than white, pleading with passersby below. They jeer and mock and spit. Someone pushes him and he topples off the snow. Two people kick him while he lies on the ground. I cannot peel my attention away from the window. The anarchy should make me nervous. Instead, it offers an odd sort of comfort. Here in Detroit, the authorities are so busy keeping people alive that I feel safely obscure.

When we finally arrive at 22 West 56th street, we ask the cabbie to wait by the curb in front of a home with a sagging roof, a warped front porch, and several missing shutters. Luka rings the doorbell and we wait outside in the bitter cold. A few seconds later, locks click—at least five of them—and the door opens just enough to show a woman's weather-worn face over a rusted chain that remains securely in place. "Can I help you?"

"Is Josiah Aaronson here?"

"Who's asking?"

"My name is Jacob. This is Lily."

She looks from me to Luka, then pulls her face away and starts to slam the door shut.

I place my hand against the wood to hold it open. "It's about Dr. Roth."

Her eyes narrow into slits. "What did you say?"

"It was nothing." Luka takes my arm and attempts to step off the porch. Mentioning the doctor's name was impulsive, not to mention highly dangerous. There's a national alert out on me, and those national alerts include Dr. Roth's suicide.

But I dig in my heels and repeat what I said. It's obvious she knows something.

"If I were you," she says. "I'd stay far away from that man."

Luka stops pulling my arm.

"You knew him?" I ask.

"Of course I knew him. He was supposed to help my husband."

So this is Dot, the wife. "Can we speak to him?"

"If you want to speak to Josiah, you'll have to go to the cemetery. He died years ago." The door slams with such force, I have no chance at holding it open. Locks click back into place. That is all the information we will get on Josiah Aaronson.

Back in the cab, Luka tells our driver to head south. He doesn't look at me the entire drive, not once.

My remorse is profound.

My careless blurting got us nowhere. Dot Aaronson could be reporting us to the police right now. Surely they will put two and two together and realize that Tess is in the city, and Luka Williams is accompanying her. I want to apologize, but I can't. Not with our cab driver within such close proximity. By the time we arrive at our destination, so much regret has pooled inside my stomach I feel waterlogged.

The townhouse at Gabriel's address is in better shape than Dot's home. The signs of wear and tear are less pronounced and offset by nice curtains in the windows and a clean welcome mat out front. Luka knocks on the door. A deep bark sounds from the other side. Nobody answers. He knocks again. The barking turns into a growl.

A gust of frigid air blows up the walkway. Luka turns back to our cab, motioning for me to go ahead of him. He stops in front of the mailbox, checks to see if the cab driver is watching, then quickly peeks inside. The envelopes are all addressed to a Miss Loraine Seymore. Wherever Gabriel lives now, it's not here.

With dwindling hope, we drive to our last stop—Claire Bedicelle. Twelve at the time she saw Dr. Roth, eighteen now. She lives in a smaller suburb further south. As we reach the outskirts of Detroit, Luka relaxes a little, as though the oppression of the city no longer drags at his shoulders. Our cab driver stops in front of a snow-covered yard and a home that reminds me of Leela's. The woman who answers the door looks like an older version of the girl's picture in the file. Wrinkles etch themselves around her eyes and mouth—the kind that look more the result of a hard life than old age.

"Sorry to bother you." Luka sticks his hands deep inside his coat pockets. "But we were wondering if Claire Bedicelle lives here."

The woman grabs the lapels of Luka's coat. "Have you seen her? Do you know where my daughter is?"

Luka totters back, alarmed. "No, ma'am, we don't."

The frantic hope on her face crumbles.

A man steps into view—a big, burly man of a man. He wears a scowl and a mustache. "Reporters are not welcome here. We've said all there is to say. Claire ran away years ago." He pulls his wife inside and slams the door shut.

Luka and I stare at nothing but the grain of a paint-chipped door.

So that's that.

Our mission resulted in three dead ends—a dead man, a missing man, and a runaway teenager. We make our way back to the hotel room, pay the exorbitant cab fare, and order room service for dinner. Luka barely speaks. In fact, he's hardly said anything since our run-in with Dot Aaronson. His silence turns my already frazzled nerves inside out. I pick at my turkey club while he sits on the bed, burger and fries abandoned by his side, scanning Gabriel's file as if he might be able to find something he hasn't already found.

"I'm sorry," I finally say. "I never should have brought up Dr. Roth's name. It was foolish." I have no idea why—maybe from the disappointment that has been today, or the weight of his growing disapproval, or the ache of missing my family—but tears gather in my eyes. I blink down at my plate and dissect a French fry.

He shuts the folder on Gabriel's dream journal, waits a beat, then opens the top drawer of the hotel room's nightstand and pulls out a thick phone book. "I think it's time to find Dr. Carlyle."

I'm not sure I'm ready to move away from my apology so quickly, but Luka is already turning to the C's. Turns out, there are thirty-five William Carlyles in the Detroit area, seven W. Carlyle's, and two Dr. Carlyle's, MD. We use the new phone we purchased at some smaller city in Iowa, not the hotel's phone, in case it's under surveillance, and start at the top of the list.

"Are you the Dr. William Carlyle who used to refer patients to a Dr. Charles Roth?"

Twenty-nine times, Luka's question is declined.

Twenty-nine times, my hopelessness steepens.

Then we reach the thirtieth.

"This is he." The voice on the other end of the line lilts up, making the statement sound more like a question than a certainty.

Luka and I look at one another. A spark of optimism meets in the center of our locked gaze.

"Hello?" The man says. "Is anyone there?"

We decided beforehand on the next question we would ask, should we happen upon the correct Carlyle. We figured this question would either be met with confusion, in which case we would hang up, or the answers we've been desperately seeking. Luka clears his throat. "Are you a believer?"

There's a long, agonizing pause. "May I ask who's calling?"

"A former client of Dr. Roth's."

Another pause—this one so stretched out that I'm positive he hung up. Or maybe he's keeping us on long enough to get a location of our phone call. I reach for Luka's hand. He needs to hang up. Now.

"Meet me at the coffee shop on Ninth and Main tomorrow morning at ten."

Before Luka can ask any more questions, there's a soft click. Dr. Carlyle has hung up. We have no idea if his invitation is a trap.

CHAPTER TEN

BEHIND THE DOOR

I'm assaulted by wolf whistles and vulgar innuendo as soon as I step outside of the cab. It's as though these street men have never seen a female before.

"Hey sweetheart, what you with him for?"

"Why don't you come over here and get yourself a real man?"

Luka drapes his arm around my shoulder, and since there's no fear in him, there's nothing from which the men can feed. They disperse. Several street vendors hassle us about buying knock-off purses and small bags of who-knows-what. I shrink into Luka's side while he gives them all a polite, but firm, "No thank you."

We head toward Ninth and Main, where a hole-in-the-wall coffee house advertises the city's best java on a dilapidated sign. Luka removes his arm from around my shoulder, opens the door, and motions for me to go ahead.

It's hot inside. Uncomfortably so. Up on the stage, a woman with the longest hair I've ever seen strums a guitar. A barista slouches behind the counter reading something on her phone. College-age students in berets and bowler hats play chess or hunch over laptops. Nobody looks twice at us in the doorway looking around for a man who might be Dr. Carlyle. The only problem is, we have no idea what he looks like. Nationality, age, general appearance—we know none of these things. He didn't stay on the line long enough to tell us.

Luka motions toward a man sitting alone at a table-for-two in the far corner—silver hair, wire-rimmed glasses, a pressed light blue button down shirt. The man stares back at us. After a short beat, he gives us a subtle nod. Luka must interpret it as an invitation, because he leads me through the clutter of tables.

The man looks older up close than he does from far away. There are age spots on his skin and his silver hair is thin on top, thicker on the sides. I'd guess him to be in his mid- to upper-sixties. "I didn't know there were two of you."

Luka pulls out the chair for me and snags one for himself from a nearby table. "You didn't give us a chance to explain."

Dr. Carlyle sets a small slip of paper on the table between us and slides it across the surface. He looks over both of his shoulders, then leans close. "The paper has an address at the top, with directions to another address below. You take a cab to the first address. Then you walk by foot to the second. Make sure nobody sees you or follows you. When you arrive, you go to the basement. At the end of the hallway, you'll find a red door. Knock on it, six times, like this." He knocks a pattern into the table. Two fast taps, pause, two fast taps, pause, two fast taps. "Keep doing that until somebody answers, and when they do, ask to speak with the captain. You can tell him I sent you."

"Who is the captain?" I ask.

"I'm sorry. That's as much as we have to say to one another." Dr. Carlyle stands, brushing his hands down his starched shirt to wipe away nonexistent crumbs. He wears pressed khaki slacks with a sharp, straight crease down the front of each leg, like he has a wife who irons his clothes and sets them out before he goes to work every day. It's what my mom does for my dad. The normalcy of it, in light of the situation we find ourselves in at the moment, makes me want to cry.

He grabs a black wool coat from the back of the chair. "How is my old friend?"

"Dr. Roth?" Luka asks.

Dr. Carlyle nods.

"Dead."

The doctor's arm pauses—half inside the sleeve of his coat, half out.

"Several days ago he was found hanging from a noose in his apartment. Authorities have ruled it a suicide."

Dr. Carlyle processes the news in silent stillness, one that is bloated with unspoken truth. We all know the authorities are wrong. Dr. Roth didn't kill himself. Dr. Carlyle slips his coat all the way on. "Please don't contact me again."

And with that, he heads to the exit, buttoning his coat as he goes.

Once we're safely inside another cab, Luka unfolds the note Dr. Carlyle slipped him across the table and recites the address. The cabbie's face twists up in disbelief. "You *wanna* go there?"

Luka double checks the slip of paper. So do I. Dr. Carlyle's scrawl is unusually tidy for a doctor—as if he took intentional care to write neatly so we wouldn't misread or second guess.

"Yes." Luka's neutral tone gives nothing away.

The cabbie isn't so good at neutrality. He shakes his head like we are a couple of fools and shifts the car into drive. "It's your funeral."

Our funeral?

What exactly are we getting ourselves into? As we wind our

way through the heart of the city, a million questions ping around inside my head. How can we trust Dr. Carlyle? What if he's leading us somewhere dangerous? Why couldn't he tell us anything? Who is the captain and what if this whole thing is one giant trap? I pull my coat sleeves over my hands to keep from scratching the inside of my wrist raw.

My window refuses to roll up all the way. The sliver of a crack lets in cold air that sets my teeth to chattering. I want to draw nearer to Luka, snag some of his warmth. Ask him to put his arm back around me like he did when we were walking to the Java Hut. But he makes no move to join me on my side and I'm too chicken to join him on his. So I shiver while the cabbie turns down a street that looks much less like a street and much more like a war zone. My shivering stops, replaced instead by gaping.

The cabbie pulls to a stop at the start of the ramshackle strip in front of what appears to be the only shop still in business. A tattoo parlor with a giant dragon on the grimy window and a neon sign that flickers. *The Dragon Den.*

Luka peers outside. "This is it?"

"It's the address you gave me. You want me to wait here?"

I'm not even sure I want to get out at all.

"No," Luka says, his tone still casual. "We're good, thanks."

"Hope the needles are clean."

I give the cabbie a weak smile, then step out into the cold. A gust of wind pushes against my body. Luka pays the driver and the cab drives away. Neither of us move until the car turns out of sight. Luka looks down at the slip of paper and motions for me to follow him.

My teeth resume their chattering. "I'm not so sure about

this."

"It's our only option." He starts walking down the street. Away from civilization. I lengthen my stride to keep up. The place may have been a business district once upon a time. But now? Now it's nothing but crumbling buildings—many only half-built—with skeletal frames and busted windows and vulgar graffiti. We stick to the shadows, avoiding the sporadic homeless man or woman warming his or her hands over a garbage can fire. Staying unseen is not difficult. The street is mostly deserted.

The closer we get, the faster Luka walks, as if propelled forward by a force I cannot see or feel. I stumble a time or two on garbage and debris, but Luka is always close by to keep me upright. Finally, he stops. "This is it."

All I see is a large abandoned warehouse that must have suffered from a fire at one point in its existence. Black stains crawl up what little remains of the walls.

"I feel something."

"What?"

"Some sort of energy."

If I weren't popping pills, perhaps I'd feel it too. It's strange, these pills. Luka thinks they protect me, but at this moment in time, I feel vulnerable. Blind, even. "Is it good or bad?"

"I'm not sure." He walks behind me as I maneuver through the rubble—close enough that should I fall, he will be there to catch me—until we're standing inside a building that is all cement and debris and rows upon rows of empty shelves. Whatever the place used to store is long gone.

"Over here." Luka leads us to an exit sign above a doorway with no door. It opens into a stairwell. I follow him down to the basement. Down, down, down. Deeper than any basement has any need to be. When we reach the last step, the air is deathly still, interrupted only by the sound of Luka's breathing and my own heartbeat. Down here in the bowels of this warehouse, I feel like Alice falling through the rabbit hole. Or perhaps I fell down that hole a long, long time ago and I'm only just realizing it now.

The dark corridor leads one of two ways. Luka pulls out the flashlight attachment on his Swiss army knife and shines it down both. The edge of the light's border reveals nothing but more hallway. He stands there for a moment with his eyes closed, then picks left. The hallway stretches on and on—a never-ending narrow cement prison without a door in sight. A few mice scamper near the edge of the wall, squeaking and skittering. When we finally reach the end, we stand in front of a steel door that isn't so much red as a faded, brownish pink.

My mouth goes cotton-ball dry. This has to be it.

Luka pivots around to face me, his shoes scritching against the floor. "I need you to promise me that if I tell you to run, you will run."

"What?"

"Before I knock on that door, I need to know that you will run if I say so."

I narrow my eyes. "Will you run too?"

"If I can."

My head begins to shake—slowly at first, then growing in fervor. If Luka is asking me to leave him behind, that is a promise I can't make. Never.

"Tess." He takes my hand between both of his and clutches my palm over his chest, dipping his chin so his gaze is more level with mine. "I can't knock on that door unless I know that you are safe."

I could never run away from him. Not in a million years. If Luka goes down, I will go down with him. If he refuses to leave me, then I refuse to leave him. But we cannot stand here forever, especially not when our answers might be on the other side of the door. I give him a small nod. Call me Tess, the liar.

Luka makes himself a shield between me and whatever potentially dangerous thing lies before us. He raises his fist and knocks in the way Dr. Carlyle instructed.

Knock, knock ... knock, knock ... knock, knock ...

Nothing happens. No sound. No movement.

Luka knocks again.

More nothing.

My breath escapes like a squeak. All of a sudden, in a moment of stunning clarity, I am overwhelmingly positive that we have lost it. Our marbles have gone and rolled away. We're standing in the basement of an abandoned warehouse in Detroit, Michigan facing a door that has nothing but empty space on the other side.

Luka wipes his palms against his jeans then raps his knuckles against the steel for the third time.

Knock, knock ... knock, knock ... knock, knock ...

One second, two seconds, three seconds, four seconds pass us by.

I shift my weight, dread sinking into the very soles of my feet. "Luka."

But he holds up his finger.

A loud click echoes into the hallway. It's followed by a groan, like rusty metal hinges. And amazingly, miraculously, the door opens. A somber-faced man with impossibly broad shoulders stands on the other side. His wide nose, bald head, and dark eyes are vaguely familiar.

Luka shifts so I am more decidedly behind him. "We're here to see the captain."

If the request comes as a surprise, it doesn't show on the man's face. His lack of expression reminds me of the sentries that stand guard outside the Queen's palace in London. It's the kind of stillness that makes me want to poke him in the ribs, just to see if he'll respond. "Who sent you?" he finally asks in a voice that is deeply baritone.

"Dr. Carlyle."

He looks from Luka to me, tells us to wait here, then closes the door in our faces.

I gape at the steel, unable to believe what just happened. I didn't actually expect that we'd find life on the other side. Yet there it was, in the form of a formidable-looking man who I can't seem to place, even though I'm positive I've seen him before. The rabbit hole just got deeper. What, exactly, have we found? Was that man one of *the others* Dr. Roth told us about? And if he—so foreboding in stature—isn't the captain, then what can Luka and I expect when we meet the man presumably in charge?

Seconds tick into eternity.

So much time passes that I begin to think I imagined the entire thing. Perhaps I'm experiencing a long, drawn-out hallucination, and when it goes away, I'll be in that white box of a room at the Edward Brooks Facility with that annoyingly sweet nurse smiling down at me, ready to feed me my medicine. How can I possibly trust a life that's morphed into something so bizarre?

The door groans open again.

I expect a man larger, more intimidating than the one we

met first. I look up and see nothing. Confused, my attention travels down, until it lands on a man sitting in a wheelchair. He has salt-and-pepper hair buzzed short like Luka's and strange skin—leathery in texture, yet deathly pale in color, as though he hasn't seen the sun in years. And his legs? The muscle has atrophied. He looks shrunken in his chair—a man with no strength at all. But his eyes tell a different story. They are every bit as captivating as Luka's, only instead of grass green, they are a silvery blue.

I've seen them before. In a picture I've been staring at on and off now for several days. I step around Luka, coming into full view. I can't help myself. It's not every day you encounter a ghost. "You're Josiah Aaronson."

His steely eyes remain steady and unyielding. "Down here, people call me Cap."

CHAPTER ELEVEN

THE HUB

J osiah—or Cap—leads us inside a large common room with
high ceilings. My shock gives way to wonder, because there's
electricity. And the vague impression of heat. And people. They
stare at Luka and me with faces mirroring my own startled
curiosity. Apparently, visitors are not a common occurrence
here, wherever *here* is.

Cap wheels further inside the room, then pivots his chair
around and spreads his arms wide. "Welcome to the hub."

I take in the arrangement of shabby couches and beaten-up
desks shoved against the walls, a foosball table off in the back
and a sizeable television attached to more wires than any
television ought to require near the front. I feel like a five-year-
old in a gadget store. My fingers tingle with the need to touch
and explore. "What do you do here?"

"Among other things, we live." Cap nods at the man who
greeted us. He stands off to the side of the door with his feet
shoulder-length apart, muscular arms crossed in front of his
muscular chest. "That's Gabe."

"Wait—Gabe? As in Gabriel Myers?"

If my knowledge of his full name comes as a surprise, Gabe
hides it well. His face doesn't even twitch. Luka takes my hand
and gives it a short squeeze, as if to silence my disbelief. But I
can't help myself. The discovery has my pulse racing. This is
Josiah and Gabriel, two of the three we've been looking for.

Two of the files marked with TG.

I glance again at the others—their faces every bit as pale as the moon, wearing clothes every bit as worn as the furniture— each one still standing in place as though they froze as soon as they heard the knock on the door and have yet to thaw. Is the third file—a teenage girl named Claire with a mother all too desperate to find her—somewhere among them?

"We seem to be at a disadvantage," Cap says. "You know us. We don't know you."

Luka steps forward and shakes the captain's hand. "I'm Luka. This is Tess."

"We met your wife," I say.

Cap's eyebrows creep up his forehead.

"She thinks you're dead."

"Tess," Luka mutters.

Josiah's face tics—with regret, maybe? It comes and goes so quickly I can't tell. All the questions that have been gathering over the past several days expand in my brain like soda in a shaken can. The growing pressure has busted apart my self-control, and my shyness too. "We went to your house."

Cap narrows his eyes. "Why?"

"We're looking for answers."

"And protection," Luka adds.

He scratches the whiskers beneath his chin, studying Luka first, then me. I catch myself pulling my shoulders back, as if to make my body taller, more impressive-looking. "I can sense the gifting strongly in you," he says to Luka. "But I sense nothing in you."

The gifting.

I mouth the two words in silent awe. It's official. These are the others Dr. Roth was talking about. Against impossible odds, we found them. I feel like a kid who just reached base in a game of tag, temporarily safe from the chaser. Only multiply the relief by a thousand. I want to melt into a puddle of it at the captain's wheels.

"She's taking medicine that masks it," Luka says. "It was the only way I knew how to protect her."

Cap cocks his head. For some reason, he looks very intrigued by Luka's confession.

"We were clients of Dr. Roth."

Movement in the periphery of my vision has me looking away from the captain's reaction. One of the onlookers slips closer, either braver or more curious than the others. A baby-faced girl with obsidian eyes and dusky skin and black, shiny hair cropped short to her chin, like mine. Besides Gabe, she's the only other person in the room with some color.

Cap spots the girl, too, and waves her closer. "Rosie, this is Luka and Tess. Luka and Tess, this is Rosie, in case you don't already know her. She's the hub's youngest resident."

Rosie lifts her chin. "I'll be twelve in five months."

Cap chuckles, then calls the others over to join us. There are three besides Rosie. Two of them—a man and a woman—are old enough to sport a fair share of gray in their hair, but don't look quite as old as Cap. The man is NBA tall and gives new meaning to the phrase *as skinny as a beanpole*. The woman has a pointy head and bushy hair that seems to grow at a thirty-degree angle. The two features together give her a triangular silhouette. I recognize them. Not from any files of Dr. Roth's, but from a news report from last night. According to the police, they are highly deranged and dangerous criminals at large in the city. If I hadn't seen the news back in California, claiming me to be the very same thing, I might be afraid. The news reporter referred to them as Mr. and Mrs. Scott and Winona Jamison, but Cap introduces them as Sticks and Non. The third is a boy who looks to be a year or two older than me. The fluorescent lighting gives his shaggy hair a ginger-like hue. He looks at us with a healthy dose of amusement, like our unexpected drop-in has brightened his day.

"And this is Link," Cap says.

"*Link?*"

My reaction to the name makes the boy smile. Seriously though, the names are weird down here. Non, I get. It's short for Winona. Sticks, I'm assuming, has something to do with the stork-like stickiness of his legs. Link, though, I can't figure out, unless it's the kid's last name.

Before I can ask, Luka quickly shifts his body so he's standing between me and whatever is to the left. I peek around him and notice that someone else has entered the room—an impossibly familiar girl. "Claire?"

She stops.

Further proof that I am right. Our third file in the flesh, only six years older, with a white-blonde braid hanging loosely down her back. She is tall and thin with wiry muscles and heart-shaped lips. While the paleness of everyone else's skin gives them a ghostly glow, this girl wears it like royalty. Even with zero makeup, she possesses a beauty I could never pull off. Her attention strays from me to Luka, and the open interest that settles in her eyes has me feeling possessive. I want to take his hand and claim him as mine. Too bad my bout of unfiltered boldness does not extend to the boy beside me.

"Come on over," Cap says to the girl. "You have some new friends."

Claire approaches warily. "I've never met them in my life."

"It is curious, isn't it?" he asks, peering up at us from his chair.

"Dr. Roth left us files," I explain, eager to dispel the distrust growing in all of their expressions. "Three of them were yours."

"That's what led us to Dr. Carlyle," Luka says.

"And then you," I add.

"Why would Dr. Roth give you files?" Cap asks.

"He was murdered. We think he left the files behind for us to find."

Silence descends in the wake of Luka's news. Dr. Roth's three former clients—Cap and Gabe and Claire—all exchange narrow-eyed glances. I never would have guessed that when Dr. Carlyle handed over his directions, he was leading us to an underground headquarters for the dead, the missing, and the highly deranged. It's all too much to process.

"Rosie," Cap finally says, "why don't you give our new guests a tour?"

Rosie takes up her role with a sense of authority too big for her small body. I look back at the adults in the room—the captain, Gabe, Sticks, and Non—conferring near the door in hushed tones. As curious as I am to see the operation they have here, I don't want a tour nearly as much as I want to stay behind and ask my questions. But Luka puts his warm hand on the small of my back and ushers me after our Arabian-looking tour guide.

"This is the common area," she says. "It's where most of the students hang out after classes and training and stuff."

"Wait—*most* of the students? How many people are here?" And they go to school?

"There's sixteen of us altogether. Anyone under age goes to class in the morning." Rosie rolls her eyes, as if she'd rather do anything but go to class, and heads down the dank corridor from where Claire came. It smells like must and cement.

"What kind of classes?"

"All the regular stuff—English, Math, Current Events. Non's *obsessed* with history. Timelines make her giddy. Sticks, on the other hand, is a big fan of independent research projects." Rosie scrunches her nose. "All I care about is The Gifting."

There. Those words again. It sounds so strange to hear them roll so easily off this stranger of a girl's tongue. I want to ask about The Gifting. I'm still not sure what it even means, but I don't know how or where to start. And I don't want to sound dumb. I look at Luka. I can tell by the stiff set of his shoulders and the quick movement of his eyes that he doesn't care much about Rosie's commentary. Unlike me, he seems unconvinced that we have reached the safety of base. "How long have you guys been down here?"

"A while." Rosie stops in front of the first opened door. The room is filled with several laptops, a large supercomputer of sorts, a police scanner, and a host of other gadgets—all wired and blinking with life. "This is the computer lab. Everything is password protected. Anybody who wants to use a computer has to go through Link first. He's the unofficial tech-head of the hub. He can hack into anything."

"What does he hack into?"

"Lots of stuff." Rosie continues down the hall, stopping at two school-like rooms as we go. There are no individual desks, but a few longer tables with old chairs and makeshift chalk-boards. Maps and a globe. A collection of outdated books.

There are, of course, no windows, seeing as we are so far underground.

"Do you ever get to go outside?" I ask.

"*I* do."

"Only you?"

"Me and Bass. We're the hubs' official runners."

"What's a runner?"

"We get to go out into the world. Gather supplies and deliver messages. We always go alone, so we don't draw attention to ourselves."

"You mean you wander around the streets of Detroit by yourself?" Surely the captain realizes how much danger he's putting Rosie in by sending her out into the city without the protection of a stronger, older adult. It makes me question his judgment.

"There are advantages to being small. And I'm tougher than I look." She flashes an impish grin, then leads us into a smaller room filled with books—shelves and shelves of them, their spines worn and faded. I spot some of my favorites. They are like a bowlful of buttery mashed potatoes, the best kind of comfort food. The next room is filled with weight machines and several treadmills. Across the hall, there's a mat room that smells like Clorox and sweaty feet. It reminds me of the dojo Mom and I went to in Thornsdale. One door down, Rosie shows us a room that is locked. Luka and I peer through the window. Except for a few chairs that resemble the chairs you would find in a dentist's office, the space is mostly empty.

"This is the training center. Nobody gets in without Cap's permission."

Luka quirks his eyebrow.

He seems to be as baffled as I am. I mean, if any room were

to be a training room, you'd think it'd be the one with the weights or the mats. "Training for what?"

"You'll see." Rosie's impish smile turns more impish as she beckons us ahead and turns off the main corridor, into an antechamber of sorts. I hear murmuring—signs of life. She points out the restrooms—male and female, complete with showers. "This is the boys' hall," she says, nodding in the direction of the narrow hallway that leads left. "And that is the girls' hall." She points to the narrow hallway to the right. "Cap doesn't like any purpling."

My brow furrows. "What is purpling?"

"Boys are blue. Girls are red." She threads her fingers together, so that her hands are linked as one and scrunches her nose again, like purpling is the last thing she'd ever want to do. "After lights-out, there's no boy-girl mingling. Claire thinks Cap's too old fashioned. She tried sneaking into Link's room once, but she got into big trouble."

I glance at Luka. He's turned into Gabe—expressionless yet attentive. Rosie said sixteen people live down here. Judging by the number of doors down each corridor, there is plenty of room to grow. She turns us around and points out yet another hallway. "This is where the adults stay, including the Cloaks. You know what a Cloak is, right?"

Luka and I shake our heads.

"They hide our location from the other side. We only have two of them and since the hub's pretty big, it's a lot of work. They keep to their rooms mostly."

My mind pops with questions. The other side? Does this mean Scarface can't find me down here? Is Luka a Cloak? Am I? *Pop, pop, pop,* until I'm standing in front of another room, not quite as large as the common area and humming with life.

We have found the rest of the hub's population. Students mill about tables of varying shapes and sizes. The noise slowly fizzles into silence as one by one each person nudges the person beside them, nodding toward me and Luka and Rosie standing in the doorway.

"This is where we eat," Rosie says. "There's a kitchen off to the side there. We take turns with meal prep and clean-up." She points toward a makeshift counter in front of an opened door, which leads, I assume, into the kitchen. "Dinner's in twenty. There're some other rooms I haven't shown you yet, but we should probably get back to Cap."

We make our way through the underground labyrinth until we're back in the common area. Cap and Gabe are where we left them. Everyone else, however, has dispersed. There must be more than one way to the cafeteria, since we never passed Sticks or Non or Claire or Link.

Cap wheels toward us. "What do you think of the place?"

"I think we'd like to stay, if you have room for two more." This is the first time Luka has spoken since our tour began. His voice rings with a certainty I rarely ever feel. It's one of the things that makes him so appealing, I think. He possesses a confidence that can't help but instill confidence in those around him.

"Where were you staying before you came?" Cap asks.

"Hotel Magnum, next to the Greyhound station."

"You need to go back. Clear out your stuff and check out. We can't have the hotel manager reporting you missing. Don't leave behind a trace that you were there."

My pulse quickens. I've never been in a hurry to leave base. As a kid, Pete and his buddies used to kick me out of the game for staying on too long. I'm no different now.

"When you come back, make sure nobody follows you."

Luka nods grimly. Some strange look of understanding passes between him and the captain. For whatever reason, it makes me uneasy. Luka slips his arm around my waist and kisses my forehead. His touch has been so sparse that the generosity of it now chases away all my thoughts. I close my eyes and melt against him, relishing the firmness of his body, the softness of his lips, the strength of his broad palm against my waist. And then he whispers something in my ear so softly the words are barely more than a breath. "Don't reveal too much."

I process the cryptic warning like a hiccup.

Luka lets go of my waist and strides to the door.

Clarity comes like a glass of ice water to the face. He means to go without me. He's going to leave me behind. I take a step toward him, but Cap grabs my arm.

Gabe unlocks the bolt.

The splash of metaphorical water morphs into a wave, or maybe a tsunami. He can't go out there alone, unprotected. "Luka!"

He turns around, his eyes full of apology. "You're safer here."

I attempt to yank my arm free, but Cap's grip is unnaturally strong. "Luka, don't leave!" Splitting up is a horrible idea. A terrible, horrible, no good, very bad idea. I have this sudden, sinking dread that he won't return. That we will never see each other again. "Luka, please!"

He doesn't look back. He doesn't seem to hear me at all.

Chapter Twelve

Rarities

C ap hands me off to Gabe. No matter how much I twist and pull, I am not strong enough to escape his unyielding grip on my arm. He drags me behind Cap's wheelchair and doesn't let go until we reach the small cafeteria. And even then, he lets go very slowly, as if gauging to see whether or not I will turn around and bolt toward the exit. I'd try if I wasn't positive he would catch me and drag me back again.

After a subtle nod from Cap, Gabe pivots around and returns from where we came. A sense of hopelessness sinks like an anchor through my chest. Base, it turns out, is no longer base at all, but a prison. One with no sunlight and no Luka. What if he never returns? What if he's caught by the police or killed by a criminal? What if he finally comes to his senses, and now that I'm safe, decides to return to Thornsdale and live the normal life I've been urging him to live? That last option should make me rejoice, but I am a selfish creature. The thought of never seeing him again turns breathing into an impossible task.

I'm so lost in my frantic storm of what-ifs that it takes several beats before I realize the cafeteria has fallen into silence. I am the new girl all over again. Everyone stares at me, sandwiched between Cap and little Rosie. The thick scent of garlic hangs in the air. I haven't eaten anything since continental breakfast early this morning. I should be past the point of hungry. But I can't drum up even a hint of appetite.

Cap rolls ahead, nodding for me to follow. When we reach the makeshift counter, he hands me a tray. The person behind the counter serves us each a tong-full of noodles, a ladle of marinara sauce, a slice of garlic bread, and an empty plastic cup. Rosie and I follow Cap as he wheels to a faucet that looks more like an outdoor hose spigot. He fills his cup, then wheels away to sit with Sticks and Non without a single word of comfort or explanation. I eye the door, wondering if now's the time to make my escape. Maybe I can slip out unnoticed and find a way to get past Gabe.

Rosie fills up my cup, then hers, and snags my attention with a nudge. I follow her to the largest of all the tables, where the boy named Link leans back in his chair, the front two legs tipped off the floor. Claire sits beside him, looking regal with her long straight nose and her white-blonde braid. Rosie takes a seat between a large, swarthy boy with a unibrow and a girl with a nose as large and pointy as a rat's. I take the open spot beside Link, which has Claire eying me like vermin just sat down at the table. It's hard to care when I'm so preoccupied with my own turmoil. Since Luka broke me out of the Edward Brooks Facility a week ago, we've only been apart once, and that was for a frantic five-minute span when I tried running away. Being without him now, his warning still fresh in my ear, has me questioning which way is up.

Don't reveal too much.

Does he not trust these people? The medicine from the pills still runs through my veins, which means he can feel and see things I cannot currently feel and see. But then, why would he leave me with people he doesn't trust? If there's one thing I'm certain of, it's that Luka cares about my safety. He wouldn't have left if he thought I was in danger. So then, what did he mean by his warning?

Link tips his chair down so all four legs hit the ground. "Where's your guy friend?"

"Um …"

"He left to check out of the hotel they were staying at." Rosie sticks a forkful of noodles into her mouth and chews enthusiastically.

I watch Link for a reaction—anything that might tell me whether or not I'm overreacting about Luka's departure, but all he does is nod toward the swarthy boy across from him. "That's Jose. And that's Jilly-bean. You already know Claire."

"It's Jill*ian*, actually." The girl with the rat-like nose gives Link a good-natured eye roll, then studies me with such exuberance, I'm reminded of Leela. How is my friend? Did she get caught helping us? I'll never be able to forgive myself if she did. "It's great to finally see a fresh face. Things can get pretty monotonous around here."

"Things were fine the way they were," Claire says.

I ignore the barb and glance at the door, willing Luka to walk through, but I know it's a foolish hope. He's probably not even reached the tattoo parlor on the street corner yet. I pick up a fork and twist noodles around my plate as the pricks and prods of curious onlookers slowly melt away.

Jillian sets her elbows on the table. "So what's your gifting?"

"Um—my *gifting*?"

"Yeah. Are you a Guardian or a Fighter?"

The question reminds me of a dream I had a long time ago. Wrestling one of those white-eyed men off the Golden Gate Bridge. He called me a fighter as we tumbled through the air. Is this what I am? "I—I guess I don't know what you mean."

Rosie swallows a big bite. Her plate is almost empty. "Up until a little bit ago, she didn't even know what a Cloak was. I don't think she really knows anything."

Had anyone besides Rosie made the statement, I would have resented it. I know *some* things. To prove my point, I start a mental list. The supernatural realm is real. Luka and I are part of The Gifting. There are others, which we have found. There are regular folk who believe, like Dr. Roth and Dr. Carlyle, who call themselves believers. I bite my lip, searching for more. Okay, so maybe Rosie is more right than I want her to be. My list is sparse.

"There's no shame in not knowing," Jillian says, wrapping her fingers around her glass. "None of us knew much when we came. But you'll learn quick enough. At least if Sticks and Non have anything to say about it."

I pull off a piece of garlic bread, roll it into a small, dense ball between my fingers, and force it in my mouth. I may be too adrenaline-logged for an appetite, but that doesn't mean my body doesn't still need sustenance. I glance at the table Cap sits with Non and Sticks. Their heads are bent close together. Luka said not to reveal much, but he never warned against asking questions.

"What are you?" I ask Jillian.

"Just a Shield."

"Oh come on, Jilly-bean. You're not *just* a shield." Link flicks some bread crust at her. It lands in front of Rosie, who picks it up and pops it in her mouth without missing a beat. "It's an important job."

"Not as important as fighting." There's no shame or longing in her words, simply matter-of-fact resignation—as though what she says is fact and there's no refuting it. "Claire and Jose are the only underage Fighters at the hub."

"Jose's not a very good one," Claire teases.

He smirks at his tray. "We can't all be like you."

Jillian forks what's left of her noodles onto Rosie's empty plate. "The rest of us are Guardians. Our role is to protect, not fight."

"I thought you said you were a Shield."

"I am. A Shield is a type of Guardian. The most common. That's what Rosie and I are." Jillian smiles at her young friend with the robust appetite. Perhaps there's something to be said about sunlight and metabolism. "With the proper training, we can shield Fighters against attack."

This explains things. Neither Luka nor I understood why our gifting manifested itself so differently. Well, now I do. We're different types—I'm a Fighter and he's a Shield. "What are the other kinds?"

"You know about Cloaks," Rosie says around her last mouthful.

"We only have two. Anna and Fray." Jillian points across the cafeteria. "They're over there."

I follow the direction of her finger. At the smallest table sits a woman with gray, coarse hair pulled back into a messy bun. It looks as though she slept on it and never bothered to redo it. A man, considerably younger, sits across from her, looking every inch his name. Neither of them talk. They both stare off into space with a dazed-sort of expression, like they've forgotten something and are concentrating really hard on recalling what it is. "What's wrong with them?"

"Nothing's *wrong* with them," Claire says. "They're working."

"They're always working." Link flicks his head, a quick

gesture that shakes shaggy bangs from his eyes. "It's why we're looking for more. It's been a tough search. Cloaks are a rarity. And dead useful, too."

I break off another piece of bread and roll it into a ball, remembering what Rosie said on the tour guide. Something about how they hide us from the other side.

Jillian leans over the table. "Imagine being constantly distracted. A part of their mind has to be aware of their job at all times. Carrying on a conversation with them can be ..."

Link's mouth curls up in the corners. "Entertaining."

I look over my shoulder and study them openly. I could probably stare for hours and they wouldn't notice. "How do they sleep?"

"Not very well," Rosie says, her eyes on my mound of uneaten spaghetti.

I scoot it over to her. "So that's it—Shields and Cloaks?"

"There's one more type of Guardian, but they're even rarer than Cloaks." Jillian's words seem to send a ripple of excitement around the table. "They're called Keepers."

"Created for the sole purpose of protecting one person," Link says. "When they find that one person, they don't have to be trained or taught. Their powers come like a reaction."

Goose bumps march across my arms.

Claire rolls her eyes. It's not nearly as good-natured as Jillian's. "Link calls them 'soul mates'."

Jillian clasps her hands beneath her chin and sighs. "I think it's romantic."

I run my teeth over my bottom lip and touch the hemp bracelet around my wrist—the one Luka put there. "Why are Keepers so rare?"

"Because," Jillian's eyes dance, "only the most powerful Fighters have them."

Jose has dish duty. After dinner, he heads to the kitchen. I stack my tray on a cart that a girl with dishwater-blonde dreads and a small diamond nose ring rolls around, then follow my dinner-mates through the hub with nerves that grow increasingly jumpy. I'm the strangest combination of bereft and giddy. It's true when they say knowledge equals power. After what I learned in the cafeteria, I feel like I have a handful of it in my back pocket.

And I want more.

My thoughts circle around the dinner conversation like hungry buzzards as we meander toward the common room. Keepers don't have to be trained. Nobody trained Luka when he protected me with that strange force field. But only the most powerful Fighters have Keepers, so there's no way Luka can be one. His ability to protect me without training is simply a matter of Luka being Luka. There's nothing he's not good at. Take football, for example. He wasn't even on the team back in Thornsdale and yet he could throw further than the varsity quarterback.

When we arrive, Jillian introduces me to the five I haven't yet met—three girls, one of whom is the dishwater blonde with dreads. Her name is Ellen. Then there's a scrawny boy named Bass (like the fish) with eyes as hard as marbles, and a fiery-headed freckled kid named Declan whose resemblance is so uncannily similar to Dustin O'Malley back in Jude I'm reminded of the séance that started everything—my family's cross-country move to Thornsdale, appointments with Dr. Roth at the Edward Brooks Facility. Meeting Luka.

I nod hello to all of them, but am unable to keep up any resemblance of a coherent conversation. Perhaps they will mistake me for a Cloak. I keep peeking at Gabe and the door, trying to guess how much time has passed. I find a spot on a couch furthest away from the hubbub and let my conflicted thoughts wander in disjointed circles. I shouldn't want Luka to come back. In light of all this supernatural talk, I should be praying him onto the next Greyhound bus back to Thornsdale. But his absence has left a physical ache inside my chest. I stare so intently at the door, I don't bother checking to see who sits next to me when the cushion sinks with weight.

"Do you have x-ray vision?" The question belongs to Link.

"Is x-ray vision part of The Gifting?"

"You have no idea how much I wish it were."

I let out a tense breath, an attempt at laughter.

"He'll be back, if that's what you're worried about."

"I shouldn't want him to be."

Link raises his eyebrows.

Don't reveal too much. Those were Luka's instructions. How can I possibly unpack my statement to Link without doing exactly that? I bury my face in my hands and attempt to recover the fumble. "He should wait to come back until morning. Detroit isn't a very safe place to wander around at night." Never mind the supernatural realm and whatever forces of evil exist within it, there are real-life, tangible dangers up there on those streets—including but not limited to muggers and gang members. "How do we know he hasn't been stabbed and robbed, left to bleed out in some abandoned alleyway?"

"Now there's a morbid thought."

"What's a morbid thought?"

I remove my hands from my face.

Jillian leans between us, her elbows propped on the backrest of the couch.

"Tess is worried her boyfriend has been stabbed to death."

"Boyfriend?" Jillian hops over the back of the couch like a female Jack-be-nimble and sits cross-legged on the other side of Link. "Tell me more so that I can live vicariously through you."

"Luka and I aren't—we're not exactly ..." A slow burn moves its way from my cheeks into my ears. "He's not my boyfriend." We may have used that excuse in Thornsdale as a cover up for our unusual relationship, but there's no reason for that here. Sure, we've kissed a couple times—a thought that makes the burn creep up into my forehead—but that's always been in the wake of an extreme bout of relief. Luka relieved to see me after we broke into Shady Wood. Luka relieved that his nightmare wasn't real. Relief and attraction are easily confused things. We spent the night together alone in a motel room, followed by an entire day, most of which was spent sitting in the same bed. He never tried kissing me then.

Jillian looks disappointed.

I scratch the inside of my wrist, then pull my sleeves over my hands. Off to one side of the common room, Rosie stands as one point of a three-person triangle, kicking a Hacky Sack into the air with Declan and Bass. Ellen sits off in the corner, reading a book. Claire and the other two girls huddle around the television. Sticks and Non pop up on the screen. Number one and number two on FBI's Most Wanted List. Link lets out a whoop, like it's a funny joke.

"So what are *you*?" I never got around to inquiring about his gifting over dinner.

"I thought you'd never ask." He props his arm along the backrest of the couch. "What do you think I am?"

I look him up and down. "You're too cognizant to be a Cloak. Jillian didn't include you with the Shields or the

Fighters ..." I shrug, at a loss. Surely if he were a Keeper, someone would have said so when the topic arose over plates of spaghetti.

"Link's a complete freak," Jillian says.

He picks up a pillow and whaps her in the face. "I prefer *one of a kind.*"

"Does your *kind* have a name?"

"Andrew."

"Huh?"

"My name's not really Link. It's Andrew."

"So why are you called Link?"

"Because that's what I do—I link people."

I must look every bit as confused as I feel, because Jillian rushes to explain. "Fighters can only cover a certain amount of area. The more powerful the Fighter, the more territory they can cover."

"Imagine it like this." Link holds out his left hand, palm up. "If Claire's here, in Detroit, she can't fight in New York. She can't even fight in Chicago. Fighters are bound by geography. But let's say you have two fighters. One in Detroit, another in Chicago." He holds out his right hand, palm up, then brings both hands together. "I can link them. That way, they can cross over into each other's territories and help each other fight."

"A lot more ground is covered," Jillian says.

"And that's only the tippity-top of the iceberg. I have many more skills up my sleeve."

Another memory wiggles into consciousness. It's from a dream not too long ago, when I watched Pete nearly lose his life in a car pile-up. Off in the distance, I saw somebody else fighting against the evil causing the mayhem. Did somebody link us? And who was the Fighter? "Are you sure you're the only one?"

"The only one down here." Link shrugs. "The best thing about being me? I'm completely under the radar. I can link to kingdom come and the other side has no idea what's going on. They don't seem to notice me as part of The Gifting at all. I'm like an undercover agent for the good guys."

"Link thinks he's invincible," Jillian says.

"I don't think, Jilly-bean. I *know*."

CHAPTER THIRTEEN

REUNITED

The longer Luka's absence, the stronger my anxiety. The news ends. The Hacky Sack circle grows. Link moves from my couch to Claire's. The two flirt the same way Luka and Summer used to flirt, back when I was the new girl at Thornsdale. Jillian scoots over to where Link was sitting and explains the hub's social hierarchy while I half-listen.

"If you thought you escaped high school ridiculousness, think again. Claire is like the queen bee and Danielle and Ashley worship the ground she walks on. If she says jump, they want to know how high. And anybody who doesn't jump along with them gets the stink eye." Jillian shifts so that her left leg is tucked beneath her. "You'll want to be careful around them."

"Why?"

"Because Link likes you, and in case you haven't noticed, Claire's not really one to share a boy's affection. Especially not one she likes."

I give her a skeptical look. "He does not like me."

"He sure is paying attention to you. I'm just saying you should proceed with caution. She gets mean when she feels threatened."

I look at Claire—the high set of her cheekbones, her flawless complexion, the perfect symmetry of her face, the fluidity of her movements. She has no reason to be threatened by the likes of me.

Jillian explains where the others lie in this odd underground hierarchy—Jose, Declan, Ellen, Rosie, and Bass—then she peppers me with questions that I mostly answer in grunts and nods. After a valiant effort on her part, she gives up on any sort of two-sided conversation and joins the widening Hacky Sack circle. Then Cap rolls into the room and announces lights out in twenty minutes. The circle breaks apart. I remain seated, gnawing the inside of my lip raw while panic rises like a searing hot ball in my throat. If Luka doesn't return tonight, I'm convinced he won't return at all. And if that is the case, how will I ever know if his disappearance was voluntary or the result of a sinister encounter up above?

Cap clears his throat. Besides him and a surly-looking Gabe, only Jillian and Rosie remain in the common area. The rest have wandered off to their rooms. "Jillian, why don't you show Tess her new room? Non set it up for her after dinner."

I shake my head. Luka's absence has me feeling like I'm back in the white room at the Edward Brooks Facility. Like I can't tell what's real anymore. Perhaps if we had a chance to say more of a goodbye. Perhaps if I had some sort of closure, something more than *don't reveal too much*, something that would speak to his wellbeing now, I'd be able to make decisions. At the moment, I can't even breathe.

Cap rolls closer, and I catch myself glaring. He's the one who grabbed my arm. He's the one who prevented me from going after Luka. He's the reason I can't breathe right now. I stand from the couch. "I need to go."

"If he doesn't return by tomorrow, we'll send Rosie out to look for him."

No offense to Rose, but it's not a comforting thought. What could she possibly do to help Luka? And if he *is* in trouble, tomorrow will be too late. I need to figure out a way to convince Cap to let me go right now. The hot ball of panic grows into a boulder. Bad thoughts perpetuate bad thoughts. It's like a torturous spiral that feeds off itself. What if Luka's in trouble? What if Luka's hurt? What if Luka's crying out for help? What if Luka's dead? Just as I'm falling into a black hole of terror, a noise sounds through the common room. A glorious, amazing, life-affirming noise.

Knock, knock ... knock, knock ... knock, knock ...

My brain says to run to the door. To sprint toward the sound. My body, however, has frozen in place. And by the time I unfreeze myself and take a few steps forward, Gabe holds up his hand with such silent authority, it freezes me all over again. I look between him and the steel door, my heart punching bruises against my sternum. Why isn't he answering? What is he waiting for?

Knock, knock ... knock, knock ... knock, knock ...

It's the second pounding that gets him moving. He un-latches the bolt with a deafening click, then opens the door. Luka stands on the other side. He's never looked more irresistible. I can't help myself. Closing the gap between us, I launch myself into his arms. He lets out a short *oomph* as my body collides against his chest, then wraps me in a hug that lifts me off the ground. His lips graze the hollow of my ear. The touch sets my skin on fire. An ocean of warmth pools in my stomach as I tighten my arms around his neck. I never want to let go.

"You okay?" he whispers in a husky voice, one that is for me alone.

I nod into the crook of his neck. I am now.

He lets my body slide down his until my feet touch the

ground, and slowly, his arms release me. Oh, but I wish they wouldn't. I don't care that we have an audience. All I care is that Luka came back. He didn't leave me here by myself. He isn't hurt or dead in an alley. We are together and I'm able to breathe again. I remove my arms from around his neck and pull down the hem of my shirt.

Cap watches us in that same way Dr. Roth used to watch me whenever I explained to him one of my strange symptoms during our weekly therapy sessions—masked intrigue, as though something about our behavior is worthy of noting.

I'm dying to talk to Luka—to ask him what happened while he was out and tell him all that I've learned since he's been away. But Cap hands us over to Non, who leads us down the length of the boy's hallway and drops Luka off at a room at the end.

"I found some clothes from storage that I think should fit you. I usually have a pretty good eye for sizes." Non looks him up and down, as if mentally measuring him again. "If they're too big or too small, please let me know. We can find you something different. Bathroom's down the hall. Breakfast is at eight tomorrow morning. Classes start after."

And just like that, we're walking away from the boy I'm desperate to speak with. I look over my shoulder at him and he looks down the hall at me, but Non moves so matter-of-factly, there's nothing we can do. Lights will turn out in a couple minutes. I'll be in my hallway, Luka will be in his and according to Rosie, there will be no purpling.

My new dormitory is closest to the antechamber with the boy-girl restrooms. Non gives me the same spiel that she gave Luka and leaves me to myself, inside a room with bare walls and sparse furniture. When her footsteps recede into silence, I sit on the edge of the naked mattress, listening to the faint drip-drip of water somewhere behind my wall. A leaky pipe, I suppose. An empty ache burrows its way inside my heart. I miss my familiar bedroom in Thornsdale. I even miss the blare of Pete's angry music across the hall. The last pill I took was this morning, which means tonight I could have dreams.

I think about sneaking down the hallway, into Luka's room. But for all I know, Cap would kick us out for breaking the rules. Now that base feels safe again—with Luka back, I'm in no hurry to get the boot. I set my suitcase next to a faded comforter and matching faded sheets folded into a perfect rectangle at the end of my bed. I make quick work of unpacking my things, setting them inside the dresser drawers alongside the clothes Non picked out for me—all as faded as the sheets. By the time I make my bed, the pressure in my bladder needs to be addressed. I grab my bag of toiletries and sneak out into the hall.

The cement floor is cold against my bare feet as I tiptoe into the darkened antechamber. I make quick work of using the restroom, then slow down considerably when washing my hands at one of the sinks. My hair grows like a weed. It always has. In just a week, my dark roots show in the mirror's reflection, and although the hair dye box advertised permanency, the vibrant honey has faded from the brown. My face is thinner than normal, which makes my navy blue eyes buggier and my pointy chin pointier. I pull my hair back with a headband and rinse my face and brush my teeth. The normalcy of the routine offers a smidgen of comfort, until I look around at the dank underground bathroom and remember how very far away from home I am.

With fear germinating in my gut, I pack up my toothbrush and face wash. I know we are safe down here. Anna and Fray have hidden our location. No white-eyed men are lurking around the corner. No big burly government officials will drag me away. No nurses are waiting to jab needles into my neck. Still, I'm a teenage girl. And this is a creepy warehouse basement. I clutch my bag and hurry out into the antechamber.

Someone grabs my arm.

I let out a shriek that is quickly smothered by someone's hand. My nostrils flare, but my fear vanishes, because I smell wintergreen toothpaste. I don't have to turn around to see who has ahold of me.

When we reach my room, Luka pauses in the doorway, as if unsure how far he can bend Cap's rules. "I want to talk to you about something."

"Only something? Because I have a hundred things."

He grins. It's the first time I've seen it since we left California. The sight makes me feel fifty pounds lighter. Luka leans against the doorframe and crosses his arms. "By all means, then, go first."

"I know why our dreams are different." I sit on the edge of my bed. "Not everyone has the same gifting. There are different ... groups, I guess?" I tell him about Fighters and Guardians. I explain that Claire is a Fighter, along with a boy named Jose, and probably me too, although I didn't tell anybody. I explain that he is probably a Shield, then I move on to Anna and Fray and the oddity that is Link. The only information I keep to myself is that about Keepers. It feels silly to even suggest it. I don't feel exceptionally powerful. I don't even feel somewhat powerful. In fact, at the moment, I don't feel like a Fighter at all.

By the time I'm finished, he stands with his hands deep inside the pockets of his faded jeans, shoulders shrugged up by his ears, furrow between his brow.

I pull at my earlobe. "What was the something you wanted to talk to me about?"

He twists his lips to the side, then steps inside the room and sits beside me on the bed. "I'd like you to keep taking the pills."

The statement comes so out-of-the-blue, it takes me a few seconds to recover. "I thought we agreed the pills were a temporary fix."

"I know, but they're protecting you."

I don't want him to worry. I don't want to tell him no. Deep down, the scared, cowering, selfish part of me would love nothing more than to give in and say yes. Just one night, in this safe place, of peaceful sleep. It seems Luka could use it, too. But at what cost? "I'm safe here. I don't need the pills to hide me anymore."

"We don't know that."

"Luka …"

He drags his hands down his face. "I'm just asking you to consider it."

"People could be dying. My safety isn't worth that."

"Unpack that statement." The gruff voice belongs to Cap.

He's sitting in the doorway. I wait for a reprimand. It's well past lights out, and he's caught us inches apart on my bed. But he wheels inside my room looking more interested than angry. "How does this medicine affect life and death?"

I glance at Luka, then back at Cap. "The pills stop me from dreaming. And when I don't dream, I can't stop bad things from happening."

"So we have ourselves another Fighter."

I pick at a loose thread on my comforter, picturing the confident, regal way Claire carries herself, the impressive length of her limbs. She's thin, but it's a thinness that exudes power. Then there's Jose—the thick set of his neck and shoulders, the largeness of his hands as he ate his dinner. Compared to them, I can't imagine I'm a very good Fighter. In fact, the other side has nicknamed me Little Rabbit. It's an animal that is neither strong nor powerful. It's an animal that runs away at the first sign of danger.

"And you?" Cap turns his knife-like gaze upon Luka.

"From everything Tess has told me, it sounds like I'm a Shield."

Cap rubs the white whiskers on his chin. It makes a sound like peeling Velcro. "Then you will train with Non. And you, Tess, will train with Sticks. As soon as the medicine wears off."

"Train for what?" Luka asks.

"Our main purpose here is not survival."

I lean forward, eager to ask what their main purpose is then. Before I can get anything out, Cap sets his hands on top of his wheels. "Social hour's over. I don't want to catch either of you in each other's rooms after lights out again."

When Luka is gone, led away by Cap, I look at my pillow. A single, white pill sits in the center. I pick it up, measuring it's lightness in my hand. Luka wants me to take this. I'm more tempted than he knows. But there's something that keeps me from giving in. Cap said there would be training. I'm not eager to meet this night, but if training will make me stronger than the demons that haunt my dreams, then this medicine has to stop. There's a drain in the center of my room. I kneel in front of it and push the pill through the grate.

CHAPTER FOURTEEN

LEFT BEHIND

My eyes open with a start, like somebody shouted my name. A couple confused seconds tick past as I stare wide-eyed at a gray ceiling through hazy darkness, trying to gain my bearings. I am not in my bedroom in Thornsdale. Nor am I locked up at a mental hospital or awake in a motel room.

"Tess, are you alive in there?"

I turn toward the feminine voice muffled by the closed door. Artificial light filters in through the crack. I lurch upright in bed. I'm in the deep, dank bowels of an abandoned warehouse. A place called the hub—a sort of underground headquarters for people with the gifting. A gifting that can be masked by medicine. Medicine that Luka wanted me to keep taking. I look at the drain in the center of my room. Did I have any dreams last night? I recall the vaguest of impressions, which I suppose, is a start.

"Tess?" It's Jillian. She's outside my door. "If you don't make like a rock and get rolling, we're gonna miss breakfast."

Breakfast—already? Without any windows, time is terribly disorienting down here. I fling the covers off my legs and open the door to a flood of fluorescent light. Jillian steps back. I'm sure I look like a real winner, with a nest of tangled hair and probably sleep creases on my face.

"Remind me to get you a clock with an alarm from storage," she says. "If you hurry, we can still snag some food."

I'm not so much hungry as eager to find Luka. I quickly get dressed, brush my teeth, run a comb through my hair, and rinse off my face. When I'm finished, Jillian leads us toward the cafeteria, I presume. The underground corridors are every bit as confusing this morning as they were last night. "Does this place always feel like such a maze?"

"You'll get the hang of it soon enough." Jillian smiles brightly. Her face might still be glowing over the excitement of having two newbies at the hub, but her skin is the color of Elmer's glue.

"How long have you been down here?" I ask.

"Nineteen months, two weeks, and three days. Not that I'm counting or anything."

"You haven't been outside in all that time?"

"Nope. No sun for me. Non has us all on Vitamin D pills. To ward off depression, she says." She must catch a glimpse of the horror I'm wearing on my face, because she rushes on to continue. "But don't worry. It's not so bad. You'll get used to it, I promise."

The words offer little comfort. No outdoors for nineteen months? No fresh air on my face? No sun on my skin? The more I think about the future, the narrower the hall becomes. I want to set my palms against each wall and push them apart. This is better than being trapped in Shady Wood, I remind myself. I'm not shackled or medicated against my will. I'm not imprisoned in a white box of a room. Plus, I have Luka. He's more vital than a thousand suns.

"So, that boy who's *not* your boyfriend?" Jillian gives me a sideways peek. "He sure was happy to see you last night."

Was he? I was so preoccupied with my own relief that I didn't really consider his.

"The look on his face was like …"

I twist his hemp bracelet around my wrist. "Like what?"

"A really amazing scene from a romance novel."

My cheeks flush. I understand why Jillian would think that. I mean, it's Luka. The boy has his own verb back in Thornsdale, created by Bobbi and her friends. *Luka'd: the act of being captivated by Luka Williams.* It happened to me on my first day; it happened to numerous girls before me; it will probably continue to happen to many more in the future. And last night, I pretty much catapulted myself into that boy's arms.

Thankfully, the hum of cafeteria chatter saves me from having to formulate any sort of response to Jillian's observation. Cap, Sticks, and Non sit at the same table they sat last evening. Anna and Fray sit at another, her hair even messier than before. There's no sign of Gabe. (I'm really beginning to think he's more robot than human. Seriously, when does he eat?) And then the rest of the tables are scattered with students. I spot Luka in line with his back to me, getting served his breakfast by Claire.

Jillian leans toward my ear as we approach the counter. "Want a name refresher?"

"Uh, sure. That'd be great."

"Jose's the muscular Mexican. The scrawny, mean-looking kid sitting by Jose? That's Bass. Before he came to the hub, he was Detroit's most infamous pick-pocket, which means you'll want to watch your stuff around him. Declan's the redhead. The girl with the dreadlocks sitting by herself reading the book? That's Ellen. She doesn't talk much, but when she does, it's usually to quote Shakespeare."

I nod, like I'm paying attention. Really though, I'd like to know what Claire could be saying to Luka to make him loiter for so long.

"I told you about Ashley and Danielle last night. They're sitting with Link. Poor guy."

Both girls stare at Luka's back and whisper behind their hands. Funny that even here—in this underground world populated by people who are not at all normal—teenage girls are still teenage girls. The closer we get to Luka, the more my skin flushes. "Where's Rosie?"

"It's her errand day." Jillian picks up two trays. The motion has Luka turning around, and the second his attention lands on me, his entire demeanor melts with relief, as if he legitimately thought I might be kidnapped in the night.

"Hey," he says.

"Hi," I say back.

I try tucking a strand of hair behind my ear, but it's too short to stay put. "Luka, this is Jillian. Jillian, Luka."

He gives her a polite nod-smile combo that has Jillian's cheeks turning the color of Leela's favorite strawberry pink nail polish. Claire gives us each a ladle of colorless oatmeal, another of canned peaches, and Jillian leads us toward an empty table in the corner, away from the prying eyes of Danielle and Ashley.

"Did you get the pill I left behind?"

I nod, keeping my gaze pinned on the back of Jillian's off-white sweatshirt, thankful we reach the table before he has a chance to ask whether or not I took said pill. Breakfast is as tasteless as it looks. The only edible way to eat the meal is by mixing the peaches with the oatmeal, and while this makes the oatmeal cold, at least it's not quite so flavorless.

Once all the trays are stacked on the cart and everyone begins filtering out of the cafeteria, Non pulls Luka and I aside to give us the rundown—explaining the cycle of daily duties and the rules for all underage students. She puts extra emphasis on no purpling after lights out, which makes me suspect Cap told her that he found Luka in my room last night. She explains that training will be in the afternoon, then leads us down the corridor into one of the classrooms, where Sticks stands up front lecturing glassy-eyed teenagers. He barely pauses as we find empty seats at a table.

While my new bean-pole-of-a-teacher talks about some obscure war I've never heard of before, Luka twirls a pencil around the tip of his thumb. I try to listen to Sticks, but I'm much more intrigued by him than his words. In all my martial arts training, I've never once seen a man as tall as him in the dojo. His slacks stop short of his ankles, acting more like high waters than pants. I'm sure he has to make do with whatever clothes they can scrounge up and these are the longest they have. I try to imagine one of his long legs doing a round-house kick, but I can't picture it. Still, he must be a good Fighter if he's the one who does the training.

The question is—what, exactly, are we training for?

Morning classes drag into lunch. Jillian invites Luka and I to sit at the largest table in the cafeteria with Link and Claire and Jose. There's still no sign of Rosie. I stuff my mouth with peanut butter and jelly sandwich and carrot sticks, as if the quicker I eat, the faster the meal will end. All it gets me is a stomachache and time to spare. Nobody besides me seems to be in a hurry to start training.

My leg begins to jiggle.

Perhaps in an attempt to calm me, Luka places his palm

over my knee. And while it's the opposite of calming, it definitely distracts me from training. My *not-boyfriend* is touching the inside of my thigh. It has me sitting up straighter. Sucking in my stomach. Impossibly aware of the subtle way his thumb moves back and forth, stirring up heat in places that don't need to be stirred. Conversation floats about—all-too-normal-teenage banter that Luka joins when prompted. Me? I'm zeroed in on other things. Like what Jillian would say if she looked underneath the table. And not letting my eyes roll into the back of my head. If this goes on for much longer, I might melt into a puddle on the floor.

Finally, Non rolls around the cart collecting trays while Anna and Fray slip out unnoticed. Jillian excuses herself for cleanup in the kitchen. Luka removes his hand, but the impression he leaves behind remains. I begin to fidget—with my napkin, with Luka's hemp bracelet, with a hangnail I've found on my thumb. Do Fighters report to one room and Shields to another? Will Luka and I be given further instruction? By the time Sticks approaches our table with his long lanky stride, I'm sitting ramrod straight, raring to go.

"Need my services today?" Link asks him.

"Not today, I'm afraid," Sticks says.

Claire and Jose exchange disappointed looks.

"I hear I'll be getting a new student soon." Sticks may tip his chin at me, but all eyes turn to Luka. Apparently, if one of the newbies is a Fighter, I'm not the likely candidate. "I look forward to seeing what you're made of, Tess."

There's a beat of shocked silence as Sticks' comment sinks in, and then …

"Wait—*you're* a Fighter?"

I look Claire straight in her disbelieving face with my chin slightly raised. I can't tell if she's more shocked or appalled. There's definitely a healthy dose of both.

"Cap says once the medicine you've been taking leaves your system, you'll join us for training."

My posture wilts. I'd hoped to join them today.

"What do you do for training?" Luka asks.

"Looks like you'll get to find out this afternoon," I say dejectedly.

"I don't mean Shield training. I mean Fighter training."

Luka's words have everyone's attention sliding in my direction. My face blossoms with heat.

"The two aren't so different. A lot of the same concepts, anyway." Sticks gives my shoulder a paternal squeeze, then nods at his young apprentices. Jose and Claire follow him out of the cafeteria. To where, I haven't a clue. Non pushes the cart of trays into the kitchen, then collects the Shields. Luka doesn't budge.

"You should go," I say. "Maybe you can finally learn how to throw that force field thing you've been trying to throw."

My words hit their mark. "Are you sure you'll be okay?"

The question rubs me the wrong way. What does Luka think—that I can't survive without him for an afternoon? He sure didn't have a problem leaving me last night. "I'll be fine."

He gives me one last lingering look, then follows after Non and the rest of them. All that remains is the clatter of trays and the spray of water coming from the kitchen, and my one-and-only tablemate. Link folds his hands behind his head and leans back in his chair. "Tess the Fighter, huh?"

"I guess."

He wags his eyebrows at me. "Care to join me for a little research?"

CHAPTER FIFTEEN

THE PLAN

L ink spreads his arms wide. "Welcome to my lair."
We are standing inside the computer lab Rosie showed
me and Luka during our tour—the room with the password-
protected computers and other unidentifiable gadgetry with
wires running every which way. "How'd you get all this stuff?"

Link plops onto a desk chair with a gash on the seat. The
force rolls him and the chair toward the *piece de resistance* in the
center of the lab. A Rubik's Cube sits by the keyboard.

"Not without a lot of effort and planning." He boots up
the large supercomputer and the screen glows to life. "Dr.
Carlyle's a big help. Rosie and Bass, too."

"I don't understand why Cap lets the two smallest and
youngest people at the hub go above ground." You'd think he'd
send someone like Jose or Gabe. I can't imagine too many
would dare hassle them on the streets. Rosie and Bass on the
other hand? It's a wonder they have made it this long.

"It's because they have the most street smarts." The screen,
now fully lit, casts an ethereal glow onto Link's profile. He
types a code onto the keyboard so quick it's nothing but a
flurry of finger movement. "And nobody's looking for them.
Bass and Rosie are wards of the state."

"Shouldn't their social workers be looking for them, then?"

"Them and a hundred other wards of the state. Before they
came here, Rosie and Bass spent more time on the street than

they did under a roof. Their social worker was never too concerned about it." Link opens up a file.

It's a database. I've seen plenty while working with my dad. Safe Guard has a database for every affluent neighborhood in the United States, including what type of security system each resident uses. I spent many Saturdays looking through them, trying to help Dad identify potential customers. I take a step closer and squint over Link's shoulder. "Who are you searching for?"

"I'm not sure yet." He punches enter. Name after name loads onto the screen. "It's a list of all the patients currently at the Detroit Rehabilitation Center. A pretty innocuous name for what it really is, if you ask me."

"What is it really?"

"Psych ward. Insane asylum. Living morgue. Take your pick. They definitely aren't doing any rehabilitating, that's for sure."

His words drum up a memory that's never too far from the surface of my consciousness. Every time I shut my eyes, I can see them—lifeless bodies hooked to machines with atrophied muscles like Cap's. "Luka and I broke into a place like that in Oregon."

Link swivels around, fascination twinkling in the honey-brown of his irises.

I tell him the story about our break-in to Shady Wood, about finding my grandmother, our quick escape, and everything else in between. When I finish, his eyes no longer twinkle—they dance.

"I can't believe you got into *Shady Wood*."

"Yeah, well, they weren't rehabilitating anyone either. Not by the looks of it."

"It's the same thing that's happening here in Detroit."

The very idea of another Shady Wood called by a different name has heat swirling inside my chest. It's inhumane. It's not right. I don't care how crazy those people may be, they don't deserve to have their lives drained away while they lie comatose on a bed. "Why don't more people know about this?"

"It's not hard to hide what people don't want to see."

"But if the public knew, if they saw, they'd do something about it."

A doubtful noise sounds from the back of Link's throat.

"You don't think so?"

"You've heard Cormack's speeches, haven't you? *Our country is only as strong as our weakest members.* The public eats it up. Everyone's been brainwashed to shun abnormality, to stomp it out at the first hint."

"And we're okay with that?" Seeing Link's amused expression at my question riles me up. "I'm serious. The public deserves to know. And if you can really hack into anything, like Rosie says, then why can't we hack into media channels and start raising awareness?"

Link is grinning at me.

"What?" I bark.

"You're going all Captain Janeway on me."

"Captain who?"

He sets his palm against his chest, like I shot him in the heart. "Captain Janeway? From Star Trek Voyager?"

I have no idea what he's talking about. I shake away the confusion, refusing to let myself be sidetracked. "A major injustice has been brought to our attention. You don't think we have an obligation to do something about it?"

"Oh, I do. I'm more on board than you know. I just think

we should teach you to fly before you captain that Starfleet." His smile widens, revealing a deep (and charming) set of dimples. "Ready for your first lesson?"

I pull up a chair and park myself beside him.

He threads his fingers together and cracks his knuckles, looking borderline giddy, as if this were some giant video game to conquer and he can't wait to get to the next level. "I've been working on identifying The Gifting. A lot of them are in mental hospitals. Hence, the database."

"How do you find them?"

"Key words, mostly. Everybody's gifting is different. Even Shields have unique abilities. But there are commonalities, too. Hallucinations, for example. Every person with the gifting sees the supernatural, or the spiritual. Whatever you want to call it. So I set up the system to pull every patient file that lists hallucinations as a symptom." He punches some buttons and types in a few codes. The database re-configures itself, shrinking by a good fifty percent. "Still a lot of names, though. So I do another key word search. Let's go with dreams."

He punches more buttons, and the list shrinks again.

"The dreams are very telling when it comes to figuring out what someone is. Fighters, for example, almost always describe their dreams as prophetic."

"Sounds familiar."

Link tosses me a mischievous wink. "Shields usually have incredibly frustrating dreams where they need to protect someone they love, but they can't remember how. Personally, I find Cloaks to be the most interesting."

"Why?"

"Anna's dreams were crawling with chameleons."

I quirk one of my eyebrows.

"She could turn people into a chameleon. She could make them change color, even shape, all to blend in with their surroundings."

"Do all Cloaks dream about chameleons?"

"No, that was just Anna. In Fray's dreams, anything he touches turns invisible."

My clammy fingers twist the small stones inside Luka's bracelet. I want to ask about Keepers. What kind of dreams do they have? But I can't figure out how to do it without sounding overly interested. "What happens after you identify someone?"

"I awaken them to their gifting."

"*Awaken?*"

Link plucks the Rubik's Cube off the desk. "Most people like us think they're crazy. I visit them in their dreams and explain what's going on. Once they're 'awake', things get very real, and a lot more dangerous."

I lean closer, like a plant hungry for the sun. "How so?"

"So far the only person we've rescued is Anna. Everyone else here came through Dr. Carlyle."

"You broke her out?"

"Of this very facility." Link nods at the computer screen, twisting the cube around with deft fingers. "It's not easy. In fact, without the skill of a very powerful fighter, it would be impossible. If we didn't have Cap, we wouldn't be able to break anyone out."

"Wait ... *Cap* is a fighter?" But he's in a wheelchair. His legs have no muscle mass.

"When it comes to The Gifting, what you see is rarely ever what you get. Cap is the only one with the skill to manipulate the physical while in spiritual form. Sticks can do it occasionally, but not consistently and when it comes to rescue missions, consistence is mandatory."

My mind hums louder than the supercomputer in front of us. "What do you mean—manipulate the physical while in spiritual form?"

"It's like this. Think of our world in terms of realms, right? There's the physical realm, which is everything we can see and touch. It's what we can prove because of our senses. We are physical beings." As if to prove his point, he sets the Rubik's Cube down and gives my hair a playful tug. "But we're also spiritual beings. Every single one of us has a soul."

"You realize that ninety-nine percent of the population would call you crazy for that statement." My dad would be the first to balk him out of the room.

"I'm well aware. But it's the truth. A person can choose not to believe it, but that doesn't make their soul go away. It's there, whether they want to acknowledge it or not. The supernatural realm is just as real as the physical one, only you can't see it. It's the realm of good and evil, light and dark. From everything we can gather, these two forces are at war, and in order to join the battle, passageways are required."

"Dreams."

Link nods enthusiastically. "Dreams have doorways. But only Fighters—and Linkers, like myself—are able to pass through them into the supernatural realm."

"What about Guardians?"

"They can't pass through unless I bring them over. It's one of my more valuable assets as a Linker." His mouth draws up on one side. "Once a Fighter enters the supernatural realm, they can fight supernatural beings, but manipulating physical things is nearly impossible. Only the most highly-skilled Fighters can do it. And even then, it's crazy dangerous."

"How so?"

"It's what landed Cap in four wheels."

"What happened?"

"He doesn't like to talk about the details. All I know is that several years ago, he crossed over and things went bad."

I clear away the dryness in my throat. Best not to dwell on that one for too long. "Okay, so how does it all work—this rescue plan you managed with Anna?"

"After I awaken a person to their gifting and explain what's going on, Cap steps through a doorway and switches out their medicine. It's important that they still act like they're medicated, so as not to tip anyone off. Once they have their strength back, we guide them out of the facility without ever being there. At least not in the physical sense."

I sit back in the chair and let out a puff of breath. "That is brilliant."

Link smiles. "Makes us almost impossible to catch."

CHAPTER SIXTEEN

SCREAMING IN THE NIGHT

An hour into research, Cap rolls into the room requiring Link's assistance, which means I'm left alone with thoughts that twist and tug in a thousand different directions. In an attempt to distract myself, I peruse the makeshift library, hoping to settle into a book. But it's no use. Outspoken Jo March, moody Heathcliff, not even Alice and her confusing tumble down the rabbit hole can distract me from the restlessness in my legs. I want to run outside, hike through the woods, roam the beach. Since I'm stuck down here, I settle for the closest thing to it.

I change into sweats and pour out my energy on one of the treadmills. I push and push and push until my lungs are heaving and my muscles are burning and sweat soaks through my clothes. Maybe if I perspire enough, the medicine will leave my system and I'll be able to join Claire and Jose tomorrow afternoon. I don't stop until my legs have become over-stretched rubber bands; then I move to the weights. After a frenzy of various sets and repetitions, I lay back against the bench with my putty-like arms dangling toward the floor. I take back my breath, clean up my sweat with a clump of paper towels, and hit the shower.

The water's not even lukewarm, but after such an intense workout, the coolness comes as a relief and the surprisingly high pressure kneads my poor muscles. I have no idea how long

I stand there beneath the stream as it washes down my body, flowing like rivulets between my toes, onto the cement floor, and down the drain straddled between my feet. Eventually, a toilet flushes. Hands are washed and footsteps fade into silence.

I shut off the water and rub my eyes. After I'm dried and dressed and combed, I head toward the common room. Lazy chatter filters out into the hallway, which means afternoon training must be finished. I give my wet hair a self-conscious tussle.

First, I notice Rosie, who has returned. She stands in the far corner of the room playing foosball with Luka. Claire stands at the head of the table holding a glass of water, laughing as Luka and Rosie twist and pull, clattering the ball around the Plexiglass field. Luka bites his lower lip in concentration and gives one of the handles a strong spin. Whatever move he tried must have failed, because Rosie whoops in jubilation, then dances about like a pixie.

"Your *not boyfriend* threw out a shield on his second try."

Jillian's unexpected voice in my ear makes me jump.

"Nobody's ever done that before," she says.

I glance again toward the corner of the room. Claire sets her hands on the foosball table and leans over it, capturing Luka's attention with words I can't hear. Nor can I see his expression, since the shift in his weight leaves me with nothing to see but his back.

"I've never seen Non so impressed."

A skittish sort of feeling flits through my stomach. I have no idea why Jillian's commentary has me feeling jumpy. Non's not the first person to be impressed by Luka, nor will she be the last. He seems to have that effect on everyone he encounters, myself included. And apparently, Claire too. "Everything seems to come naturally to him."

"I'll say."

Claire tips her head back and laughs. I narrow my eyes. "I thought she was into Link."

"When it comes to cute boys, Claire doesn't discriminate. And I'm afraid your *not boyfriend* is a walking billboard for cute boys." Jillian crosses her arms and raises her eyebrows.

"What?"

"I can't believe you didn't tell me you're a Fighter!"

Maybe that's because I'm convinced I'll be lousy at it.

"You have to promise to tell me everything once training starts. Jose and Claire are always so vague about what they're up to with Sticks. It drives me bonkers, especially since they know what the Shields do."

"Sure, I'll tell you whatever you want." My attention gravitates back to Luka.

He looks over his shoulder and a slow smile splits across his face. The brightness of his eyes reminds me of Jillian, only there's nothing rodent-like about his nose or any other one of his features. He leaves behind a gloating Rosie and a disappointed Claire and makes his way across the common room, unleashing a flurry of butterflies in my stomach.

"Hey," he says, nodding toward Jillian.

"Hi," Jillian says back.

"Mind if I borrow Tess for a second?"

"Be my guest." She wags her thin eyebrows at me as Luka pulls me out into the hallway.

When we're away from prying eyes, he takes a couple steps down the hall, then pivots on his heel. There's this triumphant energy about him that makes the air around us sizzle and pop. "I know how to do it."

"The shield?"

He turns over his palms and flexes his fingers, as if the power of throwing the shield thrums through his tendons. "I can't believe I finally know how to do it."

"That's amazing." My voice comes out off-key. A little pitchy. Like Pete's when he went through puberty in eighth grade. I tuck a strand of wet hair behind my ear, but it quickly falls loose. I have no idea why my heart is thudding so erratically against my sternum. Or why I can't seem to look up from my shoes. "Did you tell anyone that you've done it before?"

"No." Luka shuffles closer. "Why?"

"No reason."

"Tess." He hooks his pointer fingers inside the front pockets of my jeans and gently draws me toward him. The butterflies stir into a frenzy. "I know how to protect you now."

The huskiness of his voice has me looking up. For the first time since stepping onto the Greyhound bus, I don't see a trace of shadow beneath his eyes. They are as bright and green as the leaves in spring. His hand moves to my hip, his thumb finding a sliver of bare skin beneath the hem of my shirt. A feverish heat radiates from the spot and gathers in my belly. My breath catches. Because I'm pretty sure Luka is going to kiss me. He's not springing it on me in the middle of a crowded locker bay or in an alley behind a dumpster.

His hand slides to my back. He presses me closer, dips his chin …

"I'm starving!"

My heart slams into my throat.

Luka and I quickly break apart.

Rosie comes to a screeching stop, her attention sliding back and forth between us. "Were you two purpling?"

Luka tucks his hands into his pockets and smiles at the ground.

Rosie nose wrinkles in disgust. "Well, I'm going to the cafeteria to see if I can sneak in an hors d'oeuvre or two before dinner." She begins walking backward down the hallway. "Hey, Tess?"

"Yeah?"

"Your boyfriend's awful at foosball."

Luka's burst of laughter echoes off the walls, an enticing sound that makes me smile. I peek at him as he watches Rosie backpedal. Horrible at foosball. I guess there's one thing that doesn't come naturally to him after all.

I'm standing on a beach that's only ever existed in my dreams. Waves crash onto the shore. White foam creeps toward Luka sitting in the sand. Sunbeams illuminate his profile in orange as he stares toward the horizon with his thumbnail wedged between his teeth. Funny how even here—in this space between two realms—his mannerisms are the same. I scratch my wrist out of habit rather than necessity, the numbness confirming what I already know. I walk across the sand, leaving vague footprints behind me.

Once I reach him, I tilt my face toward the sun, close my eyes, and spread my arms wide, bathing in the glow as another salty wave comes crashing toward my feet. How is it possible to feel the warmth of a sun that doesn't really exist? I'm not actually outside. My physical body is sleeping at the hub. Does that mean, though, that this—right here—isn't real? If Link's lesson about realms taught me anything, it's that reality isn't as black and white as I once thought.

"You're here," Luka says.

I open my eyes and smile down at him.

"The medicine must be wearing off."

The revelation sends a thrill of excitement through my dream-world veins. He's right. If I'm here, visiting with Luka on this beach, then that means my plan to sweat out the medicine must have worked. Soon, I will get to join Claire and Jose. Luka doesn't seem to share my enthusiasm.

I sit cross-legged in the sand beside him. "You don't want me to train?"

"I'd like to know *what* we're training for."

"It's a good thing I know, then." I just haven't had a chance to tell him yet. When he brought me out into the hallway, Rosie interrupted us before I could tell him how I'd spent my afternoon and all that I'd learned from Link. We ate dinner with Jillian and interestingly, Ellen (who really does like to quote Shakespeare), and then Non handed Luka a bucket of cleaning supplies and said it was his evening for bathroom duty. Although I didn't see him again, I went to bed thinking about him. Hence, this beach.

I scoop up handfuls of sand and let them run through my fingers as I tell him everything I learned—the databases, searching for others, their rescue mission with Anna. I tell him everything but the bit about Cap and his wheelchair. Somehow, I don't think Luka will process that too well.

"It sounds dangerous," he finally says.

"Well it's a good thing you can protect me now." I give him a playful nudge with my shoulder—an attempt to keep things light—when a dragging sensation pulls at my body. It's like I'm being sucked into a straw, a feeling I've felt before. A feeling that induces panic. I try to reach for Luka. He tries to reach for me. But it's no use. There must still be traces of medicine in my system. I'm too weak to take him with me.

When the straw-sucking sensation stops, I'm standing in the middle of a familiar, rubble-strewn street. I turn a quick three-sixty, my heart hammering wildly in my chest. I'm outside the warehouse. A dome of strange light falls over the entirety of the building so that only a fuzzy outline can be seen. I reach out and touch it with the tip of my finger, expecting an electrical zap, but my hand sinks right through without any repercussions at all. This must be Anna and Fray's cloak.

Fascinating.

I move my hand over and through the luminous shield when a scream rents the night.

An awful, blood-curdling sound that has every hair on the back of my neck standing on end. It's as though the screamer is fighting for her very life. There's no time to think. No time to plan. I sprint through the rubble, toward that terrible noise, tripping and stumbling over debris. I need to get to her. I have to help her. But I don't know where she is. The scream permeates the air with horror, echoing every which way so that it's impossible to place its origin. No matter how far or how fast or which direction I run, I get nowhere.

She screams and screams and screams …

Until my body gives a violent shake and my eyes pop open.

Luka has both of his hands clamped over my shoulders. He's the one who shook me. He's here now, in my room. And I'm the one who is screaming. The blood-curdling sound belongs to me.

"You're awake. It's okay."

I shut my mouth. The screaming stops. But its echo reverberate in my mind.

Luka blinks down at me through the dark.

I push him away and disentangle my legs from the sheets. We have to go right now. Right this instant. Before it's too late. "Someone's being attacked up there. A woman. We have to help her. She's in trouble."

"We can't go out there."

"You don't understand. I think she's being ..." Raped? Beaten to death? I can't bring myself to say either, although I suspect both are happening. The very thought has bile churning in my stomach. I stand from the bed and move toward the door, but Cap is there in his wheelchair—a living barricade.

"Luka's right."

"That woman will die if we don't help her."

"We can't leave Anna and Fray's cloak. It's too risky."

Disgust swells in my throat—red and burning hot. A woman is dying out there and we're just going to sit here and let it happen? Why—because our safety means more than her life? I whip around to look at Luka, positive I will find an ally. He stands grim-faced behind me, staring resolutely at the cement floor.

"Please," I say, a plea from the very depths of my soul.

He doesn't even look up. He's probably too ashamed.

"It's time to return to your room." Cap jerks his head for Luka to follow him, wheeling his chair around so it faces the hallway. As he waits for Luka to obey orders, his silver eyes pierce mine. "Your training will start tomorrow. It appears the medicine has worn off."

It's what I hoped for. Yet in light of what's happening at this very instant, I feel far from victorious.

CHAPTER SEVENTEEN

TRAINING

The woman's screams haunt me. Through the rest of the night, through breakfast, and now through class. Thanks to yesterday's self-inflicted abuse in the weight room, I sit in class with incredibly sore muscles battling a mountain of guilt while Sticks talks about a war in the Middle East some thousands upon thousands of years ago. Luka sits beside me twirling a pencil around his thumb. Before breakfast, he pulled me aside and apologized, tried to explain why he couldn't let me go last night. I didn't want to hear it. What happened was wrong. I don't care how convincing he can be.

I prop my chin on my hand and stare at the clock, urging it to hurry up so I can eat lunch and start training already. Maybe then I can burn off some of this cloying sense of culpability over the fate of a woman I never saw, but definitely heard. Sticks drones on and on until my eyes glaze over with the irrelevancy of it all. Finally, at quarter till noon, he picks up a piece of chalk and scratches a word on the board that has me forgetting all about the screams.

Keepers

I glance nervously at Luka.

"The first recorded occurrence of a keeper dates all the way back to two thousand B.C. Very little was recorded about this particular Keeper, but what is known strongly suggests his *anima* played an integral role in the outcome of the war."

Sticks brings his hands together for a clap, his attention briefly flitting to the left of the class, where Luka and I sit. "Just to make sure we're all on the same page, who wants to explain to our newest pupils what a Keeper is?"

I shift in my seat. Thanks to my first meal here at the hub, I already know. Luka, however, doesn't have a clue.

"They're a type of Guardian," Declan says. "And they are incredibly rare."

"Why?" Sticks asks.

"Because they're created for the sole purpose of protecting one Fighter."

Luka stops his pencil twirling.

My neck turns hot.

"Only the most powerful Fighters have them." Claire's icy blue eyes gleam, as though she'd love nothing more than to be one of those Fighters.

"And what do we call this powerful Fighter, in relation to his or her Keeper?"

"The Keeper's *anima*," Rosie quips. "It's Latin for breath of life."

Luka's stare burns the side of my face.

"This brings me to our assignment. Everyone will choose a Keeper from history to study in-depth. Who were they? What circumstances brought the Keeper together with his or her *anima*? What did the pair accomplish during their lifetimes? Don't neglect to study the historical context. What was happening in the world at the time? Were The Gifting rising in number, or dwindling? I want you to become an expert on your Keeper and then I want you to write a detailed report."

Someone to my left lets out a loud groan.

"It's important to know our history, Danielle."

She twists a strand of hair around her finger. "Why?"

"Because as my dear wife likes to say, patterns in history reveal much about the future. And we don't want your brains filling up with dumb. Now, does anybody have any questions about the assignment? Luka, you look like you want to say something."

The class shifts collectively. He so easily gathers attention. It was the same way in Thornsdale.

"How does someone know if they're a Keeper?"

I shift in my seat.

"That's an excellent question," Sticks says. "Every recorded Keeper in history has been haunted by recurring dreams of their *anima*, often before they've ever met."

I've never worked so hard in my life to actively avoid someone, not even Summer Burbanks back in Thornsdale, and that's saying something. But work hard I do to avoid Luka. I would have succeeded, too, had not Non assigned me to lunch cleanup duty. With five trays left to go, Luka joins me in the kitchen. Honestly? I'm surprised he didn't come sooner.

"I don't need any help," I say, attacking another tray with the high-powered washer, ignoring the way my arm muscles scream in protest. Thanks to yesterday's workout, even holding up a tray hurts.

He comes beside me anyway and starts on the silverware. "We should talk about this."

I set the tray on the drying rack, shaking my head. The very idea that someone like me would require a Keeper is so farfetched, it's laughable. "You heard Declan. Keepers are incredibly rare."

"It's the only explanation for my dreams."

My head-shaking continues as I spray down another tray.

"It's the only explanation for the way I feel."

"So the only way you could possibly have feelings for me is if they were forced upon you before your birth?" Even as I pose the question, I don't know why I sound incredulous. Of course it's the only explanation. At least the only logical one. All along I've wondered *why*. Why is a guy like Luka attracted to a girl like me? Well, this is definitely an answer.

"That's not what I'm talking about."

"What are you talking about, then?"

"This protectiveness I feel." He grips his chest, as though he might be able to pry away the unwanted emotion. "It's consuming."

I shove another tray inside the crowded rack. "Come on, Luka, look at me. Do I look like a super powerful Fighter to you?"

He shuts off the faucet. "You're in denial."

"No, I'm not."

"*No, you're not* what?"

We both turn toward the door.

Claire has stepped inside the kitchen. Today, she wears her hair in a loose, side braid that reaches all the way down to her abdomen. I wonder if other dudes feel as annoyed by Luka's flawlessness as I do with Claire's.

"Nothing," I mumble.

She eyes Luka like a cat on the prowl, then turns her icy blues on me. "Sticks told me to come get you for training."

I turn the faucet back on, eager to finish up.

"Is the training safe?" Luka's intensity slips through.

His question makes my blood boil, especially since he's not

directing it at me. He's directing it at Claire, who looks more than a little amused by his inquiry.

"Are you afraid Tess will get hurt?"

I wait for Luka to defend me, to extend the smallest measure of faith.

He says nothing.

"You don't have to worry. Sticks won't let anything bad happen to her. She's perfectly safe." With a look of pure condescension, she flips her braid over her shoulder and saunters away.

Cap stops his wheelchair in front of the only locked room in the hub. He pulls out a key on a chain tucked beneath his shirt and lets us in. Sticks, Jose, Claire, me, and Link. I guess today, his services—whatever they are—are needed. There are six chairs inside the room that look as though they belong in a dentist office and upright trays beside each one that hold gadgets and gizmos and wires.

Link boots up the computer at the front of the room. The rest of the mysterious technological devices blink to life as well. Claire and Jose hop onto chairs, fully aware of what's about to happen. I wait for Sticks to do the same. Instead, he scoops Cap into his arms and sets him on the chair at the end.

Judging by the shocked look on Claire and Jose's faces, this is not a common occurrence.

Link begins sticking probes attached to wire onto Claire's temples. When his fingers brush against her skin, she closes her eyes. His touch lingers longer than necessary. I have no idea why it annoys me. Maybe because Claire doesn't seem like a nice person, and someone like Link ought to realize that. He adheres two probes to either side of her neck, one more slightly below her collar bone, then gets to work on Jose. Then Sticks, then Cap, and finally, me.

He holds up the wires. "Your turn."

"Aren't you going to explain what you're doing first?"

"Sleep induction, without the drugs. One hundred percent harmless, I promise." He wiggles the probes in the air. "They send electrodes to the part of your brain that's most active during sleep. The transition is instantaneous. Sort of like someone with narcolepsy. And since the sleep isn't drug-induced, everyone remains fully functional in dream world."

"So we train in our sleep?"

"Precisely."

"It's the best way to practice," Sticks says. "Our tech mastermind over there figured out a way to create a shared dream space for training purposes."

Link flashes that lopsided grin of his.

"If you're worried about your *safety*," Claire looks me up and down, "don't be. Link will monitor our vitals, just in case things get too *intense* for you."

I press my lips together. Because if you don't have anything nice to say ...

"Since I created the space, it's not actually a doorway into the spiritual realm. So you don't have to worry about accidentally getting pulled through or anything." He holds the probes up higher. "Convinced?"

More than.

In fact, for the first time since awakening from last night's awful nightmare, I feel a rush of excitement. I take the seat between Sticks and Jose. Link places the probes on my temples, his eyes catching mine as he does. There are specks of amber in the caramel of his irises, and his hands smell like soap. He pulls down the collar of my shirt just enough to attach the final probe beneath the hollow of my collarbone. "Time to see what Xena Warrior Princess can do."

Even though he's teasing, the nickname makes me feel strong.

Claire, on the other hand, shoots daggers at us with her eyes.

Link moves to the computer, where all the wires now attached to our bodies run. "Showtime on the count of three. One, two, three ..."

I open my eyes in a large room padded with mats that run up three of the walls. The fourth is one giant mirror. For a second, I think we've somehow teleported to the room beside the weight room. There are mats in there, too. But this place is bigger, with more equipment. There are dumbbells and pull-up bars, sparring pads and gloves, punching bags and jump ropes. And it doesn't smell like Clorox or feet. This is the dream space Link created.

Claire and Jose stand at one side of the room, pulling on gloves. Sticks stands on the other side next to ...

I rub my eyes, positive I'm seeing things wrong. But when I'm done with the rubbing, I see the same thing as before. It's Cap. Same white stubble. Same salt and pepper buzz cut. Same silver eyes. The only difference? This man who is Cap, but not really Cap, doesn't sit in a wheelchair. He stands beside Sticks, a good half a foot shorter, with legs as strong and sturdy as tree stumps.

"Welcome to the training center." Sticks steps into the middle of the dream dojo. "What do you think?"

"How is he ...?" My attention returns to Cap, who leans

against one of the matted walls.

"Standing?" Sticks offers.

"Yeah."

"Simple." He snaps his finger, and all of a sudden, Sticks is no longer in the center of the room; he's standing directly in front of me. I jerk back. Claire snickers. Sticks snaps again. Now he's standing in between Claire and Jose. I'm not sure if he moved so fast as to be a literal blur, or if he somehow managed to disappear and reappear. He pulls back Claire's arms, helping her stretch the muscles in her chest. "This is dream world. Our physical bodies are lying on those chairs. Physical limitations don't exist. Not here. You may be short and skinny during your waking hours …"

More snickering from Claire.

"But that has nothing to do with the amount of strength you can harness as a fighter here in this realm. Take me, for example. In real life, my height has disadvantages. I'm not very fast. But here," he snaps a third time, and in a blink, he's standing beside Cap again, "I'm as fast as I want to be."

Jose and Claire move to one of the punching bags. She holds it steady while he gives it a few powerful wallops.

"Today, we want to see what you can do." Sticks tosses me a pair of sparring gloves.

I catch them and slide them on. They feel familiar over my knuckles, and good too. I always enjoyed my Saturday morning martial art classes with Mom. In fact, I don't think I've realized until now how much I've missed them.

Sticks tosses me headgear.

"Isn't this unnecessary?" I ask, strapping it onto my head. "If this isn't my physical body, why do I need protection?"

"Why don't you show her why she wants the helmet,

Claire."

Claire couldn't be happier to oblige. She lets go of the punching bag and steps into the center of the room. I recognize her stance. We're going to spar. Determination stretches through my limbs, into my fingers. Claire might be taller and stronger, but I'm quick and scrappy. Plus, she has no clue that I have training, which means I have the element of surprise on my side. I take my stance and we circle a couple times.

She throws a few punches.

I dodge them—quick, but not as quick as I know I can be. The knuckle of her glove grazes my chin. I stumble back, then shake my head in an attempt to refocus. Something's not right. I'm more sluggish than I should be, which must mean the medicine hasn't run its full course. Claire has an unfair advantage. As if sensing my weakness, she throws a quick one-two jab. I block them both.

"You know some self-defense," Sticks says, making brief eye contact with me in the reflection of the mirror.

Claire throws a left hook.

I lean back, then do a roundhouse kick. My heel nicks her chin.

Her eyes go wide.

And in her momentary shock, I go on the offensive with a series of punches. The effort has my lungs pumping. "Why"—I throw a jab—"am I so winded?"

"It's in your head."

I block two of Claire's attacks, then take a knee to the ribs.

It knocks the wind out of me. I double over, clutching the pain in my side.

"Link figured out a way to keep the part of our brain that feels pain fully functional," Sticks says.

"Why would he do that?" I block a blow, but take a shot in the nose. There's a crack of sharp pain, then warmth trickling over my lips. When I wipe at it, my forearm comes away with a smear of red.

Sticks strolls a circle around us. "Because there's value in knowing your limits."

Beyond him, Jose wails on the punching bag.

"The absence of pain can make a person do some pretty idiotic things. It's important that we know our limits, even here."

I go on the attack, my sloppy movements stirring up more frustration. I'm panting like a dog. Sweating worse than I did yesterday on the treadmill. I try another roundhouse kick, grunting with the motion, but Claire dodges my heel by doing a backward flip that defies all sense of gravity. I stare, grudgingly impressed. Her attention slides to Cap, as if making sure he's paying attention. When it's clear that he is, she lands a strong shot in my stomach and another on my ear that makes my entire head ring.

A mass of heat builds inside my chest. I may not believe that I'm strong enough to warrant a Keeper, but I know I'm stronger than this. I curl my arm back and swing with all my might—an uppercut to end all uppercuts.

Claire catches my fist. "Looks like Xena Warrior Princess forgot to eat her Wheaties." Without warning, she sweeps my arm, flips me over her shoulder and slams me flat on my back—knocking the wind out of me for the second time. "No wonder Luka was so worried about you. You're weak. You don't stand a chance against the other side." With a smirk, she turns her back to me and starts walking away.

I jump up to my feet and throw a kick.

She spins around and blocks it, but this time I'm the quicker one. I grab her wrist, twist her around, and pin her hand against the small of her back. "I've faced the other side before."

"More than one at a time?" She spins out of my hold. "Because I don't think you'll ever be able to fight more than one at a time."

I dodge one of her jabs. "Good thing I have Luka, then."

"A lot of good he will do without Link there to bring him through the doorway."

"I don't need Link. I'll take Luka through with me. I've done it before."

Her eyes go wide.

"I can do it again." I fake jab left, then throw a right hook. I anticipate the connection—my glove, her nose. But when I make the swipe, my fist hits nothing but empty air.

Claire is gone.

I spin around.

So is Sticks and Cap and Jose. All that's left of him is the swinging punching bag. I'm standing alone in the center of the room and then suddenly, I'm not. My eyes are open on the dental chair. My ears no longer ring. My nose no longer throbs. I swipe at my upper lip, where the blood had pooled. There's nothing but dry skin. I'm not even out of breath.

Everyone is staring at me as though I just did something incredibly odd. Or maybe amazing. I can't tell.

"Why'd you all leave like that?" Link asks. "We were just getting started."

Sticks cocks his head. "Did you say that you've taken him with you before?"

I look from him to Cap, confused. "Yes."

"When?" Cap asks.

"When Luka and I were visiting in our dreams—"

Link's eyes practically bug out of their sockets. "You and Luka visit in your dreams?"

It has me shrinking back a little. I look at Claire, who stares with her mouth ajar, and Jose, whose shock doesn't manifest itself as overtly as the others, but whose quirked unibrow suggests at least a measure of disbelief. I return my attention to Link. "Is that a bad thing?"

"Explain what happens, when you visit each other."

"I don't know. It's just something we do." My cheeks burn. It's a private matter, actually. I'd rather not go into details. "One of the times, when I felt that weird pulling sensation, I grabbed his hand and took him with me."

The silence is deafening.

"Have you visited anybody else's dreams?" Link asks.

Summer. Leela. I think that's it. "A couple."

"You're a dream hopper."

"A what?"

"You're a Fighter," Link says. "But you're also a Linker. Like me."

CHAPTER EIGHTEEN

AN ANOMALY

Cap whispers something to Sticks, then tells me and Link to follow him. He doesn't say where we're going or why the discovery of my linking abilities put an end to my very first training session. The severe set of his mouth—his lips a thin, diagonal slash across his face—has me thinking it's nowhere and nothing good. Cap stops in front of the room I first mistook for the dream dojo. He rolls inside and returns a moment later with Luka in tow, who looks from Link to me with a face clouded in confusion.

I shrug.

Cap leads us down the adult corridor—where Anna and Fray, Sticks and Non, Cap, and I'm assuming Gabe, if ever he sleeps, have their rooms. At the end of the hallway we reach a door. Cap motions for us to step inside. The room is the size of a large supply closet, just big enough to fit a cheap-looking card table and several metal fold-up chairs. To my astonishment, Gabe sits in one of them, as expressionless as ever.

I turn around. "Who's guarding the door?"

"Sticks has it covered." As Cap rolls to the table, I can't seem to take my eyes off of his legs. It's bizarre seeing the shriveled uselessness of them in his wheelchair compared to their sturdy strength in dream world. "Have a seat."

Link obeys, wearing a Christmas-morning grin that never falters.

Luka, however, is not nearly as eager to oblige. "What's going on?"

Cap rubs the stubble on his pouched cheek. "Non said you threw a force field on your second attempt."

"So?"

"So it usually takes several days of intense training before a Shield can do something like that." Cap clamps his hand over the back of the empty chair beside him and pulls it out. The legs scrape against the floor. Luka still doesn't sit. "I'd like to know how you did it."

I hold my breath, waiting for him to share the theory he shared with me while I washed lunch trays. Part of me wants him to share it. Cap witnessed my fighting. Claire owned me in that dojo, which means he can laugh Luka's theory into its grave and we can all move on. But surprisingly, Luka folds his arms and shrugs. "Beginner's luck, I guess."

Cap narrows his eyes, then turns his attention to Link. "You will be taking over part of Tess's training."

Luka shifts. "Why?"

"Because Tess is turning out to be quite an anomaly." Cap takes hold of the chair on his other side and pulls that one out too. "Please have a seat and I'll fill you in."

Luka sits. So do I.

"It appears she is both a Fighter and a Linker."

"And all this time I thought I was unique." Link shakes his head in mock disappointment.

"What will this training entail?" Luka asks.

"I'm afraid that's top secret tricks of the linking trade." Link winks at me so quickly, I'm pretty sure I'm the only one who sees it. "It'll be fun."

Luka's green eyes flash. Somehow, I don't think he agrees.

Cap folds his hands on top of the plastic table. "Gabe, I'd like you to take over Luka's training."

Wait—what? My attention darts to Gabe, who doesn't even twitch at the news. "Why would he take over Luka's training?"

"Because Gabe is a Keeper." The words are like a glass of cold water to the face. Gabe is a Keeper?

"And since Luka is your Keeper, he's the best man for the job."

"You *know?*" How is that possible? Luka and I haven't said a word about his dreams.

"I had my suspicions when the pair of you arrived. They grew when Non told me about Luka's first training session. They grew again when I witnessed your training firsthand."

"But you saw me spar Claire." Cap's growing suspicion makes about as much sense as sending little Rosie out on the streets of Detroit by herself. Claire came away from that match with nothing but a grazed chin. And what did I get? A bloody nose, a full body slam, and more knees and kicks to the ribs than I care to admit. "I was weak, not powerful."

Cap sets his hands on the wheels of his chair, his silvery blue stare so invasive it's as though he's cutting me open and looking inside. Seeing for himself what I'm really made of. "My first lesson to you is this. When it comes to what's true, how we feel matters very little."

His lesson leaves me squinting, and not because I'm attempting to see better either. *How we feel matters very little?* What does that have to do with anything that's happening right now?

Luka shakes his head slowly. "So that's all it was—a suspicion?"

"Until Tess confirmed it several seconds ago, yes."

Dirty trick. Dirty, dirty trick.

Cap claimed to know something, but really, he was bluffing. If I would have reacted differently, if I would have said anything other than *you know*, nothing would have been confirmed. Cap would be none the wiser.

I look down into my lap, hating the implications. Everyone here seems to think that only the most powerful Fighters have Keepers and that Luka is my Keeper. But what if I'm the exception? Cap said so himself—I'm an anomaly. What if the reason I have a Keeper isn't because I'm incredibly strong, but because I'm exceptionally weak?

"I know this is not what you had in mind." Cap speaks the soft words to Gabe. "I hope you understand why it's necessary."

Gabe gives Cap an emotionless nod, and that's that. He's going to train Luka. As I look into his dull eyes, an incongruity surfaces. One that demands to be voiced. "If you're a Keeper, where is your *anima*?"

For the first time since I've met Gabe's acquaintance, something in his expression flickers, so fast I almost don't recognize it for what it is—pain. A deep, dark, inescapable anguish that leaves his eyes more lifeless than before.

It's all the answer I need.

Gabe's *anima* is dead.

I stare morosely at my tray—instant mashed potatoes, steamed corn, and two slices of what I suspect to be canned ham. Yum. When the impromptu meeting ended, Luka asked to speak with Cap privately. I wanted to stay too. Whatever he had to say to Cap, I should be able to hear. But Luka didn't invite me, and Gabe ushered me out of the room like a troublesome delinquent. So now I'm here in the cafeteria all by myself, the object of curiosity.

They all must know I'm a Linker. Surely Jose or Claire told everyone already. This place is like a condensed version of high school and we all know how fast word travels there. How long before they all find out that Luka is my Keeper? I stab a piece of ham and twist it into my potatoes. I hate that Luka didn't include me in his conversation with Cap. I hate that even here, in this place, I am Tess the Freak once again. The weight of it all perches on my shoulders like a heavy bird with sharp talons that doesn't release its grip, not even when a chair scoots out beside me.

I look up to find Link.

"You're really dragging down the mood in here."

He's teasing. I know this. But still, I have to bite back a sarcastic apology.

He sits down and sets his elbows on the table. "This is cause for celebration, not mourning. You're a Linker *and* a Fighter. Not only that, you have a—"

"Shhh!" My sharp hiss has him drawing back his chin. "I'm sorry, but I'd rather that not become common knowledge on top of everything else."

"Why not?"

"Because, everybody will have expectations." And I will do nothing but fail to meet them. A sudden and unexpected lump rises in my throat. Why couldn't I just be a Fighter—a regular, ordinary Fighter with no Keeper and no other anomalistic abilities? And why does the one Keeper we know have to have a dead *anima*? If Luka was obsessed with my safety before, he'll only be more so now. A tear gathers and tumbles. I drag my forearm across my cheek.

Link's excitement softens into concern. "Hey. You okay?"

Great. So now I'm not just a freak, I'm a blubbering freak. I shake my head, an attempt to downplay my embarrassing meltdown. "I'm fine. Really. I—I'm just sick of being cooped up. I want to see the sun." It may not be the reason for my tears, but it's no less true. I'd give anything to be outside, surrounded by the towering redwoods of Northern California or the lush palm trees of Florida. Even the frozen, danger-strewn landscape of Detroit sounds appealing right about now. "I miss being outside."

Link twists his lips to the side for a moment, then scoops up my tray and stands.

"What are you doing?"

"Come with me." Without any more explanation than that, he sets my plate of mostly uneaten food in front of Rosie, who brightens with gratitude. I catch a glimpse of Claire. Her animosity has reached a whole new level. Too curious to care, I follow Link out of the cafeteria.

He leads us down the main corridor, then turns down the hallway that belongs to the adults. The very one we left behind not more than half an hour ago. Maybe he means to eavesdrop on whatever Cap and Luka are still talking about in the supply-closet-turned-conference room. "Uh Link? Where are we going?"

He stops in front of a door. "Close your eyes."

"What?"

"Come on, Xena. If I'm going to be training you, you will need to trust me."

Letting out a sigh, I do as requested.

The door unlatches. Hinges squeak.

Link takes my hand and pulls me inside. The warmth on my skin has my eyelids fluttering open before Link gives me permission to look. If he's mad that I cheated, he sure doesn't look it. In fact, he's wearing that Christmas-morning grin again. So am I.

Flowers, vegetables, fruits, and lush green plants grow up from pots and planters. It smells like earth and grass. The bright lights are as warm as the sun with strategically placed mirrors to maximize the brightness. The humidity in the air reminds me not of Thornsdale, but Jude. "What is this place?"

"The hub's very own underground greenhouse. Anna and Fray are in charge of it. Non says the light and the warmth offer them some much needed fortitude."

I step in further and turn a slow three-sixty. "It's amazing."

Link leads us toward the back, where the vegetation is thickest. He lies beneath an unidentified bush with palm fronds for leaves and pats the floor beside him—unspoken code for *join me*.

There's a moment of self-conscious hesitation, barely longer than a heartbeat. The temptation is too strong to resist. I lay beside him on my back, staring up at the light as it dapples through green leaves.

Link folds his hands behind his head and gives my shoe a tap with his. "It's almost like you're outside, huh?"

The gesture wiggles its way inside my heart, pushing aside all the junk, warming me straight through. In this moment, right here, I'm no longer scared or confused or tired or homesick. I'm lying outside in the woods beside my really thoughtful, new friend. "Thanks."

"You bet."

As we lay in the silence, I do not let myself entertain questions about Gabe or his *anima*. I do not let myself think about letting everyone down when they discover I'm not as powerful as I should be. I do not think about Luka and whatever he had to say in private to Cap. I force all negative thoughts out, unwilling to ruin this moment.

"You can go outside anytime you want, you know."

"How's that possible? Gabe's always guarding the door."

"It's one of the great perks of being like me. You can go anywhere you want to in your dreams. You can dream anything you want to dream. You're the one in control."

More often than not, my dreams control me, pulling me into places I don't want to go. Link's version sounds wonderful, yet unattainable. "How is that possible?"

"How do you dream hop?"

"I don't know, I thought you were going to tell me that."

"C'mon, you know. You know even if you don't know you know. When you visit Luka in your dreams, how do you do it?"

I squish my face up, trying to recall. Luka figured it out before I did. "I think about him before I go to sleep." As soon as the confession escapes, warmth pools inside my cheeks. It feels too intimate to share with Link—that I think about Luka in bed at night. But it's true. And a glimmer of hope breaks through my sour mood. Does this mean I can visit my mom whenever I want? My dad and Pete and Leela, too? Is it really so simple as thinking about them before bed?

"Same principle applies. If you want to dream that you're outside, go to sleep thinking about being outside and you'll wake up outside. You can even create a tropical island for yourself if you want."

It sounds too good to be true. Like my own personal bedtime heaven. Can dreams really be pleasant, highly anticipated things? "Really?"

"Really and truly. You may be cooped up when you're awake, but you don't have to be cooped up at night."

I turn my head. "Is this a training session right now?"

"Nah, you'll know when you're being trained. I'm more of a teach-by-example kinda guy. In fact, I was thinking we'd have our first training session tonight."

"Tonight?"

"I'll find you while we sleep."

"Oh."

Link gives me a friendly nudge. "No reason to look worried, Xena. I promise it'll be fun."

CHAPTER NINETEEN

COME OUT, COME OUT, WHEREVER YOU ARE

I toss and turn in bed, wishing there were an on-off switch in my brain so I could turn off my thoughts and go to sleep. I'm quite positive Luka will hate this idea—me and Link sharing dreams. But then, in theory, if Link thinks about me before bed—a thought that makes my stomach kind of fluttery—he'll be in my dream whether I want him to be or not. It hits me, suddenly, how much freedom a Linker has. Dreams are often very personal things and here we have the ability to barge in on any we like. What if I end up on the beach with Luka and Link shows up? The very idea twists my muscles into knots.

I must not think about Luka. Must, must, *must* not think about him. I flip over on the mattress and force every ounce of mental energy I have on my family. The last time I saw my brother, he was in a hospital room. How's he doing now? Last I heard from Leela, my father's job was on the line. Is it still? Anytime Luka creeps into the crevices of my mind, I push him out and focus all the harder.

Pete, Pete, Pete.

I take a shovel to my memories, digging up as many as I can of my brother. Carefree, laid-back, everybody-loves-him Pete. Until we moved to Thornsdale and he changed so drastically—turning dark and taciturn and moody. Little did I know there were powers at work in his life, powers my father and most of the world would laugh off as pure fiction.

Medicine prevented me from saving my brother the first time. Medicine almost prevented me from saving him the second. How vividly I remember the man with the white scar, searing my brother's skin with that strange symbol—the same one I saw on Wren, the girl who barked at my old English teacher. If not for Luka, that symbol would have remained on my brother's forearm and the Pete I grew up knowing and loving would have been lost forever. But I brought Luka with me to fight that battle and he threw out a force field that gave the man with one scar two.

Luka, my brother's hero. Luka, the boy whose touch sets my skin on fire. Was he really created for the sole purpose of protecting me? And if that's true, how do I feel about it? I give my head a fierce shake.

Pete, Pete, Pete.

Instead of counting sheep, I count my brother. I imagine a long line of Pete clones, sitting in a large circle as I walk around them tapping their heads. Three-hundred-six Pete, three-hundred-seven Pete, three-hundred-eight Pete ...

Until my eyes grow heavy and my breathing becomes effortless and I open my eyes in a place that is every bit as dark and dank as the hub, but it's not my new bedroom. I reach out and curl my fingers around cold, metal bars. This is a prison cell. Only instead of being inside of it, I'm outside looking in, at a man huddled in the corner. A man who is awfully familiar ...

"Dad!"

It's not me who shouts the word, but the young man beside

me. He grabs onto the bars and shakes them for all he's worth, as though enough strength might bend them apart and allow my father to walk free. "Dad, look at me! Please!"

But my father—*our* father—won't look up.

I set my hand on Pete's shoulder.

He stops his shaking and spins around, his dark eyes going wide. And before I can brace myself, his arms wrap me in a hug so tight it's hard to breathe. His tall body—the one that has always grown too fast—is ganglier than usual. His bones feel sharper, more prominent than they should.

"Tess! I can't believe you're here. Where have you been?"

I lean away, wanting to see my brother's face, and as I do, the setting changes. We're no longer inside a prison. We're in the woods, the ones outside my house in Thornsdale. For one brief, unadulterated moment, I want to spread my arms wide and sprint through this familiar place. Feel fresh air on my face and in my hair. But then I remember where we came from— the image of Pete desperately trying to get our father's attention—and the woods turn dark and ominous, as if danger lurks behind every leaf.

Pete must sense it too, because he takes my wrist and begins dragging me up the path with urgent, frenzied movements that aren't like my brother at all. "I have to get you out of here."

I dig in my heels. "Wait a second."

"He's coming. He'll know you're here."

"Who?"

"The man with the scars."

Dread sinks through my stomach like an anvil.

"He's after you, Tess. He's looking all over for you."

I grab Pete's shoulders, desperate to calm him down. "Listen to me, this is a dream."

"What?"

"This isn't real. It's a dream. You're having a bad dream."

"Then how are you ...?"

There's too much to explain. Too many questions I have myself. I don't know where to start. "I found out a way to visit people in their dreams. That's what's happening right now. This is your dream and I've hopped into it."

Pete's eyes are wild and frantic, moving about inside his head as if at any minute the man with the scars will jump out and kill us both. My brother's terror is palpable. Of course it is. When a person gets as close to evil as Pete did and lives to tell about it, they know full well the danger it poses. I will get no answers unless I can calm him down. So I do the same thing I did to Leela. I pinch him as hard as I can—nails and all—on the bony part of his hand.

He draws back, a divot forming between his eyebrows.

"You didn't feel it because you're dreaming. Nothing can hurt you." At least not physically.

Pete's eyes start to clear. His fear slowly ebbs. "Leela was telling the truth. She said something about getting a message from you in a dream, but it all sounded so ..."

"Crazy, I know. Did she give you my letters?"

He nods.

A flood of gratitude washes through me. Where would I be without Leela?

"Tess, how are you? Mom's worried sick. She's not eating. She's not sleeping. And now with Dad gone ..."

"What do you mean with Dad gone?"

Pete bites his lip, as if to stop the tremble in his chin. It's a look that brings me back to our innocent childhood, when the worst trouble Pete faced was getting caught for breaking Mom's favorite vase.

"The police have him in custody."

"What?" The word tumbles out in a horrified whisper.

"There have been all these allegations that he broke into a mental facility in Eugene."

Oh, no.

"The police won't let us see him. All we know is he's being questioned and accused for a crime he swears he didn't commit. Nobody will tell us anything. But the evidence isn't good, Tess. They traced the break-in to Dad's iPad."

I shake my head, the horror in my throat spreading to my heart. When Luka and I asked Leela to divert attention to Shady Wood, we never considered the possibility that the police might trace the break-in to my father. It was his equipment we used. How couldn't we have considered it? "Pete, Dad didn't break into Shady Wood. That was me and Luka. We're the ones who broke in."

"Luka's with you? I knew he had to be, but the police aren't saying anything about him at all. It's you they're after. Mom thinks that by locking Dad up, they'll get you to come back." *But why? Why, why, why?*

The horror in my heart pumps through my veins. Every part of my body pulses with it. My father's in jail. My mom's a wreck. And Pete's having terrible nightmares. Even if my father gets acquitted, he won't be able to get a job at Safe Guard or anywhere else for that matter. Not with this on his record. Not with me for a daughter. What will happen to my family? My mind grapples for a solution. Anything to fix all that I've broken. "Listen, Pete. You need to wake up and go to the police. Tell them it was me who broke into Shady Wood. I stole Dad's iPad. It was all me. Tell them that if they let Dad out, you and Mom will promise to report me the minute you find out where I am."

Pete's eyes grow wide again. "Never. I'm not going to rat you out."

"Pretend, Pete. You have to. Get Dad out of this mess and then convince our parents that you have to move. Move far away from Thornsdale and start over somewhere else. Convince Mom that I'm not coming back." My throat closes tight, so tight I can barely breathe.

"Where are you?"

I open my mouth to tell him, to reassure him that I'm safe. But something Pete said earlier holds my tongue. "A little bit ago you were convinced the man with the scars was going to show up. Why? Has he been …?" I can't finish the question. I'm not sure I want to know. The mere thought of that man tormenting my brother while he sleeps in an attempt to get to me is too much to handle.

"Don't worry about me. I'll be okay." But it's obvious he's not, nor will he be. His face is too thin, his eyes too hollow. "I'm not sure about Mom though. She needs to know where you are, Tess. If you tell me now, we can come to you."

"I can't tell you. I'm sorry." The white-scarred man will never leave my brother alone if I tell him my location. I refuse to pull the pin and hand him such a grenade. "All I can say is that I'm as safe as I can be. Tell Mom I love her, okay? Tell her not to worry about me. Tell her to focus on getting Dad out and moving away."

An eerie whistled melody rustles through the leaves.

Pete yanks me behind a bush.

"Oh Little Raaaa-bbit. Come out, come out wherever you

aaaaare." The familiar voice turns my bones cold. "I know you're here. I'd recognize your presence anywhere."

I peek through the mass of leaves and spot him strolling through the woods like it's a beautiful summer day. "You dropped off the map, you know. Imagine my delight to sense you here tonight, in your dear little brother's dream. Hop, hop, hop, you did. I knew it was only a matter of time before you came." He walks a few more steps, pulling aside branches to search behind them. "I won't stop tormenting little Pete in his sleep. Persistence is my middle name. I will continue until you return to me, or sweet Pete goes mad. The choice is yours."

The threat makes my blood boil.

"Or maybe I'll just put that mark back on his arm—"

I jump out from my hiding spot, wanting to destroy this man. To thrust my palm up into his nose and drive the cartilage through his demonic brain.

Pete jumps after me. "Tess, no!"

The air fills with an odd song, and just like that, my eyes open.

I'm back in the hub. The stupid hub. No! No, no, no! How could I leave Pete alone and defenseless with that man? Why did I wake up?

Footsteps fall outside my room. Someone is singing.

Artificial light filters through the crack beneath my door, which must mean it's already morning. I kick the covers off my legs and fling the door open.

Danielle takes a startled step back wearing nothing but a towel and presses her hand against her chest. "*What* is your deal?"

My deal? *My* deal!? My *deal* is that she woke me up. She woke me up on her way to the shower with her too-loud singing and now I'm here, away from Pete, with no clue if he's okay.

Looking me up and down, Danielle mutters something about *somebody* not being a morning person, then makes her way to the bathroom with her song following her as she goes. I turn around and stare at my bed, my crashing heart confirmation that there will be no falling back to sleep to find my brother. I throw a sweatshirt over my tank, comb through my gnarled hair with trembling fingers, and pad barefooted into the boy's hallway. I need to find Luka. I need to tell him what happened.

I march to his door and knock. There's no answer. So I knock again. And again, and again. Until finally, a door does open. Only it's not the one I'm knocking on. Declan sticks his head out into the hallway, his flaming red hair squashed and squished in every which direction, rubbing sleep from his groggy eyes. "He's not in there."

"Do you know where he is?"

"I heard him shuffling around earlier this morning. His door opened and closed a half hour ago."

"Do you know what time it is?" Seriously, I need to take Jillian up on her offer to get me a clock from storage. It could be five in the morning or time for eight o'clock breakfast and neither would surprise me.

"Seven fifty-five."

"Aren't you going to be late for breakfast?"

"It's Sunday."

"Meaning?"

"Sunday's are free days."

"Nobody eats on free days?"

He chuckles a little. "Yes, we eat. But we get to eat whenever we want to eat. Cap thinks a full two-day weekend would give us too much idle time. He has no qualms about giving us Sunday, though. Which means sleeping in. No classes. No training, at least nothing mandatory. Eating, we still do."

"Oh. Sorry for waking you up."

"Your boyfriend already woke me up, remember? I'm a light sleeper."

I nod awkwardly.

"I'd check the library if I were you. I saw him bringing some history books to his room before breakfast yesterday."

Declan is right. I find Luka sitting in a tattered armchair—the only piece of furniture in the room. I can't tell if the yellowish color is intentional, or the result of time and wear. There's a thick book opened in his lap that reminds me of the book I saw in his bedroom that first time he invited me over for our world history project. He chews on his thumbnail and flips a page.

My fingers move self-consciously to my hair. For all I know, it's sticking every which way like Declan's. I shut my eyes, trying to blot away the memory of my brother and his dream. It's no use. Pete's gaunt face is forever seared in my occipital lobe, along with too many other disturbing images—the living dead at Shady Wood, my grandmother thrashing for freedom against the constraints that imprisoned her, Dr. Roth's limp body swinging on a noose ...

"Tess?"

I open my eyes.

Luka stands and tosses the book onto the chair. "What's wrong?"

"The man with the scars. He's tormenting Pete. He said he won't stop until I come back. My dad's in jail. The police think he's the one who broke into Shady Wood." My voice grows increasingly strained as I force the words out. "I have to go back. I can't leave them in that mess."

"You're a fugitive. Returning isn't going to make anything better."

"It could set my dad free."

"You don't know that."

"But shouldn't I try? My freedom's not more important than his."

Luka comes to me in the doorway. "You think they'll actually listen to your testimony? The second you set foot in Thornsdale, they'll throw you in Shady Wood, and then what? Your dad will still be in jail and everything we've done to get here won't matter."

Desperation eddies and churns inside of me. I don't know what to do. I don't know what's right. I just know that my dad's locked up because of me and Mom thinks the police are trying to lure me back. I don't get why I matter so much. Why—in this world where drug lords and murderers roam the streets—are they using valuable time to search for me? I'm not a murderer. Despite what the media has to say, I'm not a danger to society. My fists clench by my sides. None of it makes any sense.

Luka gently pulls me toward him. "Come here."

I resist at first, because I'm upset with him. He was talking to Cap about me behind my back. He didn't help me rescue that woman. And he treated me like a little kid in front of Claire. But his skin is warm and he smells like books and I don't have the strength to resist him. I let my body melt against his. I attempt to borrow some of his strength. "We can't go back."

They are the same words I spoke to Pete in my dream, but here, in this physical, wakeful world, they are too much. The weight of them, too heavy.

"Your parents are adults. They'll figure out a way to get through this."

Sorrow curls its fingers around my throat and squeezes tight. Since when did being grown up make a person capable of getting through anything? I take a quick step back before I leak any moisture onto Luka's shirt.

"Tess?"

I pull the sleeves of my sweatshirt over my hands and wipe at my face. "I'm fine."

"You're a horrible liar."

"It's okay. Really. I just miss my mom. And Pete and my dad. Leela." I try tucking a strand of hair behind my ear. "My hair."

"Do you miss my hair, too?"

It's grown some since I buzzed it in Motel California. More moisture gathers in my eyes. I even miss that stupid room, when it was just me and him. No Keepers or Linkers or dead *anima*. No tormented Pete or smug Claire or reasons to be angry with one another.

"You *do*. It's making you cry."

I laugh a little. "You could be completely bald and you'd still be gorgeous."

He raises his eyebrows. "Gorgeous, huh?"

I scratch my ear "What did you and Cap talk about last night?"

"You're deflecting."

"No I'm not."

"Yes, you are. I asked you a question and you changed the

subject to Cap."

"*Gorgeous, huh* is not exactly a question, especially when you already know the answer."

"You have entirely too much confidence in my confidence."

I roll my eyes. "Come on, Luka, you are well aware of the effect you have on girls."

"What about the effect I have on you?"

"I'm a girl."

"Not a typical one."

"Gee, thanks."

He smiles. "I meant it as a compliment."

"So are you going to tell me what you and Cap talked about or not?"

"My training schedule."

"*Your* training schedule?"

"What—you thought I was talking to him about *your* training schedule?"

"Sorta, yeah."

"I tried. But he's pretty set on Link training you."

The sleeping dragon inside my chest stirs. "You don't think he should?"

"I'm not sure how much I trust the guy."

"Why not?"

"You saw him last night. He was wearing this kid-in-a-candy-store look on his face, like this is all a giant game. Your life is not a game. I don't want him treating it like one."

"He doesn't think my life is a game. He just—he's not so ... intense."

"Compared to me, you mean."

My lack of response hurts him. I can tell by the way his

eyes turn down in the corners.

"Link's not your Keeper," he says.

"Maybe it's good that he's training me, then." I'm beginning to think that if Luka were in charge of my training, it would involve extensive reading and maybe some light stretches.

"I feel like you're slipping away from me," he says. "And there's nothing I can do to stop it from happening."

"I'm not slipping away."

"No?" He curls his pinky around mine. "Where were you last night?"

I look down. I'm not sure why I don't want to tell him about Link and the greenhouse. "I turned in early. Didn't really feel like socializing."

CHAPTER TWENTY

A HORRIBLE FATE

B y the time Luka and I get ready and eat big bowls of stale Cheerios for breakfast, the common room is alive and hopping. Jose and Bass play foosball in the corner while Declan watches. Ellen reads *Gone With the Wind* on a recliner that has a giant rip along one of its arms. Sticks stands beside one of the couches, running through some arm blocks with Claire while Ashley and Danielle look on admiringly. Jillian plays a game of solitaire on the floor and Rosie lounges beside her, throwing out shafts of light from her fingertips.

"Turn that up," Cap says, wheeling closer to the television.

Non points the remote at the screen. Beside her, Link sits on the edge of the coffee table with his elbows on his knees, toying with his Rubik's Cube while a recap of yesterday's Presidential Inauguration plays on the screen. My dad usually has us watch that together, too. I push thoughts of my family away and focus on a fuzzy-looking President Cormack as she addresses the nation, talking about how now—more than ever—we must be united as one. A country is only as strong as they are united. There can be no cracks in the foundation. Sacrifices must be made in the name of safety. Everything sounds so good on the surface, it's almost impossible to catch the ominous subtext simmering beneath the shiny veneer.

A flash of bright light whizzes past the periphery of my vision. Luka dodges left.

"Almost gotcha." Rosie smirks from her place on the floor.

Luka chuckles. "Better be careful there, Rose Bud. I can throw one back, you know."

"Who are you calling *bud*?"

Jillian gives me an uncertain smile. Last night she attempted to strike up a conversation while we stood in line for dinner, but I was so paranoid and convinced everybody already knew about Luka being my Keeper, I sort of blew her off. I smile back—overly bright—then slip away from Luka and Rosie's lighthearted banter so I can hear more from our dear president as she impresses upon our nation the importance of not being at war within. I take a seat next to Link on the coffee table.

"Hey," he says, spinning the cube so that one of its faces is completely white. "Where'd you go off to last night?"

He's not asking the same question Luka asked in the library. He knows very well I was with him in the greenhouse. He's talking about dream-world. I look over my shoulder to make sure Luka is out of earshot. He has no idea that Link plans on training me while we sleep. "I thought you said *you* were going to find *me*."

"I tried, but you were nowhere to be found."

"Guess you'll just have to look harder next time."

"Is that a challenge?"

I shrug imperially.

The screen pans from President Cormack to a press conference with one of our nation's senators. "The bill will give insurance companies more freedom to dispense funds wisely. If a woman refuses treatment when a fetal abnormality is found, insurance companies will no longer be obligated to cover the medical expenses that will undoubtedly accrue as the woman's pregnancy progresses. It's unfortunate that this law has become

necessary, but the burden these types of decisions have had on the medical industry have been profound and impact us all. We have overwhelming support for the bill, but there will always be a few dissenters."

The scene changes to a protest-turned-violent outside a fetal modification clinic.

Muttering under his breath, Cap rolls away from the television, punching the power button on the TV as he goes. There's a snippet of B-Trix—one of her advocacy commercials touting the numerous benefits of pregnancy screenings—before the screen cuts to black. It's obvious Cap's had enough. Whether or not he's disgusted with the bill or the protest or the pop star, I have no idea. I watch him approach Gabe. The two confer briefly, then call Luka over to join them. The entire room pauses to watch. I even catch Ellen peeking over the top of her book.

"Gabe and Luka will be needing some assistance over the next few hours," Cap calls out to the room. "Do I have a volunteer?"

I catch Jillian's eye.

"I'll do it." Claire comes forward. I want to object, but Cap nods his thanks and Gabe motions for Luka to follow him down the hallway. Claire flicks her blonde mane over her shoulder and shoots me a vindictive look before walking after them.

A monster roars inside my chest.

Mine.

Luka is mine.

I watch them disappear, so agitated by the sudden turn of events I barely notice that everyone's attention has shifted to me. They are no doubt wondering what Gabe could possibly be

doing with Luka and why an extra body is needed. It's a question I wouldn't mind knowing myself. How, exactly, is Claire going to assist? If anyone is going to help Luka, shouldn't it be *me*—his *anima*? What's worse, Claire's bound to find out that Luka is my Keeper. How much longer before everybody else knows, too?

"You look snarly," Link says.

"What?"

"Just now. You were glaring at the hallway."

"I wasn't glaring. I was looking."

"You were definitely glaring."

I can't help myself. I look down the hallway again, as if Luka might suddenly reappear and decide to use Sunday how it's supposed to be used—as a day off. We could play foosball. I could show him the greenhouse. We could lounge about in the common room reading books or watching TV or playing chess.

"Wanna help me with our next rescue mission?" Link asks.

Luka's not coming back. He'll be spending his Sunday morning with Claire. Which means I will be spending my Sunday morning thinking about Luka with Claire. A vision of the two sparring, Claire's lithe, athletic body entirely too close to Luka's, leaves a bitter taste in my mouth. Poring through databases could serve as a much needed distraction.

I follow Link to the computer lab. He shows me how to pull up lists within lists based on specific keywords and flag any individuals who might possess the gifting. Once all the patients are flagged in a database, Link pulls up their case files, which provide a lot more detail.

A half hour in, he gives me a nudge. "So what's it like?"

"What's *what* like?"

He leans back in his seat, flattening a cowlick with his

palm. "Luka's your Keeper. You're his *anima*. That has to be intense."

I focus on the screen in front of me. "Uh, yeah. Intense."

We work some more with nothing but the clacking of computer keys for noise. I find one patient to flag. When Link leans back in his chair again, I think he's going to push for more information. Instead, he pulls out a large piece of cardboard from between two of the desks. A map of the United States has been taped to one side, marked up with different colored pens. Circles within circles, to be exact—a yellow one around the city of Detroit inside a purple one around Detroit's surrounding suburbs inside a blue one around the eastern region of the state inside a green one that spans all of Michigan along with a large chunk of the Midwest. Inside the circles are several red pushpins.

"What's all that?"

"Territories. The yellow circle represents the ground Jose can cover. The purple is Claire's. The blue is Sticks', and the green is Cap's"

"His is a lot bigger."

"Yeah, well, he's an amazing fighter."

"Where's his Keeper, then? If he's as powerful a Fighter as everyone here makes him out to be, why doesn't he have one?"

"He must not be powerful enough."

I dip my chin. "You're saying I'm more powerful than Cap?"

"I don't know. Maybe his Keeper hasn't found him yet."

"Could that happen?"

"Sticks doesn't think so."

"Why not?"

"According to Sticks, the forces of light work to bring

Keepers and their *anima* together."

My forehead scrunches. A Ouija board and a séance-gone-terribly wrong brought me to Thornsdale. After the horrible things I saw all those nights ago in Jude, I can confidently say there was no light involved. "What would Sticks say if I told him that darkness was the catalyst that brought me and Luka together?"

"He'd probably say that God works in mysterious ways."

It's weird, hearing Link mention God so casually. So naturally. Logically, it makes sense. I mean, if I can see supernatural beings like angels and demons, if the supernatural realm is alive and thriving, then of course it stands to reason that there's a God. Still though, after growing up in a world—in a home—that so definitively squashed God out of existence, Link's statement sounds silly. Ingrained beliefs die hard, I guess. "So Sticks thinks *God* uses darkness to achieve his ends?"

"Confusing, right?"

Enough to make my head hurt, that's for sure. "What do the pins represent?"

"Psych wards located within our reach. Right now, we're looking through a database for a 'mental rehabilitation center' in Lansing."

"What happens if the government realizes you've hacked into their system?"

Link smirks. "I don't get caught."

We work until our stomachs growls, eat big bowls of bean soup and thick slices of sourdough bread for lunch (there's no sign of Luka or Claire or Gabe), then come back for more research. My eyes glaze over as I scan the files, trying not to imagine Luka throwing out force fields to protect *Claire*. I keep checking the hallway. How long can three people train? I find another patient to flag, my leg jiggling like a hyperactive pogo stick. "Hey Link?"

"Yeah?"

"What happened to Gabe's *anima*?"

"He lost her three years ago on a mission much like this one."

My face blanches. I can feel the color seeping away. "She died in a dream?"

"It's not a dream, remember? Not when we've stepped through a doorway into the supernatural realm. Her abilities made her a target. She and Gabe were separated, the other side got her, and when he woke up, she was gone."

"Where'd she go?"

"Her body was still there. Her heart was still beating. Her physical self was fine. But the other side killed her soul."

"So what happened?"

"She never woke up. She wasted away, and then she died."

"That is awful."

"It's about as bad as a story can get."

That's for sure. And Luka can't know about it. Not ever. If he does, he'll do everything within his power to keep me from fighting. "So is that why Gabe is so ...?"

"Tortured?" Link offers.

I roll the descriptor around in my mind. I would have said devoid of personality, but now, with this new information, I see Gabe in a different light. He doesn't have a dull personality; he simply lost his breath of life. It breaks my heart. Not for Gabe, like it probably should, but for Luka. Because if something happens to me, will he meet the same fate? Will my death be Luka's undoing?

CHAPTER TWENTY-ONE

NO RULES

Rosie was right. Non is obsessed with history—wars, in particular. So much so, she often gets lost in her own teaching. She talks about one war, then jumps to another with little warning—all the while scratching a jumbled war web on the chalkboard—stopping more than once to study her own creation, like the thing is a giant puzzle with missing pieces and the harder she squints, the more she'll be able to make out the complete picture.

"History is always connected to the present," she mumbles to nobody in particular.

I'm beginning to wonder if it matters at all that we're here, in these chairs. I'm not convinced she's teaching us as much as she's trying to figure something out for herself and we're stuck observing.

She scratches the back of her head, momentarily flattening a section of her gray, bushy hair. "It's curious, isn't it?"

Luka and I exchange a look—the first bit of normalcy between us since he disappeared with Claire and Gabe yesterday. His dark mood afterward reminded me all too much of Pete. I ended up leaving him alone with his fat history book, and instead hung out with Jillian. She beat me in mancala three times in a row, but I came out the winner, since I managed to evade her questions about Luka's new training schedule by monopolizing on her curiosity about Fighter training. I told her all about the dream space Link created and what it was like sparring Claire. I may have even embellished and exaggerated just to keep us safely on topic.

Our teacher is muttering something to her fist when Claire raises her hand high into the air. "I have a question about Keepers and their *anima*."

My muscles tighten.

Luka shifts in his seat beside me.

Non blinks several times, as if batting away her reverie. "What about them?"

"I was trying to figure out who I'm going to pick for the research assignment Sticks assigned. And I got a little confused. Link's always calling them *soul mates*." She rolls her eyes at Link, who rolls his eyes back. "But that implies romantic love, which can't be true, right? I mean, how could it be? Gabe's *anima* was his sister."

"What?" The word tumbles out in a shocked gasp before the filter in my brain can censor it. And with the word comes a pool of heat in my cheeks, because everyone turns to stare at me.

"You're right, Claire. Gabe's *anima* was actually his *twin* sister."

"But his file said he had recurring dreams of a woman he'd never met before." Again, the filter in my brain fails me. The heat in my cheeks grows hotter.

"That's correct, also. Gabe and his sister were separated at birth and adopted into different families. Six years ago, Gabe's sister found out she had a twin brother and went looking for him, hoping to find out if her biological brother saw the same unexplainable things she saw. You can imagine that Gabe was quite surprised when she showed up on his doorstep."

"So they don't have to be a man and a woman ... *in love?*"

"No, Claire, they don't."

The smug look Claire shoots me makes one thing crystal clear. She knows very well that Luka is my Keeper. I try not to imagine the two of them talking about it—talking about *me*—during their training session with Gabe yesterday.

Lunch comes and goes. I find myself filing after Jose toward the training room with hands clenched into fists. I cannot wait to get to the dojo, put on my sparring gloves, and knock that smug look off Claire's face. The news that Gabe's *anima* was his sister throws me for a bigger loop than I care to admit. If romantic feelings are not part of the Keeper-*anima* package, than why did Luka kiss me? The one-worded explanation deflates some of my anger.

Relief.

Both times Luka kissed me, he was in the middle of experiencing a surge of relief—an overwhelming emotion that could easily be mistaken for something more. But what about Friday? If Rosie hadn't interrupted us, I'm positive he would have kissed me. My anger deflates even more. On Friday, Luka had been feeling euphoric over his success with throwing a force field. Combine that feeling with his innate desire to protect me and anyone could get carried away. This connection we share? It's not like Luka chose it. It's more like the universe forced it upon him. Literally stuck me next door. And now, because of feelings he never asked for, he's living underground in Detroit, Michigan. Away from his family. Away from the ocean and surfing and everything else he loves by choice.

I shuffle inside the room after Sticks but stop suddenly. We have an unexpected guest.

"What are you doing here?" I ask.

Luka doesn't answer for himself. Cap does. "I've been convinced that it would be a good idea for Luka to observe today."

"The dojo's getting crowded," Jose mutters.

Is this what Luka talked with Cap about in the makeshift conference room on Saturday? Or did he arrange it just now, on his way out of the cafeteria? Either way, I'm left feeling betrayed. And childish. Like I'm a little kid who needs supervision. I take a seat in one of the chairs, my deflated anger blowing back up again. By the time Link reaches me, the last of the group, my hands have balled up into white-knuckled fists.

"Already drawing a crowd, Xena." Link pulls down the collar of my shirt and attaches the final probe beneath the hollow of my clavicle. "Maybe someday I'll get to watch you fight."

I can feel Luka's stare, but I don't give him the satisfaction of eye contact.

"All right," Link says, moving to the computer. "Blast off in three ... two ...one."

I blink once and I'm there, in the dream space. Luka is too. He looks around, taking in every inch of the training center before his attention lands on Cap, standing in the center of the room. I know I saw it on Saturday, but it's just as shocking today. Judging by Luka's widening eyes, he's feeling the same.

"You're not in Kansas anymore, Toto," Claire says, brushing her body against his as she walks past. Her tank top shows off long, toned arms. Her yoga pants reveal equally long, toned legs. She's like a graceful lion, seductive in her prowl. I don't miss the way Jose admires her. It's the same way Jared used to look at Summer, as if a string of drool might stretch from his bottom lip at any moment. I'm afraid to look at Luka, lest he wear the same expression.

"The deal was, you don't interfere," Cap says to Luka.

I look between them. "What deal?"

Neither answer.

Unlike our last training session, Cap takes a more active role. He asks Sticks to run through some drills with Jose off in one corner, then tells Claire and me to take our positions in the center of the mat for another round of sparring. Despite my anger and irritation, I'm terribly distracted. Every time I catch a glimpse of myself in the mirror, I'm struck by how foolish I look blocking Claire's blows—like a little girl fighting a woman. As she attacks and I do my best to defend, I can't help but think that she is the one who looks like Xena Warrior Princess. She is the one who deserves a Keeper.

My muscles begin to burn as I dodge and duck and block. She jukes with her left and kicks with her right. Her foot connects with the side of my head and my ear explodes with a high-pitched ring. She jabs me in the ribcage. I double over.

"Come on, Tess," Cap says. "Focus."

How can I, though, with Luka watching me make a fool out of myself?

Claire holds up her gloves and circles me. "I thought Fighters with Keepers were supposed to be powerful. There goes that theory." She does a low roundhouse kick, sweeping out my legs from beneath me. And just like that, I'm on my back with all the air knocked from my lungs.

Claire cocks back her fist, but before she can strike there's a flash of bright light. An intense wave of heat and somehow, Claire gets knocked onto her back too.

"Luka!" Cap barks.

Luka has stepped away from his place against the wall. "She was about to—"

"I have this under control. You interfere again and you're out of here. Got that?"

It came from him. Luka threw out a force field. He threw out a field because I couldn't handle myself. Because I was weak. The realization has me jumping to my feet. I will not let Claire humiliate me again.

The two of us take our positions, and this time, I don't let the mirror distract me. Dream world is not reality. Claire's reflection might look stronger and taller and more athletic, but we're not really here. I know I'm stronger than this. And the traces of medicine that slowed me down on Saturday no longer remain. I am strong, I tell myself. I have a Keeper. I've trained in martial arts since I was five. And this isn't real. I do a round house, leveraging the quickness of momentum for power and connect so strongly with Claire's jaw that she reels back, clutching her cheek.

She looks up—furious, incredulous—and comes at me. I dodge every single one of her blows. I am quick, like lightning. Quick, like a rabbit. I can feel the truth of it pulsing inside of me. She can't touch me. She's too slow. She's too sloppy. Claire throws a punch, but I grab her arm. I twist it around and push her elbow up, forcing her to her knees. I keep her there for a moment, making it clear that I am the one in control before pushing her away.

With rage in her eyes, she comes at me again. Three more times she tries to take me down. Each time, my power grows. I will not let her embarrass me like that in front of Luka ever again. I duck and spin, then pop her in the mouth.

She stumbles back, wiping blood from her lip.

"Time for a break," Cap says.

Humiliation flickers across her face. It's obvious the break

..or her. But as quickly as it came, her expression changes. She steps close, so only I can hear. "How does it feel needing a babysitter?"

I narrow my eyes.

"That's how he sees himself, you know. He told me so yesterday. Little Tess's babysitter. How pathetic." She pulls off her gloves and saunters away, as if she were the victor. As if I didn't just take her down five times in a row. She picks up a water bottle beside Luka—one that wasn't there before—and takes a long drink.

Babysitter? Did he really say that? I whip around to face Cap. "Is this all training is going to be? Because I already know how to fight."

He tosses me a water bottle.

"Where'd this come from?" I ask, twisting off the cap.

"Dream world, remember? You're not actually holding anything. It's all in your head."

The bottle disappears—up and vanishes from my hands. "What the …?"

Cap points to the ceiling. The water bottle rests on a beam high above our heads. "In dream world, if you want something like a ladder? You think it into existence." A ladder appears in front of me, one that leads straight up to the beam overhead. "The second you realize you're dreaming, you can do whatever you want to do." He points to his temple. "It's all in here. Your body's still in the dental chair."

Behind me, Claire laughs. The sound might as well be sharp nails on a chalkboard.

"Think of something you want right now. Whatever you want, you can make happen."

What I want is for Claire to be gone. What I want is to

make Luka realize that I don't need a babysitter. What I want is to get stronger so I can figure out a way to fix the gigantic mess my life has become. I want to become as powerful as Link and Cap think I can be. So powerful that we don't have to hide in a basement anymore. I want to free all those people locked away in insane asylums, like my grandmother. And there's only one way I can do that. "I want to learn how to impact the physical when I'm in spiritual form."

Cap studies me for a moment. "We're not there yet."

"When will we get there?"

"That's level ten. You're at level two. Let's get the basics down first, shall we?"

I look at Cap, standing in front of me when he shouldn't be able to stand. I recall the training session on Saturday, when Claire did a flip that defied gravity. I look up at the water bottle on the beam. This is what I want—to show Cap that I don't need to work on the basics. I tell myself there is no gravity. Not here. The rules don't apply. In fact, there are none at all. I coil my legs and I jump. And just like that, I am dangling from the beam, high up in the air. I take hold of the water, and without giving myself time to be afraid, I let go. My stomach drops as I fall. I land on both feet right beside the base of Cap's ladder, twist off the cap, and take a drink.

The room has gone silent.

Jose and Sticks have stopped their drilling. Claire no longer whispers flirtatious nothings into Luka's ear. I turn to Cap. His arms are crossed. His face is serious. But there's a faint flicker of pride in his eyes as he gives me a small, subtle nod of approval.

CHAPTER TWENTY-TWO

SITTING DUCKS

After my exhibition with the water bottle, Cap had me face off with Jose. Luka was not pleased. I could understand his concern. Jose has the body of a linebacker. I thought that after all the sparring, I wouldn't have any energy left. In reality, I spent two hours lying on a chair. I wake up restless and head to the weight room for another vigorous work out. Luka joins me. I ignore him and my protesting muscles as he spots me on the bench press.

On my fourth set, final rep, I have to strain every muscle in my body to lift the bar one final time. As soon as my elbows lock, I let the weights clank down and heave out a breath. I wipe away the beads of sweat trickling down my temple, then sit up and grab the bottle of sanitizer.

"You're mad," he finally says.

"You think I'm weak."

His eyes flash. "What—you're some kind of mind reader now?"

"I don't have to be a mind reader to make a safe assumption." I spray the bench and wipe it clean.

"Well, your assumption is dead wrong."

And yet Claire's words circle my mind like a vulture—*little Tess's babysitter.*

"Your strength is one of the things I see most clearly."

I crumple the wet rag in my hand and scold my fluttering

heart. It is too eager to hope. At least where Luka is concerned.

"It's quiet. Unassuming. But it's there; this undeniable thing. I saw it the first day we met in Thornsdale. And before then, every night in my dreams. I see it better than anyone." Luka steps closer. Takes the spray bottle from my hand. "Don't tell me I think you're weak, when it's your strength that scares me."

"Why?"

"You heard Sticks. Only the strongest Fighters have Keepers."

"So?"

He looks at me like I'm crazy. Like I don't get it. "So there's a reason you were created with one specific person to guard you. You're a walking target. And now Cap wants to train you, even though whatever he's training you for landed him in a wheelchair."

So he knows. I'm not sure who told him. Maybe Cap himself. Or maybe Claire. It doesn't matter how Luka found out. What matters is he knows the danger that's involved in fighting. How long before he learns how Gabe's twin sister died?

"I can't let anything happen to you. I won't."

"*If* Sticks is right, and I'm destined to be some super powerful Fighter, then you don't have to worry. I have you. You'll protect me." I want to comfort him. I want my words to erase some of his torment, but they only seem to haunt him more.

"You don't see what I see."

"Tell me what you see, then."

A world of fear festers in the grass green of his irises.

"Please, just tell me."

But he doesn't, and I'm left with nothing but my own speculations.

That night my dreams are a hodge-podge of nonsensical things—my father walking to the gallows, angry protests outside fetal modification clinics, the prisoners of Shady Wood buried alive inside mass graves, and dead rabbits everywhere. I can't find my family, and Link must not be able to find me.

By the time me and my aching muscles arrive for breakfast, Claire has already taken the seat next to Luka. And since I don't want to sit by Claire, I end up at a table with Jillian and Rosie, listening as Claire giggles and slaps Luka's knee playfully, like they are good buddies. What's worse? Luka smiles at her. It's the first real one I've seen since Sunday morning. And Claire is the one who gave it to him.

Our first class of the day with Non is more of the same, only instead of wars of the past, she's moved onto events in the present. Her bushy hair waves about as she scribbles dates and names and seemingly obscure, unrelated events on the chalkboard, connecting them in the same web she used yesterday—a disjointed map of crisscrossing lines. I think we all leave more confused than when we came.

We're given ten minutes to stretch our legs and use the restroom before our last morning class with Sticks. He asked us to come with the name of a Keeper we want to research, but I haven't even started looking yet. So I forgo the bathroom and head to the library. Maybe I can grab something that will at least look as though I've put some effort into the assignment. Inhaling the comforting smell of books, I make fast work of perusing the shelves. Toward the top, I spot a clump of spines that look more like composition notebooks than book-books. Curious, I stretch up onto my tiptoes in an attempt to reach them.

Warm breath tickles the back of my neck. The minty smell is familiar. Luka reaches up and easily retrieves them, so close behind me goose bumps prickle my skin. "I guess things aren't as easy to get in real life."

He's referencing the water bottle in the dojo, of course. I take his offering and give them a cursory assessment, feigning indifference to his all-too-close presence directly behind me.

"It was Gabe's suggestion, you know." The words feel like a peace offering.

"What was?"

"Watching you train. He wanted me to see what you're capable of. I guess he figured that if I'm going to be in awe, it's best if that happens when your life isn't in danger."

I turn around. "*Awe?*"

"I was a little afraid, to be honest. You're like a ..." His attention slowly moves from the tip of my feet to the crown of my head, making my skin flush with warmth. "A tiny, lethal ninja."

"I can take Claire, that's for sure."

"Think you could take me?" He holds up his fists in a mock fighting stance. "Come on Karate Kid, put down the books and show me what you got."

My left cheek pulls in with the makings of a smile. I set the notebooks on the tattered, yellow armchair. "I could take you. I'm a powerful Fighter, remember?"

Luka does an arm drag, so quick I don't even see it coming. The motion is light and playful. It puts my back against his chest and his lips near my ear. I spin out of the hold, but this is real life, where I'm small and he's strong and before I know it, he's wrestled me to the ground and I'm pinned beneath him.

"You're lucky we're not dreaming," I say, attempting to

squirm free.

"You think you could take me in a dream?"

"You saw me fight Claire and Jose."

"But I'm your Keeper, created to protect you, which means I must be stronger. Otherwise, who are we kidding? And besides, you haven't seen *me* train."

I stop my struggling. "Claire has."

"Why *Miss Eckhart*, is that jealousy I detect in your voice?"

"I'm not jealous."

"You are." He releases my wrists and gives my forehead a quick kiss. "It's cute."

Cute? Cute is for little kids. Cute is for bunnies. Cute is not what I want to be to him. With the element of surprise on my side, I flip around and pin *him* beneath *me*.

He flashes me a dazzling smile, and whatever threat Claire posed this morning ebbs away. She might have gotten Luka's first smile of the day, but I got the bigger one, and his lips have never looked more enticing. I'm suddenly very aware of the fact that I am straddling him. I'm straddling Luka and he's not exactly objecting. In fact, his hands move to my thighs, then slowly slide up to my hips.

Before I can process what's happening, a frantic scream for help splits through the hub. I scramble to my feet. Luka and I exchange a look of alarm, then take off running toward the noise. We don't stop until we're standing in the doorway of the greenhouse. Anna is the one screaming, tears streaming down her face as Fray lays unconscious at her feet. Luka slides to his knees and presses his ear to Fray's chest. "Tess, get Cap! Hurry!"

He folds his hands over Fray's sternum and begins administering CPR. I stare in horror, because we're too late. We have to be. Fray already looks dead.

Another image permanently seared into my memory—Luka resuscitating a lifeless, gray-skinned Fray on the greenhouse floor. For obvious reasons, Cap couldn't call 9-1-1. But he did call Dr. Carlyle, who gave him specific instructions regarding Fray's care until Dr. Carlyle himself arrived. Non helped Anna calm down so she could focus on casting a cloak, and Sticks shuffled me and the rest of my gaping classmates into the common room, where a somber mood has descended.

The rest of morning classes have been cancelled. Afternoon training, too. We all sit on the couches and chairs, scuffing our feet, looking down at the ground, unsure what to say. My attention alternates between the entryway, waiting for Luka to appear, and Gabe standing guard at the door to the hub, anxious for Dr. Carlyle's knock to announce his arrival. What's taking so long? Doesn't he realize a man's life is on the line?

Luka shows up first and we all come to the edge of the couch cushion.

"He's alive."

A loud exhalation fills the common room—a collective sigh of relief. I didn't even realize I'd been holding my breath.

"Where did you learn CPR?" Claire asks.

"I was a lifeguard at the beach last summer."

It sounds so normal. A thousand lifetimes ago.

"Good thing." Jillian shudders, as though imagining what might have happened had Luka not known CPR. Surely one of the adults would have stepped in.

Luka nudges Rosie's foot with his shoe. "You doing okay there, Rose Bud?"

She sits on the floor with her knees tucked to her chest, hugging her shins. It's the first time I've seen her look every bit the little kid that she is. She looks up at Luka with those deep, obsidian eyes. "Do you think he'll be okay?"

"Hopefully Dr. Carlyle will be able to figure out what's wrong."

"What happens if he can't?" Ashley asks.

"Ash," Declan warns, his attention shifting to Rosie.

"It's a legitimate question." She looks around—wild-eyed. "Anna can't keep the cloak up twenty-four seven. It was hard enough with two of them."

Nobody has a response for this. We all just look at one another, as if waiting for someone else to offer a solution, or maybe at the very least, a bit of comfort. I find myself watching Luka, taking my cues from him. But his only movement is the muscle ticking in his jaw, as though he's grinding something between his teeth.

A quick *knock-knock*, pause, *knock-knock*, pause, *knock-knock* fills the common room.

Gabe doesn't wait for the person on the other side to knock again. He unlatches the bolts and the steel door groans open. The man we met at the hole-in-the-wall coffee shop in downtown Detroit steps inside with a black medical bag and an air of distinct authority. Gabe doesn't even have to point him in the right direction. Without a second glance at any of us—not even me or Luka, who you'd think would draw his attention—he heads down the hallway.

Luka peers after him, then turns to Gabe and asks if they can pick up where they left off on Sunday. There's an urgency to his question, as though learning how to protect me will somehow cure Fray of whatever made him stop breathing.

"I have to stay here," Gabe says, his baritone voice devoid of inflection. "But you and Claire can continue where we left off."

Whether to irritate me, or to escape the heaviness in the room, she quickly and gladly stands from her seat to follow after Luka. As they disappear together, I push out a frustrated breath and grab the stack of composition notebooks I brought with me from the library. I tuck them beneath my arm and separate myself from the group like Ellen, only I'm not reading *Gone with the Wind*. What I'm reading doesn't make any sense at all.

They are journal entries—recordings of dreams and real-life battles, lists of names, locations, even a few obscure hand-sketched maps of places I don't recognize—with dates stretching all the way back to the 1300s. Which sort of refutes everything in them, seeing as composition notebooks didn't exist during medieval times.

I flip to a page dated 1756 with *Fire Heart, Shawnee* transcribed above it. I know enough about American history to know that the Shawnees are a Native American tribe, and judging by the odd wording of the passage, which I think is a recording of a strange dream on the eve of battle, it was written by Fire Heart himself. I'm fairly certain, though, that if this were authentic, Fire Heart wouldn't be writing in English. I'm squinting at the neat, black-inked penmanship, trying to make sense of it all, when Link and Jillian join me on my couch.

"What's got your brow all furrowed?" Link asks, peeking over my shoulder.

"Some notebooks I found in the library."

Jillian picks one of them up. "I've seen these on Non's desk before."

"Really?"

"I'm almost positive."

Link untwists the cap off his water bottle. "We need to find another Cloak."

He's right. Even if Fray recovers completely, his collapse today made it abundantly clear that two Cloaks are not enough to keep us safely hidden. Without them hiding us, we are ducks sitting in the wide open. It's only a matter of time before the other side finds us.

"Link and I are going to pore over the databases," Jillian says. "See if we missed anything the first time around. We thought you'd want to join us."

"Yeah, I do." It's better than sitting here trying to decipher meaning from journal entries that could very well be Non's work of fiction. I collect the notebooks into a pile as Jillian starts walking toward the computer lab.

Link takes my hand and helps me up, then leans close to my ear. "Stop hiding from me, Xena. Training has to start tonight."

CHAPTER TWENTY-THREE

A JUMP OF CRAZY PROPORTIONS

I open my mind to Link. I don't think about my family or Luka or Fray's fragile condition. Even though I want to see my mom, convince her to do whatever she needs to do to bail Dad out of jail and move far away from Thornsdale, this has to come first. I need Link to teach me everything he knows, because maybe then I can help awaken more of The Gifting. And once they're awakened, we can break them free. And once they're free, we'll have more people fighting on our side.

I lay in bed with my eyes closed, thinking about Link—his shaggy hair and the light spray of freckles across his nose, the fast way his fingers navigate a keyboard or twist his Rubik's Cube, his lopsided grin, the mischievous twinkle in his eye whenever he calls me Xena and everything he told me the evening we lay under a plant in the greenhouse.

When I wake up, I'm surrounded by trees. Not the impossibly-tall redwoods that grow up from the ground outside my home in Thornsdale. But oak and ash and birch. This wooded area is so generic it could be anywhere.

A twig snaps behind me.

I turn around and Link is there, leaning against a tree with his hands in his pockets and a grin on his face. "I found you."

"That's because I made myself easy to find."

His grin grows wider. "Can't give a guy a little credit, huh?"

A gnat buzzes by my ear. I swat it away, then remember that this is dream world. There doesn't have to be gnats. Or ants or spiders or any other creepy crawly thing that makes people like Leela prefer the indoors. I look up at the canopy of leaves above, where birds chirp and a squirrel scampers across a tree limb. It's the perfect environment. "So *Teach*, here I am. What's first on the training agenda?"

"Whatever you want to be first. There's dream hopping, dream linking, dream spying, dream searching, scouting—"

"Wait—dream *spying*?"

"It's one of our most valuable assets. Dreams are incredibly revealing, you know. They tell you a lot about a person's emotional state. Their fears, their weaknesses," Link ticks each item off on his fingers, "their secrets."

"How do you do it?"

"The only difference between dream hopping—which apparently, you've already done—and dream spying is that when you enter somebody's dream, you don't reveal yourself. You stay hidden and you observe."

I tuck that morsel of information away for later. "Okay, so what's scouting?"

"The lack of a modifier there was intentional, just so you know. Scouting isn't actually done in a dream. It's done after crossing through a doorway and it comes in handy when you want to scope out a specific location while remaining unseen by the physical eye."

"Dream searching?"

"Ah, that's how I awaken those with the gifting. At least it's how I awaken the ones in medically induced stupors. It's not easy. Anna's mind was so mired in the medicine that was being pumped into her system, that it was almost impossible to access. I had to go very deep. When you finally find the person, you explain what's going on. It's the first step to freedom, since a lot of times, they aren't even aware. Searching's also useful when someone's being hijacked."

"*Hijacked?*"

"Controlled. Possessed. Whatever you want to call it."

"Does that happen a lot?"

"It happens enough."

"What happens to the person who's being hijacked?"

"They're like an oblivious hostage. Stuck in dream world, with no idea that they're actually stuck. Which isn't good, because when they're oblivious to what's happening, they can't fight the entity that's hijacking them."

Out of habit, I scratch the inside of my wrist. "Are they trapped in dream world forever?"

"Not likely. Usually, the entity uses the person they are hijacking to accomplish something specific and once it's accomplished, the entity leaves. Except for some gaps in memory and the fear of Alzheimer's, the person who was hijacked remains completely clueless. I have some suspicions, though, that some people in power are being hijacked indefinitely."

A puzzle piece clicks into place—the government official who shot me in the neck with the needle, the one who dragged me out of Mr. Lotsam's Current Events class and called me Little Rabbit. It's a name I've only ever been called by one person. Was he possessed by Scarface? My mind spins around the thought. Who else might darkness be using to do their bidding? If I can find a way to search for them, awaken them, get them to fight their hijacker ... then surely this will give our side the upper hand. Being a Linker is more than I ever hoped it could be. Maybe even more useful than being a Fighter.

"So what do you want to try first?"

"My grandmother," I blurt.

"Huh?"

"I want to awaken her." I couldn't save her when I was younger, like she hoped I could when she wrote in her dream journal all those years ago, but maybe I can save her now. Maybe rescuing her is the first step to restoring my broken family.

"Your grandma is in Shady Wood."

"So?"

"Shady Wood is in Oregon. We are in Detroit. There's a limit to how far we can hop, remember?"

"I thought that was only for Fighters. I thought the limit only applied to the supernatural realm. This is dream world."

"There's always a limit. Same rules apply here. You can't hop into someone's dreams when they're so far away."

"I can."

"Whoa there, cocky."

"No, for real. The other day, you asked where I was. Well, I was in California. I hopped into my brother's dream."

There's a long pause. A few birds, perhaps unhappy with the sudden silence, flutter away from a branch, up into the sky. Finally, Link crosses one of his ankles over the other. "You must have been constructing."

"What do you mean?"

"Just like you can construct a place, like this, you can construct people, too. You thought it was your brother, but it was just a construct of your brother. You made him appear in your dream because you were missing him."

"It wasn't a construct of Pete. It was Pete."

"Show me, then."

He might as well have thrown down the gauntlet and said *prove it*. He doesn't believe me. But I know I'm right. The Pete from the other night was too real to be a construct of my own imagination. "I don't know how to show you."

Link's cheeks pull in, like he's sucking on the dilemma. "There's a way to tell whether you're constructing or hopping."

"Okay."

"When you hop into somebody else's dream, you can't control it. You're a visitor. What happens is up to the person dreaming. Take right now, for example. This is your dream. You can do what you want. Create what you want. I can't, since I'm a visitor. So if you want to know whether you're hopping or constructing, you do a test."

"Try to create something."

"Exactly."

A tree grows up from the ground beside us. Up, up, up into the air. A towering redwood in the midst of lesser things.

Link looks up at it.

"Now what?"

"Can I make a suggestion? Next time, make your test something a little quicker. Like a penny appearing in the palm of your hand."

"Okay, fine. A penny. Now how do I prove to you that what happened the other night wasn't my own construction?" In the past, whenever I've hopped, I've woken up in the place I've hopped to. I have no idea how to do it when I'm already inside my dream.

Link steps closer and threads his fingers with mine. His hand is smaller than Luka's, his palm smoother. "Close your eyes," he says. "Focus all your thoughts, all your attention, on the person whose dream we're jumping into."

Okay, so who will that person be? I'm not eager to visit Pete again, not after seeing his nightmare first hand. There's no way I'm bringing Link to my mom or my dad. But what about Leela? My heart twists at the thought of seeing her.

With my mind made up, I squeeze my eyes tighter and focus on everything I know about my friend—her obsession with pink, the way she squeals in terror at the mere mention of spiders, the warmth of her brown eyes, the way she hardly pauses between words when she's talking about something that excites her. Her hugs, her bubbly handwriting, her busy room—every inch of wall space covered with posters of her favorite musicians. The way she used to blush whenever Pete paid her any attention.

Leela, Leela, Leela. I want to see Leela.

I repeat her name over and over in my mind until my stomach drops—like I missed a step. The wind no longer rustles the leaves and the birds no longer chirp. I open my eyes. Link and I are standing inside my old high school. We're in the upstairs hallway, right outside of Mr. Lotsam's classroom. There are familiar faces—Bobbi and Chet and Serendipity. For a moment, I forget myself and wave at them. They walk right past, like I'm not there. But really, they're the ones who aren't there. They are figments of Leela's dream. I spin in a circle, searching for my friend.

The hallway clears and there she is, walking and talking with ... Vick Delaney? Yep, it's him. Vick Delaney, former boy band singer turned heartthrob actor for some zombie show that won him more MTV people's choice awards than anybody else has ever won in a single night. *Oh, Leela.* I hate to interrupt her moment with him, but I can't help myself. I push through the crowd, pulling Link with me, and wrap my arms around her neck.

"Oh my gosh!" She hugs me back in one of her tight Leela hugs. "I can't believe you're here. Tess, this is Vick Delaney. Like, *the* Vick Delaney. Can you believe he transferred to Thornsdale?" She looks from me to him, a swoony-sort of expression on her face. "I'm his ambassador."

I decide to go with it. There's no reason why I have to ruin this moment for her, not when she thinks Vick Delaney will be her new classmate. Leela's attention drops to my hand, which is still holding onto Link's.

"Who are you?" she asks him.

But Link doesn't say. He's too busy gawking at me. "Try it," he says. "Do the test."

I close my eyes, only instead of imaging a redwood growing up from the ground, I imagine a penny appearing in my palm. Nothing happens.

"Are you faking?" Link asks.

"Why would I fake?"

"To impress me."

I roll my eyes.

His go ever wider. It is officially the biggest kid-in-a-candy-store look I've ever seen. I'm convinced Luka would hate it. "Holy crap! You weren't lying."

Leela's eyebrows squish together. "Lying about what?"

"Tess, this is *insane*. You just jumped to California."

"Jumped to *California*?" Leela turns to me, her eyebrows still decidedly squished. "What is he talking about? Where's Luka?"

Before I can answer, Link grabs my hand and starts pulling me away.

"Hey, what are you doing?"

But he doesn't let go, and he doesn't explain. We sprint away from Leela until she fades away and I'm sitting up in bed, back at the hub.

What just happened? Why did Link do that? I stuff my arms into the sleeves of a hoodie, open my bedroom door, and run into the very boy I had planned to go looking for.

"That was insanity!" he says, grabbing my arms.

"Why did you do that? We just got there." I wanted to talk to Leela. See how she was doing. Maybe have a couple minutes of normalcy back at Thornsdale High.

Link, however, is not concerned with what I want. He grabs my hand and pulls me down the hallway. I have no idea what's gotten into him, or where we're going. Especially when we head toward the adult dormitories. He stops in front of the second door on the left, throws it open, and turns on the light. Cap pushes himself up. "What in the world do you think you're doing?" he roars.

"Tess just dream-hopped to California."

More lights go on in the hallway. Doors open.

"Cap, I'm telling you. She just brought me with her to freaking California."

"*What?*"

Only it's not Cap's voice responding to Link's excited declaration. I yank my hand away from Link's and turn around. But it's too late. Luka already saw. "You're visiting Link in your dreams?"

"Luka ..."

He doesn't wait for an explanation. Luka turns around and walks away.

CHAPTER TWENTY-FOUR

HICCUP

"From now on, I'll be training you." Cap's unblinking stare makes me fidget. "We start today."

A glob of Claire's grilled cheese plunks onto her plate.

I glance at Luka, but he refuses to make eye contact. If he's concerned or alarmed by Cap's lunch-time announcement, I can't tell. All day he's ignored me. He won't give me a chance to explain. Last night, Link and I were training. It's not like I went looking for him in my dreams for the fun of it. It's not like we share a beach of our own.

"When you're finished eating, meet me in the training room. Claire and Jose, you'll be training with Sticks in the mat room this afternoon." Cap rolls away.

As soon as he's out of earshot, Claire whips around, a blue vein throbbing in her neck. She glares at me like training alone with Cap was my idea. But I didn't ask for this. I didn't ask for any of it. I wait for her to say something spiteful. I wait for her to goad me in some way. Or maybe flirt with Luka. She seems to realize this pushes my buttons more than anything. Instead, she snatches up her tray, dumps her food into the garbage, and stalks out of the cafeteria.

"Hey, I would have eaten that," Rosie calls after her.

Jillian scoots what's left of her lunch—strips of crust and a few stray peas—across the table to Rosie. "Private lessons with Cap now, huh?"

"I guess." I can practically see the cogs spinning in her brain. If there was any question regarding the speculation surrounding Luka's status as my Keeper before, there won't be any now. Gabe, the hub's only trained Keeper, is training him, while Cap, the hub's most powerful fighter, is training me.

Luka stands so abruptly the legs of his chair scratch loudly against the cement floor. He sets his plate in front of Rosie, whose face lights up with delight. He's barely touched any of his food. Without even glancing my way, he exits the room, too.

A pit forms inside my gut as I watch him go. I envision him finding Claire, being comforted by Claire, commiserating with Claire, and what's left of my appetite vanishes. Looks like Rosie will eat her fill today. I leave my leftovers and head toward the training room, passing Anna and Fray's empty table on the way. It was empty over breakfast, too. From what I've gathered, something is wrong with Fray's heart and Anna's caring for him until Dr. Carlyle can return later this evening.

"All right, Xena," Link says after hooking me and Cap up to the probes. "Take it easy on the captain in there. He's getting weak in his old age."

I can't even manage a smile.

His finger depresses a button on the computer and I find myself standing in the dream dojo. It looks bigger somehow, with just me and Cap. I shift my weight nervously. "Is what Link said last night true? Does dream hopping to California mean I can *fight* in California?"

"I'm not sure." He slides on a pair of gloves and tosses a pair to me.

I soon find out that sparring with Claire and Jose was child's play. Cap is insane—one place one second, another place the next, defying gravity, moving in ways I can't even follow with my eyes let alone mimic. He doesn't sneer at me like Claire or remain detached like Jose. He coaches me, insisting that I work harder, focus harder, fight harder. He conjures up distractions, all sorts. They fly at me in the midst of our sparring. Cap demands that I concentrate. That I get my head in the game. I should be better than this. The odd combination of provocation and pride growing in his eyes gets under my skin. I'm increasingly motivated to prove to him that I can do this. That I'm as powerful as I'm supposed to be. That this attention he's giving me is not undeserved.

He keeps pushing—harder and harder. And I push back. Until we're both spent, dripping sweat as we sit on the mat and guzzle water.

I squirt the liquid onto my face. "Did I pass the test?"

He knows what I want to move on to. If he teaches me how to impact the physical when I'm in spirit form, then I can help. I can make a real difference. Link and I can awaken people with the gifting. Cap and I can set them free. Together, we can make our side stronger. It's the only way I know how to help my family.

"It will involve leaving behind the protection of Anna's cloak."

"I'm okay with that." More than okay, actually. I'm chomping at the bit.

"When you open yourself up to the physical, you put yourself in physical danger."

"I'm not worried." But even as the confident words rush forth, I picture Cap in his wheelchair and I'm not so sure.

He studies me in that piercing way of his, a way that indicates I'm about to undergo another test. "First, you need to learn how to startle."

"Which is …?"

"The ability to wake yourself up from a dream. I can't take you past Anna's cloak until you have it mastered."

"How do I do it?"

He crosses his legs and sits up straighter. His eyes roll back in his head. His body gives a small shudder. And *poof.* He's gone. I twist around, as if I might find him behind me. But he's nowhere.

How did he do it?

I stand up and pace, waiting for him to come back and show me. Seconds tick into minutes. My pacing grows frenzied, impatient. What's taking him so long? And then I stop, comprehension dawning. He's not coming back. He's waiting for me to wake up. All on my own, without any clue as to what I'm doing. Eagerness stirs to life. This is another chance to prove myself. To show him I'm capable.

Okay, Tess, think. What did Cap do?

I try rolling my eyes in the back of my head. I even force a shudder through my body. Nothing happens. I'm still in the dojo.

Wake up, I tell myself. *Wake up, wake up, wake up!*

Before I realize it, I'm screaming the words so loud they echo off the high beams overhead. When my screaming stops, I'm still here. Alone. With nothing but embarrassment to keep me company. Who in the world was I screaming at?

I resume pacing, thinking about last night. Link grabbed my hand and sprinted far away from Leela until I was awake in my room. It's not much help. Sure, that's how Link woke us up from Leela's dream. How in the world, though, do I wake myself up from my own?

What usually wakes a person up from a dream, other than an alarm clock? Two things come to mind—fright and death. Seeing as I can't exactly frighten myself, I settle on the second. But how? I'm not about to conjure up a noose or a gun, not when the images they elicit make me so nauseous.

Without thinking, as though my subconscious figures it out for me, I suck in a mouthful of oxygen and hold it captive. I count off the seconds. At forty-five, my lungs start to burn. At seventy, my vision blurs. At eight-two, the room darkens. At ninety, my eyes close and then I'm gasping for air, sitting in the dental chair while Link and Cap stare at me.

"Told you she'd be out in under ten," Link says with a smile.

I gulp in gobs of air—over and over again—until my lungs are satisfied. "I could have done it in five if I hadn't spent the first half waiting for Cap to come back."

Link's smile turns into laughter.

"I'm so glad this is entertaining you."

He's unfazed by my scowl. His smile doesn't even falter. Cap says again, and with the push of a button, we're back in the dojo.

"What was your method?" he asks.

"I held my breath."

"That's no good. You need something that will wake you up instantaneously."

"Tell me what you did."

"It's called a hiccup."

"How does it work?"

"What do you do when somebody jumps out at you?"

"I'm not sure what you mean."

"That moment, when somebody JUMPS—" He shouts the

word, clamping onto my arms at the same time. And I'm awake in the dental chair again, sucking in a sharp breath.

Cap is awake too.

Link lets out a whistle. "A minute thirty. Not too shabby."

"Now you need to figure that out without me."

Link sends me back into the dojo alone. I focus hard on the way my body reacted when Cap startled me. My muscles clamped tight. My lungs seized. A jolt of cold shock crackled down my arms into my fingertips. I squish my eyes closed, simulate the reaction, and I'm awake on the chair.

"Fifteen seconds, Cap." Link slaps him on the shoulder. "That's a record."

We do it again. And again and again and again. Until I'm in and out in under two seconds. Link is about to put me under once more, but Cap holds up his hand to stop him. He stares for an extended moment, then gives me a barely-there nod.

I want to jump out of the chair and do a victory dance. Instead, I give him a barely-there nod in return. I passed the test.

CHAPTER TWENTY-FIVE

CAP'S ORDERS

"Your move, Tess."

Jillian's words are muffled. I hear them without really hearing them. Link and Jose and Claire toss a football near the entryway to the common room—where Luka exited a second ago. An entire day has gone by without us talking, an entire day with us in this weird spot. "Ground control to Major Tess? It's your move."

I blink away the glossy film over my eyes and focus on the board. I move my rook up four spaces and capture one of Jillian's stray pawns.

"That's really your move?"

"Sure."

Jillian shrugs, like it's my funeral. She moves her knight to capture my rook and lets out a sigh. "Check mate."

Sure enough, Jillian's right. Thanks to her queen and now the placement of her knight, my king is trapped with nowhere to go. I knock him over.

"Man, Tess, I never win at chess." Jillian starts arranging the board again, as though we're going to play another game. "Even Danielle beats me most of the time and she's not the brightest bulb, if you know what I mean."

Claire shrieks delightedly. She has the ball. Link has his arms wrapped around her waist and he's attempting to tackle her to the ground. I look at the spot where Luka disappeared.

He didn't even ask about my training with Cap. On Sunday, he said he felt like I was slipping away from him. Today I think we can both agree that *he's* the one slipping away from *me*.

I twist the stones inside his hemp bracelet that's still on my wrist. I want to ask Cap when he will start teaching me how to impact the physical while in spirit form, but he's been MIA since our training—conferring with Dr. Carlyle in Fray's room. I caught a glimpse of Anna after dinner. She looked as though she'd aged ten years in the span of twenty-four hours. She's now having to cast the cloak without any help from Fray. One thing's obvious—she can't keep it up. Either Fray needs to get better or we need to find another cloak. The entire ordeal makes me want to crawl out of my skin. I have to do something. This place is making me claustrophobic.

I stand abruptly from my spot on the floor.

"You don't want to play one more game?" Jillian asks, looking at her watch. "We have forty minutes before lights out."

"I think I'm gonna call it a night." If only I didn't have to walk in between Link and Claire and Jose's football game to do it. I make a beeline for the door and right when I'm about to exit, a ball flies at my face. I attempt to dodge it, but I'm not quick enough. It pegs me in the shoulder.

"Whoopsies." Claire raises her eyebrows and shrugs. "Didn't see you there."

Yeah, right.

"I guess your reflexes aren't as quick in real life."

My teeth grind together. What are the chances that I'd be stuck with a prettier, stronger version of Summer Burbanks in the basement of a warehouse in Detroit, Michigan? I pick up the ball and throw it back at her—hard, hoping she will fumble. Claire catches the ball with all the grace of a star receiver and throws it in a perfect spiral to Link.

"Hey Xena," he says. "You hop to me tonight, all right?"

"Why?"

"We're gonna try something."

I lift my shoulder—a *whatever* acknowledgement, slightly mollified by Claire's twitchy glare. Apparently, she doesn't like the idea of Link and I sharing dreams any more than Luka. I want to go to his room. Purpling is only forbidden after hours and it's not yet after hours. I want to march up to him and force him to hear me out. Link and I are not having nighttime dream rendezvous for the fun of it. He's *training* me. But then, maybe he doesn't care. Non said so herself—keepers primary concern is for their *anima's* safety. What if he's not jealous or upset? What if he's simply realizing that the best way to keep me safe is to let me train with Link and Cap?

The thought is depressing.

I lay in bed, rubbing my thumb over the strange symbol in the upper left corner on the cover of each composition notebook I found yesterday. I've never seen the symbol before. It's definitely not the same one Scarface nearly marked on my brother. I flip through the pages, trying to make sense of them. Together, they paint a historical portrait of The Gifting. I need to ask Non about them, see if they are legit. When my eyes grow heavy, I drop the notebooks on the floor next to my bed and picture Link. The next thing I know, I'm standing in the center of some large, futuristic looking space ship.

Link sits at the helm, looking amused.

"What is this place?"

"Your very own star fleet."

"Why?"

"I talked to Cap after dinner."

My attention perks.

"We both want to see how many people you can link at once."

As far as I know, I've never linked anyone. There was the one time when I brought Luka with me into the spiritual realm, but I'm not sure if that's considered linking. "I don't know how to do it."

"Sure you do. It's the same concept as hopping. You hop to someone's dream, like mine, and we're linked. Then you anchor yourself to my dream, think about the person you want to link me to, and voila. We'll be linked. The most I've ever done is three. It took me all night and I woke up with a splitting headache."

"So what—I'm supposed to pick someone?"

"Anybody you'd like."

"Do we have to hold hands or something?"

"You can grab whatever you want to grab in here." There is a flirtatious gleam in his eye. "If you want that thing to be my hand, I won't object. Just make sure you keep yourself anchored to my dream when you travel to someone else's. I'd start with Claire."

I raise my eyebrow at him. "Why?"

"I've hopped into everybody's dreams here in the hub. Claire's mind is easiest to access."

I have a feeling that's because she's incredibly open to Link entering. I'm not so sure the same is true for me. But whatever. I grab hold of the seat Link is sitting in, close my eyes, and focus all my thoughts on the girl I don't like. Her ice blue eyes. The hungry way she looks at Luka. The graceful way she fights. The air around me seems to shift, like a gust of wind and when

I open my eyes, Claire is here.

"A star fleet, Link. Really?"

"Would you expect anything less?"

She sits in the co-pilot seat, hooking her long, slender leg over the armrest. The way she takes the situation in such stride has me suspecting that Link told her what we would be up to tonight. Eager to get somebody else here, I tighten my grip on the chair and think of Jillian next. Her large, pointy nose. The friendly way she smiles. The slightly dorky way she words things. Again, the air shifts—widens somehow—and Jillian is there, not quite so prepared as Claire.

Her attention shifts from me to Link.

"Take a seat, Jilly-bean." Another seat appears on Link's other side. "We're seeing how many people Xena can link up."

"Oh, fun." Jillian sits in the chair Link conjured up for her. By the way she's looking at me, I think he ought to conjure her up a bag of popcorn too.

"Why don't you get Luka next?" Claire asks. "We can see if he's as hot in Link's dreams as he is in mine."

My grip tightens on Link's seat back. This time, I focus on Rosie. The darkness of her hair and her eyes. Her tiny frame and dusky skin and impish smile. But it's harder somehow, like my mind is crowded, and it takes longer too. I squish up my face in concentration. This time, I hear our new guest before I see her.

"Whoa!" Rosie grabs hold of the steering shaft. "Where are we going, commander?"

"I'm not the commander tonight." Link nods at me, a fascinated twinkle in his eye. "You might want to link to Cap next. His dreams are pretty callused."

I close my eyes and think of the captain. My brain feels

even more crowded than before. Heavy. Easily distracted. But I force myself to concentrate on everything I know about Cap and just as his wife's face swims into focus, he's there making a tally of everyone here—Link, Claire, Jillian, Rosie, and now him.

"You seeing this, Cap? She just linked five of us without breaking a sweat." Link's fascinated twinkle has turned into a glowing fire. "Who's next?"

"Luka," Cap says. "I'd like you to link to him before you try anyone else."

It's not a request. And it makes me wonder why. Why should Cap care if I bring Luka into this ship? And how will Luka feel when he shows up and sees I've waited so long to invite him to the party?

"Think you can do it?" Link asks.

I know I can. Unlike the others, Luka is a snap away. A breath. The second I close my eyes, before my heart can even beat, he's already there. I know before I see, because my whole body feels his presence. The ship is warmer, brighter somehow, and the ache that's taken up residence in my chest expands. I hate that there's so much distance between us. When I open my eyes, he's looking around with coiled muscles. His body shifts, as though shielding me from non-existent danger.

Link slaps his knee. "This is crazy town!"

But I'm not finished. I manage to pull in Declan, Jose, and Ellen, too. My brain feels squished, like I'm in a submarine at the bottom of the ocean without anything to control the pressure. Luka wants me to stop. Link insists I keep going. I spend a good fifteen minutes trying to think about Ashley or Sticks or Non, even Anna and Fray, but it's a no go. The Starfleet is officially full.

Cap begins inspecting the ship, searching for who knows what.

My breath comes more quickly than it should in a dream. Not only does my brain feel squished, so do my lungs. Thankfully, now that I'm no longer grasping onto the seat or trying to pull another person in, the pressure begins to stabilize.

Link boots up the control panel. "Where am I flying this thing, Cap?"

"Outside the warehouse. I need to check on Anna's cloak."

I stand up straight, every nerve-ending on high alert. The pressure has gone completely away. "Are you going to teach me how to do it?"

"Your job," Cap says, "is to *walk* through the doorway. Don't let yourself be dragged."

"How?"

"Close your eyes. Focus on your center. You should feel a pull."

He's right. I do. It's like a tiny hook behind my belly button, tugging me to the left.

"Don't let it pull you. You walk with it. *You* remain in control."

I tune everything else out—Jillian's questions, Claire's sarcastic commentary, the tension radiating off of Luka. I walk to the left, with the pull, like Cap instructed. And the more I walk, the more intense the tugging becomes.

"Resist it, Tess. Don't let it pull you."

I walk some more, drumming up every ounce of self-control that I can muster. The tugging has turned into an all-out yank, a force that is almost impossible to resist and I know if I step one step further, I won't be able to. I open my eyes. I'm standing in the back of the ship. "The doorway is right here."

Cap nods.

"Now what?"

"Now we walk through."

Luka steps forward. "You didn't say anything about walking through any doorways."

I was right. Luka and Cap *did* talk about this.

"I can't show her how to impact the physical while in spirit form without going through the doorway, Luka."

Claire stands up. "Take me with you. I want to learn how to do it, too."

"We can't risk it. The less people who walk through the doorway, the better. Otherwise we'll draw attention to ourselves." Unfazed by the mottled color of Claire's neck and face, Cap turns from her to me. "When I tell you to startle, you will startle."

"What if—?"

"That is a command. If we run into the other side, you do not fight. This is not a fighting session. I need your full cooperation before we walk through. Do you understand?"

"Y-yes."

Cap comes closer. "You don't hesitate. You don't ask questions. You startle the second I give the word or else our training is through."

"Okay. I got it."

Cap steps beside me, where the tug is almost impossible to fight.

"I'm going with." Luka's voice holds as much authority as Cap's.

"We aren't going to fight. I promise you, Tess will not be in danger."

Luka's jaw tightens. "She's leaving Anna's cloak, which means I am going."

"I need you to trust me, Luka."

"I do trust you. Just not with her life." He steps forward and takes my hand. Heat shoots through my palm, up my arm, filling the hollow ache in my chest until it's nothing but warmth and energy. Cap must decide it's not a battle worth fighting, because he takes my other hand and gives it a squeeze.

"Step through. Don't let yourself be dragged."

With a deep breath, and a whispered prayer, I step.

We're no longer in Link's ship. We're standing outside the warehouse, surrounded by darkness in front and the faint, otherworldly glow of Anna's cloak behind. Cap lets go of my hand and begins examining it. It flickers like a light bulb about to burn out. I don't know much about cloaks, but I can't imagine this is a good sign.

Frowning, Cap nods toward another flicker of light—this one in the opposite direction—and we walk toward it. Luka and I follow. I don't let go of his hand. If he wants to stop holding mine, he will have to be the one to let go first. As we approach a homeless man warming his hands over a fire in a garbage can, Luka's grip only tightens and the warmth in my chest grows warmer. My senses sharpen. I actually feel like a rabbit—whiskers twitching, ears perked. As far as I can tell, there isn't any evil in sight. No Scarface or white-eyed men. It's just us and this homeless guy and his crackling fire.

"This isn't dream world. You can't think things into exist-ence here." Cap prowls around the homeless man and stops next to the garbage can. The dancing flames cast moving shadows along his jaw line, turning his eyes into shining rings of gossamer. "But when it comes to your ability to fight, the same rules apply. You are in spirit form right now. The strength of your spirit has nothing to do with the size of your physical body. Or your ability to do this." And just like that, he nudges the garbage can.

The homeless man takes a skittish step back and looks about.

"How'd you do that?"

Cap steps aside and extends his arm, inviting me to give it a try.

I let go of Luka's hand and touch the can in the same way Cap did. Nothing happens. I try touching the man, but my hand is like vapor. It passes right through him.

"It comes from your core, and it's fueled by strong emotion."

"What kind of emotion?"

"That's for you to decide. What fuels me won't fuel you. All that matters is that the emotion is strong." All the muscles in Cap's face tighten, and I wonder what emotion he's letting himself feel. Just as it seems to reach its crescendo, he reaches out again and touches the homeless man's shoulder.

"What the—?" The guy jumps back, batting at the spot Cap touched.

I shuffle through the list of emotions I've felt at one time or another. I'm not sure why. Maybe because Claire is still so fresh in my mind, but jealousy jumps to the top. It's definitely an intense emotion. As much as I don't want to, I let myself go to a no-good place—where Luka's hands are in Claire's hair, his lips on her skin, her arms curled around his neck. The feeling is intensely strong. I let it ball into a fist in the center of my chest. Then I reach out and try shoving the garbage can.

Nothing.

"You're going to have to work up something stronger than that," Cap says.

I look at the fiery glow flickering across Luka's face and I let myself feel today's frustration—the agitation, the helplessness—over the growing chasm between us. I let myself feel the full brunt of his dismissal today, then I try again. The can doesn't budge. I let out an agitated growl.

Cap folds his arms. "The *strongest* emotion you know."

The strongest emotion …

I think about the way I felt when I watched Pete fly out of the windshield in my dream all those nights ago. The way I felt when Luka and I were running for our lives out of Shady Wood, and then through back alleys after we found our only ally hanging dead from a rope. I think about the nightmares I have had and my father in a prison cell. I think about something bad happening to Luka. My entire body turns cold with fear. As I reach out to jab the man in his chest, I can't imagine feeling a stronger emotion.

He doesn't react. Not even a twitch.

I grind my teeth. Clench my fists. I'm failing, and instead of feeling closer to success, I feel further away. Drained and weak. "What am I doing wrong?"

"You're not focusing."

"Yes, I am." I squish the words between my teeth. I couldn't focus harder if I tried.

A scream splits through my frustration.

The homeless man spins around and peers down the darkened street. Every one of the hairs on my arms stand on end. Unlike the scream I heard before, this one doesn't belong to a woman. It belongs to a kid. And it pierces my heart like a sharpened blade. What is a kid doing here—in this place? I take several quick steps toward the terrified cries, barely able to make something out. Familiar black tentacles swirling around a little boy, a street kid like Rosie or Bass. And the fear I drummed up moments ago comes on its own, rushing forth without any effort required. We are not alone.

"Startle."

I spin around. "What?"

"Startle." Cap's voice is firm, demanding. A reminder of the stipulation he gave on Link's Starfleet. If I don't obey orders, he will stop training me. And if he stops training me, what good will I be then? Shutting my ears to the boy's cry for help, I grab Luka's hand and I follow Cap's orders.

When I open my eyes, I'm alone in my bedroom with tears sliding down the side of my face, into my hair.

CHAPTER TWENTY-SIX

BREAKTHROUGHS

The next morning before breakfast, I gather the notebooks into a pile and go searching for Non. I find her in the greenhouse with Anna, whispering soothing words into her ear, petting her hair as Anna repots lavender with shaking hands. The stalks quiver as Anna shakes, but increasingly less as she takes deep, calming breaths and inhales the scent of the purple petals.

"That's it," Non says gently. She catches sight of me in the doorway, but her voice continues in its comforting cadence. "Let your muscles relax. Let your mind relax. Soak up the warmth."

When Anna's shaking has turned into a light tremble, Non joins me in the doorway. "Did Cap send you to get me?"

"Oh, um, no. He didn't."

Anna hums a sad, haunting melody and repots more lavender with her eyes closed.

"Is she going to be okay?" I ask.

"She's still shaken up about Fray. We need to get her to calm down. The more relaxed she is, the less energy she's expending on worry, the easier time she'll have casting the cloak." Non's attention dips to the stack of notebooks in my hands. "What do we have here?"

"I was hoping you would know. Jillian said she saw them on your desk once."

"Jillian would be correct." Non takes one off the top and turns it over. "You're the first student who has shown any interest in these."

"I found them in the library the other day, when I was looking for a Keeper to study for Sticks' research assignment."

She flips through the pages. "Have you read them?"

"Bits and pieces."

"So what's the answer to your question?"

"They seem sort of like an historical account of The Gifting. But they don't really make sense, because the journal entries are dated all the way back to medieval times, and these notebooks didn't exit back then, so unless they've been transcribed ..."

Non flicks her eyebrows. In approval, it would seem.

"So they're transcribed? These are all *real*? But they're all in English."

"Which means ...?"

"They must have been translated as well."

Non touches the tip of her nose. "I met a believer once, early on in my years. Right after I figured out that I wasn't crazy. She was born into a long line of believers, dating back as far as her family tree could go. Her family's life work has been collecting these journals throughout the years, translating them, preserving them, and transcribing them. Believe it or not, these are only a portion of the ones she had."

"Where are the others?"

"Where they should be—with the believer and her family. See, these are the ones I had with me when I had to go underground. Which is how they ended up here. And a good thing, too."

"Why?"

"So someone like you could study them. In fact, I think I'd like to give you an assignment. I'll even have Sticks give you a pass on his Keeper project. You study these journals instead." Non gives the notebook a tap, then makes her way back to Anna. "When you think you have it figured out, we can talk."

My eyebrows pull together. "Have what figured out?"

"The connections. The pattern." Non holds up her finger. "There's always a pattern."

Life at the hub slips into a routine with little to no downtime. I spend the mornings in class, the afternoons training with Cap, and evenings poring over databases with Link and anyone else who wants to help. Thanks to my jumping abilities, the number of databases we have to search have increased exponentially. Fray's condition worsens. Dr. Carlyle insists he needs medical treatment that he cannot provide in the basement of our warehouse. He needs to check into a hospital, so Link works on getting Fray a fake identity. It's his only chance of survival.

Except for the occasional glimpse of her in the greenhouse, I don't see Anna much. Every time I do, my sense of alarm grows. In my opinion, she looks worse than Fray. Luka spends his afternoons training with Gabe, and whether motivated by Gabe's training style or the nightmares he keeps hiding from me, he's turning into an incredibly powerful Keeper. When he joins us in the dream dojo, nothing and nobody can touch me. Claire, Jose, Cap—they all take turns trying to get at me. Sometimes all three of them will try at once. But Luka can throw a shield that is impenetrable. Not only that, Gabe has taught him how to cloak me. Once, he even prevented me from dreaming. It required so much energy it made him physically ill.

I forbid him from doing it ever again.

I'm too busy at night to afford dreamless sleep. I've learned how to dream hop, dream link, and dream spy. I've learned how to sense and find doorways and walk through on my own volition. According to Link, my territory is unheard of. I can jump to California, and I can jump to New York. I can jump as far north as Adak, Alaska and once, I even made it to Mexico City. Link was practically beside himself when he added another circle to the map—bright red, around the entirety of the United States, plus a substantial chunk of Canada and Mexico.

My bi-colored hair grows to my shoulders. Dark at the roots, then two inches down, a wall of lighter brown. My already pale skin grows paler. I forget what the sun feels like against my skin. All of the physical training makes me stronger. And Claire's resentment grows darker. According to Jillian, she was the hot shot before I came, the promising one. The drastic shift in attention hasn't been easy on her.

The evening news has been odd. Either President Cormack's new initiatives are seriously doing the trick or the Chief of Press finally had enough and started popping Prozac. The crime rate and unemployment rate has dropped significantly and the U.S. dollar is worth gold. Cormack, of course, uses the statistics to fuel her increasingly popular campaign—eradicate weakness, unite as one. Now more than ever. She's the first president in a long time who's not only adored domestically, but internationally. A true friend of refugees and immigrants. She's even appointed Secretary General of the United Nations and takes the lead in negotiating a potential cease-fire in North

Africa. It all seems great. Grand, even.

And yet several times, I've caught Non muttering at the television screen.

Every night before bed I pore over the journals. They've become a bit of an obsession. I have a list of each journal writer in chronological order tacked on the wall above my dresser. The first on the list is *Fire Heart*, a Shawnee Indian whose entries span from 1755 – 1762. He helped the French in the French Indian War. There are plenty of other entries before his, but the authors are unknown. Next on the list is a young Ukrainian man who wrote from inside Kiev jail. He recorded several frantic entries in 1929, of fellow *kulaks* being pulled from their cells at night and shot in the head. Judging by the way his writing stopped so suddenly, I believe he became one of them. There are a string of entries from a young Jewish girl who wrote from the hell that was Auschwitz in the early 1940s. She met several other Jews like her and wrote about them, too.

Next was a Chinese man living in Cambodia in 1975, where he and his people were starved and worked to death and separated from their children. I circled the phrase "what is rotten must be removed"—a phrase touted in Cambodia during his lifetime—startled by how similar it sounds to our own president's slogan today. The most recent entries date back to 2005 and were written by a Darfuri woman who lived in West Sudan and told of unspeakable horrors done to her and the rest of her village—so many raped and slaughtered by what she called "devils on horseback".

It's not easy reading.

The first connection I come up with is that they are all fighters. When I bring this up to Non, she looks disappointed and tells me to dig deeper. So I do. Google becomes my best friend and I repeatedly come across names like Stalin and Hitler and Pol Pot and the Janjaweed—names that might not mean much had Mr. Lotsam not been my teacher back in Thornsdale. It was the project Luka and I worked on together in World History—the one on genocides of the past.

I flop my research notes onto Non's desk. "Each one was a victim of genocide."

"Interesting, isn't it?"

"I guess. Yeah." Although I'm failing to see why it's relevant. In fact, I'm much more interested in something I ran across the other night—a reference to some prophecy. I pored over the rest of the notebooks, but couldn't find anything more about it. "Do you know anything about a prophecy?"

"I know many things about many prophecies."

"I'm talking about one in particular." I scratch the inside of my wrist. The dry air down in the hub has been irritating my eczema. "I think it relates to The Gifting. I think it might be mentioned in one of the other notebooks. Did you ever read about it?"

"Maybe I have." Non picks up my research notes and hands them back to me. "Make sure to look for the connections."

Non speaks in riddles.

Later that evening, I'm curled up on the couch in front of the TV, looking through a printed-out database for a rehabilitation center in Phoenix when an anchor for CNN catches my attention with the results of a boring national survey. "And finally, the number one profession on the rise in America is the mental health industry, most likely due to the dramatic increase in mental rehabilitation facilities."

An image comes—one that is never too far from the surface. Rows and rows of patients in medically induced comas, all in the name of *rehabilitation*. Non's words from earlier wiggle like a puzzle piece attempting to shift into place.

Cap, Luka, and I stand outside the warehouse, Anna's flickering cloak a constant reminder that I need to learn this already. I try kicking a pile of rocks, but my foot passes right through.

"Why is this taking so long?" I hate failing. I hate even more the relief in Luka's eyes every time that I do. He doesn't want me to master this skill. No, he's never come out and said it, but he doesn't have to. My failure means that I am still relatively safe, and my safety means everything to Luka. Another point of frustration. I try kicking the rocks again. Nothing. "What if I never figure out how to do this?"

"You will," Cap says. "Now focus."

"I *am* focusing." Harder than I've ever focused on any-thing. Figuring out how to do this is essential. Not just to add another Cloak to our number, but to get my family back. I have no idea how they are doing. I haven't allowed myself to visit them since the night I hopped into Pete's nightmare. I'm too afraid of what I will see.

There's a tug behind my belly button.

I pull my shoulders back and cock my head. I know a doorway when I feel one. It's not very often one opens up when I'm already in the spiritual realm. And this one is strong, intense. It fills me with the oddest sense of urgency. I take a couple steps in the direction of the pull.

"Tess?"

A scream fills the night, only this isn't from a lady down

the street or a young boy fighting off black mist. This is a scream that comes from the doorway. I've only heard my mother scream once in my life, when I was in third grade and Pete fell off a tall set of bleachers. The horrified cry left an indelible mark on my memory, so much so that I recognize beyond a shadow of a doubt who is screaming now.

Horror propels me forward.

Cap raises his voice. "Do not take another step."

As if realizing what I'm about to do, Luka grabs my arm. Cap lunges for my ankle. But it's too late. I've already jumped through, and I'm dragging them both with me. When we tumble out, we're nowhere near the warehouse. We are on the floor of my parent's bedroom, in my old house back in Thornsdale.

And we aren't alone.

Scarface is there, black mist coiling from his fingertips and wrapping around my mother's head. She arches up in bed and screams as though she's in unbearable pain. My heart careens out of control. She needs to wake up. This pain she's feeling isn't real, it's in her mind. This man is putting it there. But my father isn't here to wake her up and somehow, my mother's door is shut and locked. Pete is on the other side banging, banging, banging. To no avail.

"Stop!" I yell.

The man does. He stops and he turns and he looks at me with unhinged triumph. He barely takes a step toward me before Luka throws out a shield that slams him back into the wall. My mother arches up again. Her body twists—an awful, unnatural twist.

Love swells inside of me—hot and white and fierce. I dive onto the bed and I shake her. I actually shake her.

Her eyes flutter open.

Luka must be as shocked as me, because his shield falters. Scarface recovers and runs toward me. But it's too late. I do what Cap is shouting for me to do. I startle awake.

CHAPTER TWENTY-SEVEN

UNFORTUNATE CONSEQUENCES

E xhilaration and terror are two very odd emotions to feel at the same time, but these are what hit me. In fact, they slam into me with such force, I can barely breathe. My mother, being terrorized in California. Me, shaking her awake when my body was here in Detroit. I grabbed a hold of her shoulders and I jarred her awake.

There's commotion in the hallway. My bedroom door bangs open and the light flickers on. Cap wheels inside, his hair a mess, his white whiskers thicker than normal. "You disobeyed a direct command."

Luka walks inside behind him wearing a pair of sweatpants and a white undershirt. "Cap, it was her mom."

The captain rounds on him, and although he's pointed at Luka, I catch myself shrinking back. "She never should have gone through the doorway." He spins his chair and jabs the air with his pointer finger. "Never again, do you hear me? Never. Again."

I swallow, unable to respond—not with words, not even with a nod.

Cap mutters a curse, then wheels back out into the hallway. He didn't comment on the fact that I finally did it. That seeing my mother being tortured was all the emotion I needed to accomplish what I've been trying and failing to do for weeks now. Nor does he tell Luka to get back to his room. This, more than the former, proves just how irate he is about me disobeying orders.

"Are you okay?" Luka asks.

I open my mouth to speak, but the terror and the exhilaration has rendered me mute. I take a deep breath and try again. "My mom."

The corners of his eyes crinkle with concern. He moves to take a step toward me, but before his foot even hits the ground Cap bangs on the wall. "Get back to your room! We're done for the night."

Luka doesn't budge.

As much as I long for his warmth, his embrace (it's been much, *much* too long), I think it might be my undoing. "You should listen to Cap's orders before he kicks us both out."

He fists his hair at the crown of his head, a world of conflict raging in his eyes.

"I'll be okay." I manage the weakest of smiles. "I promise."

When I go back to sleep, I find Link in his dream and tell him exactly what happened.

Cap cancels our afternoon training the next day. He doesn't even tell me himself. I show up to the training room to find Link attaching probes to Sticks, Claire, and Jose. No sign of Cap at all.

"Sorry Tess, I thought he told you," Sticks says. "Dr. Carlyle is here to run some tests on Fray. Cap said he wanted to oversee the appointment."

I have a feeling that had last night not happened, Cap wouldn't have felt so compelled to oversee anything. With nothing else to do, I head to Link's lair and boot up his computer. I've been spending enough time in here that I know his password. I type it in, pull up the database for Shady Wood, and study my grandmother's case while fiddling with Link's Rubik's Cube. I can never solve it. He can in less than thirty seconds, no matter how much I twist it around.

Patient: *Elaine Eckhart,* **Age:** *72,* **Diagnosis:** *Paranoid Schizophrenia,* **Symptoms:** *advanced psychosis,* **Medication:** *olanzapine & lorazepam,* **Treatment:** *ECT, psychotherapy.*

I pull up the calendar and attempt to figure out how many days it's been since Luka and I broke in and saw her. The more days I count off, the more my guilt festers. How could we just leave her there, after everything we saw? I want to get her out of that prison. I want Elaine Eckhart to be the next patient we break out. But she's not a Cloak. Cap would never approve it. I don't even think Link would go for it. The only hope I have of breaking her free is by finding a cloak at Shady Wood. Maybe then, Cap would agree to rescuing my grandmother, too. Since we'd already be there.

I search the Shady Wood database all afternoon, poring over every detail of every file until my eyes sting and my shoulders ache from hunching. With twenty minutes to go until dinnertime, I find something that makes me sit up straighter.

Patient: *Clive DeVant,* **Age:** *46,* **Diagnosis:** *Obsessive Compulsive Disorder,* **Symptoms:** *Claims to hide important items in his dreams, compulsively looks for items during the day, unable to stop ...*

"What you doing on my computer, Xena?"

I spin around. Link stands in the doorway of the computer

lab. Sticks must be finished training Claire and Jose for the day. I wave him over and point at the section I've highlighted—*hides important items.*

Link leans over my shoulder and peers at the screen. "I think you just found us another Cloak."

Link and I make a beeline for Fray's room, throwing each other excited, disbelieving looks as we go. After Link pulled up Clive DeVant's individual file, there could be no denying it. On top of having dreams where he hides things so well he can never find them again in real life, his therapist reported that Clive could see things nobody else could see, and he often insisted that demons were responsible for everything he had lost. We missed him the first time around because Shady Wood didn't tag hallucinations or delusions as a main symptom. After weeks and weeks and weeks of desperate searching, we finally found another Cloak.

Fray's door is ajar.

When I peek inside, my excitement loses its sparkle. Fray lay in bed looking even grayer than the day Luka administered CPR, painfully thin too. Thanks to Dr. Carlyle, he wears a cannula hooked to an oxygen tank and there's an IV that needles the vein in his bony hand, providing medicine and nutrients. It's not enough, though. He's creeping closer to death every single day.

Link raps lightly on the door. Fray doesn't move, but someone does in the corner of the room that the door blocks from view. A second later, Cap appears.

"Tess found a Cloak," Link blurts.

Cap doesn't react. He stares up at us from his chair, then

wheels out into the hallway, closing Fray's door behind him.

"I need you to train me some more tonight so I can get the hang of it."

His lips draw into a thin line; his silver eyes turn to steel. "No."

"What?" Surely, he can't mean it. He's upset that I didn't listen to him, I get that. But this is bigger than hurt feelings. This is bigger than Cap's sense of pride. "I had a breakthrough last night."

"You disobeyed a direct order last night."

"It won't happen again."

"I'm making sure of that."

"If you're upset because—"

"I will not bring an insubordinate soldier onto the battle field. Nor will I bring an impulsive one. Impulsive is what got me in this wheelchair. Impulsive is what killed Gabe's sister. I can't have you risking your life and the lives of everyone else all because you're feeling impulsive. There will be no loose cannons here."

"Come on, Cap, it was only one time."

The captain rounds on Link, his eyes flashing like bolts of lightning. I've never seen him look angrier, or more imposing. "Once is all it takes."

With that, he wheels down the hallway, toward the cafeteria for dinner.

I shove both hands through my hair and kick the wall. Pain stabs my big toe. "I need to practice *tonight*. Not tomorrow or the next day. If I wait, I might forget how I did it."

A slow smile pulls up the corners of Link's mouth. "Cap said he wasn't going to train you tonight."

"I know!" It's nothing to smile about.

"He never said you couldn't train on your own. Or that I couldn't join you."

I find Link sitting in the stands of what appears to be an ancient gladiatorial arena. I quirk one of my eyebrows.

"I thought you should have your own arena. I've never actually been to The Coliseum, but I've seen lots of pictures. I think I did a pretty good job, don't you?"

"Yes, excellent." I close my eyes, eager to feel the tug of a doorway.

"Aren't you going to get Luka first?"

"I thought we'd give him the night off."

Link makes a sound.

I open one of my eyes. "Do you have something to say?"

He shrugs a shrug that speaks volumes. He knows I'm not concerned with giving Luka the night off. I'm more concerned that he'd put a stop to our plans the second I pulled him into this arena. He's not comfortable with my training when Cap's around. I can't imagine he'd be too thrilled to learn that I made plans with Link to do that very same training without Cap's supervision.

I push thoughts of Luka out of my head and focus on the tugging. I step to the right and the thin pulse strengthens. Another step to the right and it turns into a pull. "You feel that?" I ask.

"Sure do."

We clasp hands and walk through together. When we step over the threshold, we aren't where we normally are—directly outside the warehouse. We've gone further than usual. We're standing outside the rundown tattoo parlor, the one with a dragon painted on the window. It sits on the corner of the street that leads to the warehouse, and another street that's not quite so abandoned. A scantily-dressed woman hangs out kitty-corner across from us, showing off long legs and crooking her finger at a car that drives past. The vehicle slows to a stop. The woman climbs inside and the street is deserted again.

"Can you feel that?" I ask Link.

"The cold?" He rubs his hands together. "I never understood why we can feel cold when we're not in our physical bodies."

No, not the cold.

It's a heaviness. As though something dark lurks around the corner. It makes me uneasy. I step closer to the tattoo parlor, next to a bolted-down garbage can (just in case someone's in the mood to pilfer a garbage can, I guess). A crushed beer can sits on the ground beside it. I close my eyes and let myself feel the emotions I felt last night—the fear and the anger, and most of all, the love. My mother, the woman who raised me. I think about the way she played with my hair whenever I had a nightmare as a little girl. The motherly way she peppered me with questions the minute Pete and I walked through the door after school. The embarrassing tour she gave Leela of our house. Her happiness when I started making friends in Thornsdale. What it must have been like for her when she had to pack a bag for me and send it with Luka. I miss her so terribly it feels as though all the world's gravity takes up residence in my chest. I let it swirl and build until I can't handle it anymore, then I swing back my leg and kick the can.

It whizzes past Link's nose.

My eyes widen. I did it. For the second time now, I have moved something in the physical realm without being there in physical form.

Link looks from me to the can. "Do it again."

So I do. Again and again and again, until I'm exhausted, replete, absolutely wrung dry. And just as I'm learning some control, just as I've gotten to the point where I don't send the can sailing, but scoot it a few subtle inches with my toe, the sound of clapping breaks through my concentration.

"Well done! Well done, Little Rabbit."

I whip around, dread crawling up my throat.

He's here in Detroit, grinning like the Cheshire cat.

It's so startling that my eyes fly open in bed. I sit upright and look about, as if the man is here in my room. How did he find me? How did he get from California to Detroit? Last night, when I finally obeyed Cap's orders and startled, it was only after Scarface lunged at me. Did I give him enough time to grab on? To travel through the door and find us here?

If this is true, I've put everyone in serious danger. Anna's cloak is failing. It's only a matter of time before he finds us.

CHAPTER TWENTY-EIGHT

THE PROPHECY

N ever mind purpling, I have to talk about what happened. Besides, it's four fifty-five, which makes it more early morning than middle of the night. I step out into the darkened antechamber, prepared to head down the boys' hallway when a light flickers to life down the corridor that leads to the cafeteria.

Is Link already up and about?

After a couple months here at the hub, I've learned many things about Link, one of which is his affinity for sleeping in. If he could make up the schedule, breakfast would be at ten every day. Not only does he enjoy sleeping in, he can sleep through almost anything. Once, Bass and Declan were in a full-out wrestling match—complete with body-checks against the wall—right outside Link's bedroom and he slept right through it.

I tiptoe toward the mumbled conversation and scratch the inside of my wrist, just in case I didn't actually wake-wake up and this is still a dream. The spot burns. When I reach the entryway, I stand against the wall and force my breathing to come as silently as possible.

"Couldn't sleep either, huh?" The gruff voice belongs to Cap.

Whoever he asks doesn't reply—at least not verbally.

"Still having the nightmares?"

My ears perk.

"Some nights are worse than others." It's Luka. He's the one who is awake.

I peek around the corner and see them sitting at one of the tables. Cap pours coffee from a pot into the mug in front of Luka, then fills his own as well.

There's a long stretch of silence. So long I start to feel silly, standing here in my pajamas, listening to the pair of them drink their coffee. I should make myself known. Shuffle out from my place against the wall and join them.

"Did you train Tess tonight?"

I press my shoulder blades against the wall.

"I'm trying to teach her a lesson, but something tells me she took matters into her own hands."

So Cap knew I would go anyway? And Luka suspected that whether with Cap or not, I wasn't going to bring him with me this time. I close my eyes. Luka's primary concern may be about my safety—he may, in fact, feel as though he's forced to babysit—but my feelings for him go so much deeper than that. And although he drives me crazy with his over-protective ways, I miss him. So much it leaves an empty ache in the pit of my stomach.

"Do you think she figured it out?" Luka asks.

"If I was a betting man, I'd say yes."

"So where does this leave us?"

"We have some time before we need to move. I have an eye on Anna's cloak. She's holding up better than we think. I'd like Tess to have a couple more weeks of training under her belt before we enter into life-or-death situations."

Another couple weeks? How can Cap possibly think Anna's cloak will make it that long?

A rhythmic scritching sound, as though someone is slowly spinning their mug against the surface of the table, fills the silence. And then, "It took me two years before I learned how to do what she did the other night. I've been training Sticks for three. Tess managed to figure it out in a little less than three months."

My brow furrows. I had no idea it took Cap that long.

"Why her? Why can she link *and* fight? Why am I her Keeper?"

Luka's frustrated questions pull at the corners of my mouth, turning them downward. Worry is a gnawing emotion. It's no fun to feel, not even when that feeling is our choice. I can't imagine how awful it must be to have the emotion thrust upon you against your will. I'm like a thorn in his side. One he can't escape. One he never asked for.

"There's a prophecy."

A prophecy? Is this the same one I came across in the journals?

Cap clears his throat. "It was made many, many years ago. Given by a believer during the fall of Rome in 476 A.D. Recorded on a scroll, the whereabouts of which are unknown."

"What does it say?" Luka asks.

"I don't know all the details, nor do I know how much has been embellished over the course of time. But I do know the main points."

There's a torturous pause. I press my lips together, silently urging him to continue.

"Those with the gifting were created to keep the powers of darkness contained. The prophecy tells of a time when The Gifting will face extinction, and in defense, there will be One who arises with a gifting that manifests itself differently than ever before. This person will have the power to save us from extinction and contain the forces of darkness until the day they can be eradicated altogether."

Goose bumps break out everywhere on my skin. I swear I even have them on my palms.

"You believe this prophecy is truth?"

"I didn't used to," Cap says.

"But that was before you met Tess."

"She doesn't realize the potential inside of her, Luka. She doesn't see it in herself. I've never seen anyone with a gifting like hers."

"If you're right, if she's the One, what does that mean?"

"It means a war is coming. And Tess is going to lead us."

I lay beneath a row of tall spinach plants hoping nobody will find me. I don't want to be in the hub anymore, and while Link is right and dreams enable me to escape for a time, they also come with doorways I don't want to step through. Doorways that lead to my mother's screams. Doorways that lead to a man who relentlessly hunts me, like he won't stop until he has me. I'm sick of doorways and I'm sick of being stuck in a basement.

So I came here, with Anna, who waters a row of tomato plants on the other side of the room, unfazed by my presence. She goes about her business like my behavior is completely normal. Like people come to the greenhouse and lay on the ground all the time. I inhale the scent of green and earth, imagining wind rustling through the leaves overhead, pretending the bright artificial lighting is the sun on my face, trying not to replay Cap and Luka's early morning conversation.

But it's no use.

Cap—and, I suspect, now Luka—believe the prophecy is about me. My own grandmother called me the "key", something I've been able to brush off as medicated nonsense. Until now. Still, it's the most ridiculous thing I've ever heard. Even more ridiculous than angels in ceramics class and dream hopping and doorways into the spiritual realm and every other ridiculous thing I have seen and heard and experienced since that séance in Jude changed the whole world.

The question I've wanted to ask ever since I found out I was "powerful" enough to warrant a Keeper rises to the surface. *Why me?* Why am I able to fight and link? Why can I jump to California and New York when Cap can only jump to Northern Missouri? Why, why, why? They bounce around inside my head like the balls inside that Powerball machine I've seen on TV, except there's no exciting lottery to be won. There's nothing but too much pressure and a world of crazy expectations crushing me beneath their weight.

"Tess."

My eyelids flutter.

Cap looms above me in his chair.

So much for hiding.

"You're missing class," he says.

"I don't care about class." The words escape as dry as winter air, devoid of all emotion. I used all of them up last night while honing my skills with Link. Really, though, what does class matter? Anna's cloak will fail. Scarface will find us. And I will prove to Cap and Luka and everyone else that the prophecy chose wrong. The "key" is a dud.

"Link tells me the two of you had a little adventure last night."

I wait for the reprimand, more of what he handed to me last evening—that I'm insubordinate. A loose cannon. Not to be trusted. But Cap says nothing. He just sits there in his chair staring down at me.

"I don't understand."

"What is it you don't understand?" he asks.

"Look at me. I'm below average in height. Slightly above average in intelligence. And utterly average in every single other way. I'm nobody special." How ironic that I spent the majority of my life wanting nothing more than to be the very thing that taunts me now—average. Normal. A person who flies under the radar. The wish mocks me. I sit up and set my elbows on my knees. "I overheard you talking to Luka this morning. But you're wrong. I'm not powerful enough to lead anyone. Especially not an army."

"I agree. You're not powerful enough."

I pull my chin back. "But I thought—?"

"Your gifting isn't something you earned or deserved. It was given to you. It's a gift, the size and value of which says more about the giver than the recipient. By definition, it doesn't come from you at all."

"Where does it come from, then?"

"The one who created you. The one we're fighting for."

"You mean *God*?"

Cap bows his head in concession, but I shake mine. Why would this *God* give someone like me such a gift? It doesn't seem like a very smart move. It doesn't clear up my confusion at all. "All of that you just said? It still leaves me with the same question. *Why me?*"

"Why *not* you?"

Is Cap really asking that? Because if he wants them, I can

give him a million reasons.

"Sometimes, the most ordinary people are given the most extraordinary things. Who knows *why* you were chosen. You're dwelling on the wrong question."

"What's the right question, then?"

"The gift is yours. You can bury it if you want. You can deny it or ignore it. Or you can embrace it. *That's* the question, Tess. What are you going to do with the gift you've been given? It's something only you can decide."

Chapter Twenty-Nine

Rogue

*W*hat am I going to do with the gift I've been given?

The answer came almost immediately after Cap finished asking the question. It comes so easily, so obviously, like something I've known all along. I'm going to do what I should have done months ago, when Luka and I broke into Shady Wood. I'm going to break my grandmother out of that prison. I try to drum up a sense of urgency in Cap, but he thinks we have time. He says the reason they rescued Anna successfully was because they didn't rush. They planned; they researched. But what more do we need to research? Clive is a Cloak. My grandmother is a Fighter. Cap may think I need a couple more weeks of training, but I don't. Two more weeks won't change anything for me. It could mean life or death for them. I've waited long enough. I've let my grandmother languish in that place long enough. The time is now.

The question is, how do I start?

Link has taught me everything except how to awaken someone. I could perhaps go to him and tell him what I'm thinking. He's my best bet for an ally. But something tells me that even he—rules-don't-apply-to-him Link—will be wary of starting without Cap's permission. Various plans spin about in my mind. All of them start at the same place. First, before we can awaken my grandmother or Clive, I need to make sure I can find her. And dream *searching* is something I already know how to do.

That night in bed, I focus on everything I know about my grandmother. I close my eyes and create a mental picture in my mind—her white hair, my father's eyes, the same prominent nose, her gaunt face. I picture her handwriting in the dream journal. I think about her gnarled fingers curling around mine when Luka and I broke into Shady Wood. Her raspy voice, as if it had long gone out of use. The frenzied look in her eyes when she said I was the "key". I play the entire scene on repeat until my mind drifts into slumber.

When my eyes open again, I'm in a mass of hazy white. I'm standing in a cloud. There's nothing but fog and mist, above me and even below my feet. I turn in a circle, trying to gain my bearings. This has never happened before. What if I dream hopped somewhere I shouldn't have? What if I can't escape? I shake my head. It's as though the fog is seeping into my own mind.

"Grandma?" I call.

Nothing.

I walk forward a few steps, squinting through the white. I call for her louder this time and keep walking, trying to ignore my swelling sense of panic. I cup my hands around my mouth to form a megaphone. "Elaine Eckhart! Are you in here?"

There's movement up ahead—a small, slight stirring.

I run toward it. The fog gets thicker, so much so that I bat at it with my hands. It's so hard to see now that I stumble over her—my grandmother, sitting in that way Rosie sits when she's feeling scared, with her knees drawn up to her chest, rocking back and forth. I crouch beside her. "Elaine?"

Her rocking stops. She looks up from her knees and her paper-thin eyelids quiver with the tiniest flicker of recognition.

Or maybe it's not recognition at all. Maybe she's just incredibly startled to see someone here, in this cloud of a place.

"Do you know who I am?" I ask, maintaining eye contact.

She shakes her head.

"My name is Tess Eckhart."

"Teresa?"

A seed of hope sprouts inside my soul. She remembers me. She knows me. "Yes, my name is Teresa Eckhart."

She reaches out her trembling hand and touches my cheek, as if to make sure I am real. "How do I know you?"

"I'm your granddaughter. I came to visit you once, not too long ago."

"You came with a boy?"

I nod, faster. She's more lucid than it would seem.

She presses her hands against the vaporous floor and looks about, as if realizing for the first time that she is somewhere very odd. "Where am I?"

"We're in your dream."

"A dream?"

I nod, unsure how much I should tell her. She looks so fragile. Like one too many words will turn her back into the curled-up pill bug I ran into a few seconds ago. And what if the things I tell her now make her say suspicious things when she's awake? Now that I know I can find her, I need Link. I don't know how to do this. "You're in Shady Wood."

"What's that?"

"It's the place where you live." If living is what it can be called. I press my lips together. Do I tell her that she's on medicine? Do I tell her that's why her dream is like this? Do I tell her that we are going to break her out and that she cannot, under any circumstances, arouse suspicion in the doctors or nurses? It all sounds so complicated. Much too complicated for the state she's in right now. And who's to say she'll remember any of it when she wakes? I can't afford to mess this up. "Would it be okay if I came back again to visit?"

"Here?"

"Yes, here." If I got here tonight, then I can get here again tomorrow. "I'm going to bring a friend. Is that okay?"

My grandmother nods. "I—I think I'd like that."

The second I wake up in bed, I kick off my covers. The clock reads 4:27 a.m. I need to find Link. I suppose I could go back to sleep and hop into his dream. He always leaves them wide open to me. But there is no way, short of being hooked to those probes, that I will fall back asleep again. Not with all this adrenaline coursing through my body.

I peek out into the hallway to make sure the coast is clear. Unlike yesterday morning, there's no light or murmuring voices coming from the cafeteria. I creep through the empty antechamber, down the boy's hallway, and gently knock on Link's bedroom door. When he doesn't answer, I knock again—just as quietly, but quicker—and press my ear against the wood.

Nothing.

With a here-goes-nothing breath, I grab the handle on his door, let myself inside, and march through the dark room, bumping my shin against something on my way to his bed. "Link," I hiss, clutching my smarting leg.

He mumbles something incoherent and turns over.

I grab his shoulder and give it a good shake. "Link!"

"Xena?" His voice is croaked. Unlike me, he doesn't get

extra sleep during the day. While I can easily get by with four hours since I spend three of them sleeping almost every afternoon while training with Cap, Link needs a good six. He sits up, the covers falling to his waist in a crumple. It's not so dark that I can't tell he's not wearing a shirt. "What's going on?"

"We need to talk."

He pulls the covers off his legs and finds the light switch.

I've never been inside Link's room before. When my eyes adjust, it's like I'm sitting inside an inventor's den. There are gadgets everywhere. Smaller ones that look like remote controls and tracking devices, slightly larger ones that look like computers and cable boxes, even security alarms. Most are half-finished. Some are completely disassembled. "What are you doing with all this stuff?"

"Tinkering." Link shuts the door.

The click is soft, but the sound echoes. I've been alone with Link multiple times over the past couple months. There's no reason to feel awkward now. But this isn't a dream, and well, he's half-naked. And well built. I blink away from his bare chest. "I found my grandmother."

"What?"

"She's highly medicated, but I found her and she recognized me. Do you think you could put on a shirt?"

He grabs one off his floor and pulls it over his head.

I stand and begin a short-routed pace between his bed and a computer tower beside his dresser. "I didn't know how to awaken her. I was afraid of saying something that would make things harder, or—"

"Wait, wait, wait." Link holds up his hands as if to slow down my words, then sits on the edge of his bed and pinches the bridge of his nose. "Hold on a second. I'm still waking up here. You found your grandmother?"

"I want to break her out."

"Does Cap know what you're up to?"

"He wants me to train for a couple more weeks. And even if he was ready and willing to start a new rescue mission right now, you and I both know that my grandmother would not be included in that mission." My grandmother is a Fighter. We're not looking for another Fighter, we're looking for a Cloak. Cap has never been in the business of making emotional decisions. He has to think logically and strategically, with the safety and good of the entire hub in mind. I'm sure he will see too much danger in rescuing two people at once. But if the plan is already under way and my grandmother is already awakened … well, then. I don't see how he'll say no. "I'm not going to Shady Wood without breaking her out. I left her once. I won't do it again."

"You think you can unhook her medicine without being detected?"

"Yes."

"Cap will be livid if we go rogue like this, you know. And we're going to have to tell him eventually. I mean, we can't break them out without the whole team."

"I know. I'm not planning on it. I just need to get it started first." The question is, is Link crazy enough to get it started with me? "You've seen Anna's cloak with your own eyes. It's failing every day. It's only a matter of time before it goes out altogether."

And then what? How long before we are found? How long before all of us are arrested and thrown into jail, or worse, put into a place like Shady Wood? I imagine myself strapped to a bed, medicine needled into my neck against my will. Luka too. They will put us in isolation. They will convince us that the other doesn't exist. I remember the feeling all too well—not knowing what's real and what isn't, thinking Luka was a figment of my imagination, thinking my grandmother was dead. Thinking I was crazy. I can't let that happen to me, and I definitely cannot let that happen to Luka. The only way I can pull this off is by convincing Link to help me get the plan rolling. "You saw that man last night. You know how close he is."

"Yeah. Who is that guy?"

"Nobody good."

Link rubs his eyes and peers up at me. "You know this will be highly dangerous?"

I nod.

"Anna wasn't our first mission, she was just our first successful mission."

"What happened to the others you tried to rescue?"

"They didn't make it."

Fear presses against my shoulders, but I stand up straight beneath its weight. I've been given a gift unlike any Cap has ever seen. He said so himself. It's up to me to decide how I will use it. Well, I've decided. I'm going to break my grandmother out of Shady Wood and I'm going to give the hub another Cloak. "I can do this, Link. I know I can. But I can't do it without your help."

A wicked grin pulls in his cheek. "Count me in."

Chapter Thirty

AWAKENED

"**I**'m surprised you didn't ask to train last night," Cap says as we wait in line for our oatmeal. The comment comes with a healthy dose of suspicion.

Luka hands me a tray, silent but attentive.

I tuck a strand of hair behind my ear. "I assumed you were still teaching me a lesson."

"I hope the lesson has been learned. If so, we can pick up where we left off."

I focus my attention on Declan, who doles out a large scoop of steaming oatmeal and another scoop of fresh raspberries—courtesy of the greenhouse—to everyone who passes by in line. I'd rather not look Luka or Cap in the eye when I say what I have to say. Luka, especially. He will see right through me. "I'm going to train with Link tonight."

The tension that radiates from the boy beside me is instantaneous.

Cap frowns. "Like you trained with him the other night?"

"No, not like that. I need to—um—fine-tune some linking skills." This is technically the truth. Awakening someone *is* a linking skill I have yet to learn. Who better to practice it on than my grandmother? But the suspicion in Cap's eyes grows.

He watches me throughout the day. Him and Luka both. I don't ease their misgivings at all when I recommend that Cap and I train in the mat room for the afternoon so Claire and

Jose and Sticks can have a turn in the training center. There's no getting around it though. I need to be exhausted tonight if I'm going to get to sleep, which means I can't take a three hour nap on a dental chair in the middle of the day. Luka seems slightly mollified when I ask if he'll join us.

I can't spar with Cap in the mat room, so he coaches while Luka and I spar. I may be quick and well-trained, but Luka is significantly faster, stronger, and taller. He's toying with me, I can tell. I work up a sweat. He barely breaks one. But his grin makes it all worth it. It's been a long time since we've had any fun. Once my muscles can go no longer, Luka practices casting his shield. I stand in the center of the room while Cap throws things at me—gloves, five pound dumbbells, a whole bucket of tennis balls—while Luka uses a force field to block every single one. When we're finished, I head to the weight room and push my exhausted muscles further on the treadmill.

Luka watches from the squat rack.

I increase the incline and keep going. I can only manage two miles.

At dinner, I scrape my plate clean (sorry Rosie). I always have an easier time falling asleep on a full stomach. I play Jillian in several games of mancala, then excuse myself to my room to turn in early. Luka's hot stare follows me from the couch all the way until I step into the hallway, out of sight. I shower, brush my teeth, get into my pajamas and lay in bed with the composition notebooks, looking for anything I missed, hoping the reading will make me tired. Around midnight, my eyes grow heavy. I set the journals aside and think about Link.

This time there is no Starfleet and there is no Coliseum. Just Link in a generic room, dressed in army fatigues.

"What took you so long?" he asks.

"What do you mean?"

"I've been waiting forever. I was beginning to think you were gonna stand me up."

I scratch my temple, not exactly sure. From my vantage point, I fell asleep and then I found him. Why would he be waiting forever? I quirk my eyebrow at his ensemble. "What's up with the outfit?"

"We're going into battle. I thought I should dress appropriately."

"This isn't a joke."

"I know." He dips his chin and nudges me with his elbow. "But it sure is fun."

I roll my eyes and grab his hand and pin every ounce of my mental energy on my grandmother. There's that familiar feeling—a drop in my stomach like I'm falling without really falling at all. When I open my eyes, I'm in the white cloud again with Link's hand in mine. Only somehow, the white cloud is denser than before.

Link coughs and bats at the vapor. "How could you find anyone in this place?"

"It wasn't this thick last night." I tighten my grip on his hand, afraid that if we let go, we won't be able to find each other again.

"They must have upped her medicine."

"Why?" But even as I ask it, I know the answer. My grandmother must have done or said something that aroused suspicion. Somebody is on to us. I walk forward, pulling Link along with me, shouting my grandmother's name. We walk for what feels like an eternity, until finally, Link yanks me to a halt. "Tess, this isn't going to work."

"She's in here somewhere. I know she is." I call out her name again and stumble over something. It's her. Curled up into a ball. I bend over and shake her, worried that she's somehow dead. That I waited too long and now it's too late. "Elaine!"

I can feel the tug of a doorway. It would be so easy to step through it and unhook her medicine. Make some of this blasted fog disappear. Link must feel it too, because he holds tighter to my hand. "You can't unhook her medicine. If she starts acting coherent before she knows she's not supposed to act coherent, then our mission will fail before it begins."

I grip her shoulder and give her an aggressive shake.

Her head lolls. Her eyes stay closed.

I look up at Link. "What do we do?"

He nudges me aside, grabs my grandmother beneath the arms, and pulls her up into standing. Then he pushes her. Hard.

"Link!"

My grandmother stumbles back. Her eyes fly open. He catches her hand before she falls. "I'm startling her. Because of all the medication, she won't wake from the dream, but it will make her coherent inside of it."

Grandma's eyes begin drooping again. Link gives her another hard push and her eyes open even wider this time. She looks left, then right. Whatever Link did, it worked.

"I'm Teresa Eckhart," I say. "Do you remember me?"

"You—you were here before …"

"You said I could come back. You said I could bring a friend. We want to help you."

She looks at me like my offer to help is a shard of jagged glass that will tear open her skin. I need her to understand what's going on, but I don't know how.

Link grabs her by the arms and gives her a violent jolt. "Elaine Eckhart, we are inside your dream." He waits a couple beats, then gives her another rattle, as if to physically shake the meaning of his words into place.

Her confusion ebbs.

Link doesn't let go of her. He speaks loud and slow. "You are being medicated." He gives her another jolt. Her head wobbles like a bobble head. "You are a Fighter." Another rattle.

She's staring at him now, almost fully attentive.

"But you are trapped inside a mental facility called Shady Wood." Another shake. "You cannot trust the doctors or the nurses." More shaking, harder this time, as if really rattling that truth down deep inside the crevices of her brain. "We are here to help you. We're here to get you out."

Shake, shake, shake.

I watch, wondering how in the world Link learned this. If he never met another Linker before him, then how did he figure this out? I have to imagine it took a lot of time and a lot of educated guessing and probably a lot of help from Cap.

"You cannot tell anyone what we are doing." Shake.

Her eyes are as wide and round as ping pong balls now. My grandmother stares at Link with utter concentration. The cloud is every bit as thick around us.

"We will get you off the medicine." Shake. "But you have to act like you know nothing. When the doctor comes into your room, pretend you are sleeping." This time he shakes her so violently, I think her head might snap off.

I take a step forward. Enough is enough.

He holds up his hand to stop me, then slowly lets go of her arms.

She stands on her own without even swaying.

"Do you understand what you have to do?" Link asks her.

She nods.

"Tess, you can go." He points in the direction of the tugging without breaking eye contact with my grandmother.

I walk toward the doorway, until the tugging is a knock-down-drag-out sensation that is impossible to resist. Taking a deep breath, I close my eyes and step through. When I come out on the other side, I'm standing in the same white room Luka and I broke into months ago. My grandmother sleeps on the bed, constrained by thick leather straps. I spot two needles sitting on the tray beside her IV. One is labeled AM, the other PM. These must be the drugs the nurse injects into her IV to keep her sedated.

Okay Tess, you can do this.

I think about my mother and my father and Pete. I think about how terribly I miss them. I picture seeing them again. Running to them in the light of day and falling into one giant family hug. I imagine the feel of my mother's happy tears wetting my hair and my father's strong arms wrapping us all up tight. Emotion swells so strongly that I can barely breathe and just when I think I can contain it no longer, I pick up the syringes. I squirt the liquid medicine into the sink and fill the syringes with saline fluid, which they'll unknowingly put in her IV tomorrow. I set the needles exactly in the place they were before, then find the doorway back into the dream world.

In and out in under two minutes.

Link and my grandmother are where I left them. He tells her the plan once more, promises we will return soon, then takes my hand and together, we focus on the little we know about Clive DeVant from his file. Age forty-six. Divorced with two sons and no visitation rights. Kicked out of the marines when his OCD and delusions reached their peak. Admitted into Shady Wood a couple years ago.

There's a shift in the air. Another dropping sensation.

I open my eyes in what appears to be the same white cloud, only my grandmother is no longer there. Instead, a middle-aged man with a square face and hair cut to army-regulation stands at attention in front of us as though he's been waiting for this very moment for the past two years. While I'm shocked, Link doesn't miss a beat. He takes the man's shoulders and does the same thing to him that he did to my grandmother. Clive doesn't object. In fact, he focuses on Link in a way I've never seen anybody focus before—like a soldier trained for combat, one who has prepared his entire life for this very moment.

This time, when I step through the doorway, I'm not alone.

Someone is standing guard.

My sudden presence has that someone looking up with eyes that are completely white. No irises. No pupils. The demon comes at me, but I am well trained. I am stronger. I block his attack and kick him so hard in the chest, he flies through the wall. Positive he will be back any second, I make quick work of emptying the syringes. I fill them with saline and jump back through the doorway.

As soon as I'm through, Link waits for my nod and we both startle awake.

I blink up at my ceiling. We did it. Our next rescue mission is under way.

CHAPTER THIRTY-ONE
AN IMPOSSIBLE REQUEST

If I thought hopping to Shady Wood to awaken my grandmother and Clive DeVant was frightening, it's nothing compared to what I'm walking to the cafeteria to do now. It's Sunday, which means the cereal bins are available from six in the morning until ten. Cap, I know, will show up closer to six. Now that Link and I successfully started the mission, it's time to bite the bullet and fill him in on our plans. The sooner, the better.

My heart thuds heavily inside my chest. He's going to be fuming-hot mad, maybe so much so that he will kick me and Link out of the hub. And if I'm kicked out, Luka will feel compelled to come with me, and then what? In my fervor to rescue my grandmother, I didn't fully think through the repercussions. I was exactly what Cap accused me of—impulsive. I didn't think ahead to this moment, right here.

When I step inside the cafeteria, there is only one person sitting at a table. Sure enough, it's the man in a wheelchair, the material of his shirt so threadbare I can see the outline of every muscle and saggy spot of his back. I look down at my own pair of jeans, which have holes in both knees. We could all use some new clothes. A mug near Cap's left hand breathes steam into the air and an old newspaper, courtesy of Dr. Carlyle, lays open in front of him. It's outdated, but Cap reads it anyway. I suppose he figures week-old news is better than no news.

I take a few steps closer and clear my throat.

"You're up early," he says, not even turning around.

"Yeah." My voice comes out shaky, the same way it sounded whenever my family moved and teachers asked me to stand at the front of the class to introduce myself. I try to inject some confidence into my posture as I close the rest of the distance between us and take the seat across from him.

Cap studies me while tapping a slow, steady rhythm against the tabletop with the tip of his pointer finger. My heart beats triple-time for each one of his finger-taps. "Are you going to tell me what you and Link have been up to?"

"How do you know we've—?"

"Been up to something?" He raises his eyebrows. "Tess, I'm the captain of this ship. I make it a point to know when members of my crew are up to something."

I wring my hands in my lap and look at the door, as if Link might step through and offer some help. But it's a foolish hope. Link will not be in here until nine forty-five. Fifteen minutes to grab a bowl of cereal before Non shuts the bins. "I was hoping the three of us could meet in the conference room later. Link and I have some information to share."

Cap takes a sip of coffee, peering at me over the mug's rim. "Don't you think Luka ought to be part of that meeting?"

"I'm not sure we need to burden him with this yet." And burdened he will be, against his will. A compulsion of his spirit, one he can't control. Like hunger or thirst. Only his is a consuming need to ensure my safety.

"He's your Keeper. I think that warrants his involvement, especially when it's in regards to something of this magnitude."

"Magnitude?"

"Awakening a mental patient who is part of The Gifting."

Warmth drains from my face. Cap isn't a dream-hopper. There's no way he could know, unless ... Did he somehow overhear my conversation with Link early yesterday morning when I snuck into his room? Of all those gadgets, it would be easy to hide a bugging device in one of them. "How did you know?"

"I didn't."

I press my lips together, annoyed with myself for falling for the same trick Cap played before. On me and Luka, when we tried hiding from him the fact that Luka was my Keeper. I can't believe I fell for it again. Why, if he strongly suspected what we were up to, did he let us go through with it? I wait for his wrath to descend. I wait for him to grab me by the scruff of my neck and wheel me to Gabe, who will then kick me out.

He takes another drink of his coffee. I find his calm demeanor more unnerving than his outrage. "Luka deserves to know," he finally says. "Ten o'clock. Make sure he's there."

I scoot my chair away from the table and turn toward the exit. As much as I don't want to, I need to find Luka. After everything I've already done, I'm not about to disobey another one of Cap's orders.

The already-small conference room feels even smaller with so many of us stuffed inside. Cap invited Sticks and Non, who wear matching looks of intrigue. Luka sits to my right, looking green in the face. It's the same way I found him earlier, when I told him about the meeting. It's as though he's battling a strong bout of wooziness. Link sits to my right, half-awake. I had to drag him out of bed to make it to this meeting on time and if the yawn splitting his face has anything to say, it's that he's not going to be much help. Besides, all eyes are on me. I'm the one who called for the meeting.

I take a deep breath and dive in. "Last night, Link and I visited two patients at the Shady Wood Mental Rehabilitation Facility in Oregon."

Luka's chair scrapes against the floor. "That's impossible."

I hadn't planned on looking at him. In fact, the less I look at him, the easier it will be to plow through all I have to say. But his words are so strange they grab a hold of me. The pallor of his skin. The tremble in his hands. His refusal to eat breakfast earlier. Suddenly, his flu-like symptoms make sense. He tried to keep me from dreaming last night. It's why it took me so long to find Link. He tried to keep me from dreaming even though I strictly forbade him from ever doing it again. I can't believe him.

"Apparently, it wasn't impossible. We visited Elaine Eckhart, who is a Fighter. And Clive DeVant, a Cloak." I glance at Cap, who wears that same calm expression from before. I keep waiting for an explosion of anger, more harsh words about my insubordination. But it doesn't come. I guess technically, I didn't disobey orders. We just didn't ask for permission. "Link awakened them both."

Sticks' eyes go buggy.

One corner of Non's mouth pulls up a little.

And the muscle in Luka's jaw tick, tick, ticks into the silence.

"You should have seen it," Link says. "Tess was in and out in under two minutes. Got them both off their medication like it was nothing but gravy."

Cap's nostrils flare.

Here it comes.

"You mean to tell me that you tampered with the physical *without* your Keeper?"

I lift my chin, feeling justified. If Luka was trying to keep me from dreaming last night, then it's obvious he never would have gone along with the plan. Never.

"Do you have any idea how dangerous that is?" Cap growls.

"She wasn't in any danger," Link assures. "I'm telling you, Cap, she's unstoppable."

"No, she's not!" Luka smacks the table with his hands, then stands so abruptly that his chair topples backward. "She is *not* unstoppable."

"Luka," Cap says.

"You know it and I know it, Cap. But this guy here." Luka jabs an accusing finger toward Link. "He doesn't know it. Because he's never been in danger before."

Link's expression clouds over.

"He's just a Linker. He's not a Fighter. He has no idea what he's talking about!"

Luka's outburst sets a tremble in my hands. I sit on them to hide the shaking. "We need to continue this rescue mission right away." I might as well come out with all of it, now that so much is already out in the open. "The other night, Link and I ran into the man from my mother's bedroom. He must have followed me through the doorway. Link and I saw him outside the Dragon Den."

Cap's lips pull into a thin, straight line.

"With Anna's cloak flickering in and out the way it is, it's only a matter of time before he finds us."

"Isn't Shady Wood located in Oregon?" Sticks asks. "Even if we can break them out, where will they go when they escape?"

"I have a friend named Leela. She helped Luka and me when we needed to get out of Thornsdale. I can visit her tonight. I think she would help again."

The air inside the small room crackles with tension, most of which radiates from Luka, who has yet to right his fallen chair and sit back down. It stirs up a desperation that will not remain inside. "Cap, you said it yourself. I've been given an extraordinary gift. Only I can decide how I will use it. Well, I've decided. *This* is how I'm going to use it—to awaken and free as many people as I can. I started this, and I will finish it. But I'd really like to have you on my side when I do."

Everyone turns to look at the man in charge.

I wait with bated breath. His answer determines the fate of this mission. If he's on board, then everyone else will be too. But if he's not ...

"Cap." Luka squishes the name between his teeth. "You know how dangerous this is."

He looks at Luka.

He looks at me. "You've decided?"

"Yes."

"Okay, then. I'm in."

Luka kicks over an empty chair, then stalks out of the room and slams the door behind him. It rattles the walls. It rattles my soul.

I have the courage to battle white-eyed demons, to break my grandmother out of the highest security asylum in the country. Yet when it comes to finding Luka after his display of outrage, I'm paralyzed with fear.

The only way I know how to fight it? Convert my fear to

anger. Anger at this ever-widening chasm between the two of us. Anger that he continues to treat me like a helpless child. Anger that out of everyone here, his support matters the most, yet he refuses to give it. Anger that he tried stopping me from dreaming last night. I gather it into a hot, dense ball and fling open his bedroom door without knocking.

He sits up in bed, his hair sticking straight up, as though he's pushed his hands through it a few too many times.

"I have the chance to get my grandmother out of Shady Wood. You of all people should know how important that is." He saw the atrocity of that place right alongside me. The images have to be just as seared into his memory as they are into mine. "I can't let her stay there. Not when I have a way to get her out." We have a plan, and if he would have stuck around instead of storming off, he could have heard it with his own ears.

Luka works that same muscle in his jaw. It pulses like an angry heartbeat.

"Please, I need you to believe that I can do this."

"Just because you can jump to California does not mean you can do this."

"What was all that crap about believing in me, then? About seeing my strength? You said it with your mouth, but you don't act like it. Sometimes it's like you *want* me to fail."

Luka shakes his head.

"You tried to stop me from dreaming last night."

"To protect you."

I run my fingers back through my hair and laugh—a fed-up, slightly hysterical sound. "You didn't see Link last night. He knows what he's doing. And he believes that we can do this." If only Luka could believe the same.

"Link doesn't know what it's like to be in danger. Link can't see the things I see."

"Nobody does, Luka. Because you won't tell anyone."

"You want me to tell you what I see?"

"Yes!"

He stands from the bed. "Fine. Every night in my dreams, you're killed. Is that what you want to hear? You die, and I can't save you. You're leading a freaking army, Tess. *An army*. And every time you die. Over and over and over again, you die. If that's what you want to know, then okay, there it is. That's what I get to live every night when I close my eyes. So excuse me if I don't have the same confidence as your friend, Link."

"Luka … they're just dreams."

"You and I both know they're never *just* dreams."

I hold out my hands and shrug, at a complete loss, because where does this leave us? "What do you want me to do?"

"I want you to stop being reckless. I want you to think before you jump into things. And I want you to stop leaving me out of your plans."

"I leave you out of them because you won't let me do what I need to do." Last night was proof. Claire's words come—*little Tess's babysitter*. And my anger swells. "If I could figure out a way to release you, don't you think I would? But I don't know how, and I can't wait in the shadows of safety while people die all for the sake of making your burden easier to bear."

"What are you talking about?"

"This overwhelming obsession you have with my safety. I know you didn't ask for it, but I didn't ask to be a powerful Fighter, either." Looks like we were both given burdens we're not too thrilled to carry.

"You think that's what this is about—*your safety?*"

"Isn't it obvious?"

Luka takes a step toward me, his eyes narrowing. "If this was only about your safety, then why would I kiss you?"

"I don't know. You were confused. You were relieved." And it's been a long time. "You heard what Non said in class. The relationship between Keepers and their *anima* has nothing to do with romantic feelings."

"Last I checked, Non's not a Keeper." He takes another step closer.

"Claire said you felt like my babysitter."

"Claire doesn't know anything." He takes one final step, closing any smidgen of distance between us. "If you want to know what it's like being your Keeper, you should ask your Keeper."

But I can't. He's standing so close I can barely think.

Luka tucks a strand of hair behind my ear.

My heart takes off. *Beat, beat, beat*—faster than the wings of a hummingbird.

"It's like fire and oxygen." He traces my jaw with the pad of his thumb. "I touch you and everything ignites. You walk into the room and every single one of my senses comes to life." He takes my wrist and places my hand against his chest. His muscles are hard and warm beneath my palm. "You push me away, and it's torture. You hurt, and I'm in agony. You smile, and it's like I've won the world. Don't even get me started on your laugh."

I can't breathe. My lungs have officially stopped working.

"*Anima*, Tess. *Breath of life.*" Luka curls his fingers around the back of my neck. "It's not your safety I care about. It's your being." He crushes me against him, his lips melding with mine, and I think my hummingbird of a heart might lift me off the ground altogether. His free hand moves to my back, where he grabs a fistful of my shirt. He smells like wintergreen and he tastes like butterscotch. His grip is firm and his lips? An impossible combination of hard and soft. By the time he's through, my entire body hums. The world spins. And tears sting my eyes. Because his words? That kiss? They are too good. Impossibly, euphorically good.

Luka cups the sides of my face with his hands, presses his forehead against mine. "Please Tess, I'm begging you. Don't do this."

And just like that, I come crashing down to earth. "You're asking the impossible."

"No, I'm not."

I take his hands from my face and hold them together in front of my heart. "You're my Keeper. Nothing will happen to me."

"Gabe was powerful."

"So?"

"So, he lost his sister anyway. And now he can hardly bear to live."

"You're just going to have to trust that what happened to her won't happen to me. I *have* to do this."

He pulls away. Shakes his head. He looks two seconds away from spitting at the floor. "Then you're going to have to do it without me. I cannot watch you march to your death."

CHAPTER THIRTY-TWO

UNDERWAY

L eela sits on top of her comforter—one leg tucked beneath her, the other bent in front of her—painting her toenails with a bottle of bubblegum pink OPI nail polish, but the strangest thing happens. As soon as she brings the brush to her nail, the color comes out black. Muttering under her breath, she twists on the cap, gives it a nice shake, and tries again. More black.

"That's weird."

Leela looks up at the sound of my voice, her face brightening. She clambers off the bed and hugs me. "You're here! I can't believe you're here! Did you see this nail polish? It must be a defective bottle."

"Or you could be dreaming."

She squints at her toe.

"Think about it, Leela. How else could I be here? I haven't been in Thornsdale since you picked me and Luka up from that motel. We're on the run, remember?"

She rubs her fingers over the spot on her arm I pinched the first time I visited her dream, when she thought she was at a football game with my brother.

"How's my family?"

Leela scuffs her toes against the floor. They smear the carpet with streaks of black.

It was hard enough to ask the question in the first place—

I'm so afraid to hear the answer—but now that it's out, I'm not letting it pass by without a response. "Leela, I have to know."

"They aren't doing well."

Emotion knots inside my throat.

"Your dad was moved to the California State Penitentiary."

"*What?*"

"The judge refused to release him while he awaits trial."

Every last drop of warmth drains from my face. "How can they do that? It was just a break-in. He didn't murder anyone." He didn't even commit the crime. And now he's in a state penitentiary? My *dad?*

"I'm so sorry, Tess."

"What about my mom and Pete?"

"All I know is that they put your house up for sale. Pete hasn't been at school much."

I sink onto the edge of Leela's bed.

"Luka's parents moved, too. It finally came out on the local news a couple weeks ago—that Luka aided and abetted in your escape, that he used to be a patient at the Edward Brooks Facility."

I shake my head. It doesn't make sense. Why wait so long to out Luka? The only logical explanation I can think of is that they always knew of his role in my escape and were attempting to lure him back to Thornsdale with a false sense of safety, and when it became obvious that wasn't working, they switched tactics. Or maybe his father simply ran out of influence.

"As soon as it all came to light, Luka's parents packed up and moved away. Nobody knows where." Leela eases down beside me. "Are you really in Detroit? Is it as dangerous as everyone says it is?"

Looking back, I never should have told Leela where we

were headed. We're lucky that didn't come back to bite us. "I can't say."

"Are you and Luka still together?"

I nod, trying to push the news of my father aside. I can't think about that right now. If I do, I'll start coming unstitched, and now is not the time. So I shove it inside a box in my brain marked *later* and focus my attention on Leela. "I came tonight because we need your help."

She crosses her legs and grabs onto her shins.

I absolutely hate dragging her into this more than I already have, but she's our only viable option. The police are no doubt still trailing my mom and Pete. There's no way they could get within a hundred mile radius of Shady Wood. "What I'm about to ask you to do is really dangerous, and I want you to know straight off the top that you can say no. You really can, Leela. If you have any misgivings at all, there won't be any hard feelings. I promise."

"You sure are making a hard sell."

I smile sheepishly. Maybe Luka's concerns got to me more than I thought.

"I don't care if it's dangerous, Tess. What's happening right now to you and your family? It's not right. I want to help in any way that I can."

This should come as a huge sigh of relief, because Leela is in and she is a huge piece to our rescue mission puzzle, but all her willingness does is exacerbate the pit in my stomach. Luka doesn't want to watch me march to my death. Am I asking Leela to march to hers? "It involves Shady Wood."

"The place your dad's been accused of breaking into?"

"The one and only."

"Okay."

"We're going to break out two patients who are there, but shouldn't be there." I'm not actually sure any of the patients should be there, but since we have to start somewhere, my grandma and Clive will be that starting point.

"Who is *we*—you and Luka?"

"And some others. I can't go into the details of how it's going to work, I just need you to trust me that we can get them as far as outside the gate. What we can't do is drive them away, which is where you would come in."

"When?"

"Tomorrow night." It's incredibly fast notice, I know this. But Cap agreed that now that we've started, the quicker we can finish, the better. Two nights of no medicine for my grandma and Clive should be plenty. Any more would arouse suspicion, any less and they'd still be too groggy. "Do you think you can get there?"

Leela nods.

I give her the address. She picks up a pink gel pen to write it down, but I remind her that this is a dream. If she doesn't remember when she wakes up, she'll have to Google it. "You'll need to arrive by midnight."

"Where am I taking them?"

"The closest Greyhound station. There will be two tickets waiting for them." Thanks to Link's hacking abilities, all they will need to do is step up to the automated ticket booth, punch in a code, and their tickets will spit right into their hands. "If they aren't outside the gates by one, then leave. We failed. I'll find you as soon as I can to explain what happened."

"Got it."

"Tomorrow morning, a man named Dr. Carlyle is going to call you. He's going to ask if you remember what you're supposed to do. He knows the plan, so if any of these details are vague, you can ask him."

She nods again. "Dr. Carlyle. I won't forget."

"Leela?"

"Yeah?"

"Thank you."

She gives me her thousand-watt smile and wraps me in a hug once more. "I miss you," she whispers.

I squeeze her back, because I miss her too. More than she could possibly know. And then I close my eyes and I think about Link. When I open them again, I'm no longer being hugged by Leela inside her bedroom. I'm standing in front of Link in an understated dream space, at least for him. Probably because he had to use all his mental energy on linking Cap and Sticks, who are already here. When I admitted to Cap that someone from the other side was standing guard inside Clive's room and that I had to fight him off before switching out his medication for IV fluid, he was adamant about him and Sticks coming tonight, as well as a Guardian, in case there are more this time. I didn't argue.

"Is she in?" Link asks.

"She's in."

"All right then, on to phase two." He grabs my hand, since there's not much of anything for me to anchor myself to but him.

I close my eyes. The room shifts, widens. And just like that, there's Non.

"I thought you were getting Luka," Cap says.

"He didn't want to come." Even as I say it, I know he didn't mean it. I know he regrets the words he spoke in anger. He's not more than a blink away, a breath. As though he's willing me to find him. But he made his wishes clear. And besides, we have a Guardian. Seeing as Link and I did this on our own the night before, and we're just popping over for a very quick medicinal switch, I think we are more than covered.

Cap grumbles something that I ignore. I can't think about his disapproval right now, or Luka's absence. Right now, the only person I need to think about is my grandmother. The five of us join hands. I'm not linking my grandmother's dream to Link's, I'm actually hopping to her dream and taking these guys with me. It's not something I've tried before with this many people. Gripping Link's hand so tightly he grimaces, I close my eyes and think.

The world drops.

And we're there. Standing in a very light fog, nothing at all like the night before. What's even better? My grandmother's waiting for us with a world of hope in her eyes. "You came back," she says.

"We promised we would."

She looks from me to the four standing behind me. "You brought friends."

"They want to help, too."

"Do you think the doctors or nurses suspect anything?" Link asks.

"I don't think so," she says.

I let out a sigh of relief, then tune into the tugging behind my belly. I take a step toward the doorway, but Cap grabs my arm. "Sticks and I will pass through. Link will take Non. I'll change out the medicine. You will stay here. As long as you maintain our link, we'll be able to come back through just fine."

"Why can't I go?"

"Because if there was someone standing guard in Clive's room last night, there are bound to be more waiting on the other side right now, and Luka is right. You have a giant target on your back. You are being hunted, Tess. It's best if we don't make you easy to find."

Something in me cries foul. I started this; I should finish it. And besides, I'm supposed to be the strongest Fighter. Why would I stay back here while Cap and Sticks and Non and Link put their lives in danger? "I want to go."

"It's not a request. You're staying here." Cap lets go of my arm. "Your presence isn't necessary."

"But—"

"I've let a lot slide. Please do not test my patience right now."

The two of us have a brief face-off in the middle of my grandmother's dream—his silver-eyed stare meeting my navy-blue one, and as much as I don't want to, I stand down. Cap is the alpha here. Although I may be more powerful in theory, he's calling the shots. He's been calling the shots for a long time now. It's best if I learn to respect that.

I watch as Cap, Sticks, Link, and Non stop in front of the invisible doorway. Link takes Non's hand and the four of them step through. There's an odd sort of tugging sensation, as if my link with them is trying to pull itself away. I grab hold of it with my mind and begin counting the way I was taught to count seconds in kindergarten, when we lived in Missouri, right along the Mississippi River. One-Mississippi, two-Mississippi, three-Mississippi. I get all the way to seventy-eight Mississippi's before the four of them return.

"Did you run into any problems?"

"None," Cap says. "It was a little suspicious if you ask me."

"You think the other side should have been there?"

"Yes."

Well, best not to dwell on it right now. We have to get to Clive. Link explains the full plan to my grandmother, then the five of us grab hands and I envision the man with the army haircut, standing at attention like a bona fide soldier. My stomach drops. There's a bit of a swish. And he's there, waiting for us just like he was before. He doesn't even ask about the extra people.

Cap, Sticks, Link, and Non pass through again and I wait, counting Mississippi's while Clive watches me. When I reach eighty-Mississippi, I start to get nervous. I find my feet creeping closer and closer to the doorway, until I'm so close that the tugging is officially a yank. It would be so easy to step through and make sure everything is okay.

Ninety-five Mississippi, Ninety-six Mississippi …

Seriously, why is this taking so much longer?

I'm just about to step through at one-hundred-eleven Mississippi when Non comes crashing through and tumbles right into me, followed close behind by the others. I scramble up off the ground. "What happened?"

"There were three waiting for us," Sticks says.

Cap rubs his hand along his piqued brow. He looks nearly as gray as Fray. "I think the distance is getting to me. It doesn't normally take me that long."

"Are you going to be okay?" I ask.

He bats away my concern then says the magic word— *startle.*

I wake up in bed, a whole host of emotions tumbling about like clothes in a drier. Luka will be happy to know that I'm back, safe and sound. I was never in any danger at all.

CHAPTER THIRTY-THREE

THE BEST LAID PLANS

The next day, Cap gathers everyone into Non's classroom after breakfast—even Anna and Gabe. The only person missing is Fray. Judging by the silent stream of tears sliding down Anna's cheeks, he's doing even worse.

Up until this point, the plan had been on a need-to-know basis. The only people who knew were those in the conference room yesterday. Today, Cap lays out the plan in a room that's as silent as a morgue, but far from dead. Everyone leans forward in their chairs, a mixture of excitement, anticipation, wariness, and fear. I find myself studying Claire the most. She wears Gabe's poker face. For the life of me, I can't figure what she's thinking.

After everyone knows, we begin poring over Shady Wood's layout and fine-tuning our plans. I can link eight of us. All four of the Fighters. Three Guardians—Non, Gabe, and then surprisingly, Ellen, who wouldn't be my first choice, but according to Non, casts one powerful force field. The last member of our ragtag army will be Anna. If there were three enemies waiting in Clive's room last night, there will be even more waiting for us this night. Anna can hide us, which means she needs to rest today. Cap orders her to put down her cloak while Rosie and Bass stand guard for the day outside the warehouse with walkie-talkies to radio us should they catch a glimpse of anyone from the other side. It's a dangerous move, but a tactical one too. Cap is right. If Anna's coming with us tonight, she needs her rest. Her cloak cannot flicker.

Declan will take Gabe's post and stand guard at the door and Link will be at his supercomputer, hacking into Shady Wood's security system to turn off the alarms and feed the security camera feed into his own computer. As soon as he sees Clive and my grandmother at the gate, he will hack into the system and make it open. The only three without specific jobs are Jillian, Ashley, and Danielle—so they do their part by preparing three hearty meals, looking after Fray, offering words of encouragement and interjecting with the occasional suggestion. Jillian's eager cooperation, I expect. Ashley and Danielle's come as a very pleasant surprise.

The only one who remains uninvolved is Luka. He avoids us all, spending the bulk of his time burning off energy in the weight room. Cap isn't happy about Luka's decision, but there's nothing I can do about it. He's made his choice and I'm doing my very best to avoid his brooding, even if he does wear it appealingly. We don't speak at all. We barely even see one another. Until after dinner. He finds me sitting on a couch in the common room, looking over a printed-out map of Shady Wood with Cap.

Luka clears his throat and asks if we can have a word. I'm about to say no, but Cap practically pushes me off my cushion. When we step out into the deserted hallway, he pushes the fingers of his left hand into his hair and balls them into a fist at the crown of his head. "You're really going to do this?"

"You know the answer to that."

"What if I tell you that last night's dreams were the worst they've ever been?" He takes my hand and pulls me close, his eyes so haunted they make my stomach pucker with guilt.

"Please, just listen to me. This isn't going to work. I've had an awful feeling all day and I cannot get rid of it. It keeps getting worse."

"I'm sorry, but I have to do this." Even if I wanted to back out now, which I don't, I've gotten too far. I can't leave my grandmother or Clive or Leela or the rest of our team high and dry, not when the plans are coming together so well. And my dad can't stay in the box marked *later* forever. He's innocent. My grandmother is innocent. I've had enough of innocent people rotting away in captivity.

"I don't want your apology."

"It's all I have to give. I can't give you what you want, Luka. I'm going."

"Then so am I."

"What?" I shake my head. We've already made the plan. Three Guardians will come tonight. Luka won't be one of them. "I promise, it's fine. I'll be fine. I understand why you don't want to be there."

He laughs a laugh devoid of all humor. "Tess, you don't understand anything. If you're going, I'm going. I can't stay behind and let anything happen to you."

"Nothing will."

Luka brings his lips to my forehead, then wraps his arms around me in a cocoon of safety and warmth. It's in this place that I want to close my eyes and exist forever, here in Luka's arms. My entire body aches with the longing.

I love him.

The realization doesn't just sink in, it bursts forth. So powerfully I have to bite my lip to keep the words from pouring out. When he pulls away, his eyes search mine. "Will you do me one favor?"

Yes, a thousand times over. Anything and everything for this man who holds my heart. This man who has given up so much for me.

"Tonight, when you fall asleep?"

"Yeah?"

"Find me first for once." He brushes his lips against mine, then walks toward his room, leaving me breathless in the hallway.

I fall asleep thinking about Luka, bringing to mind the most random of things—the broadness of his palms, the scar on his right elbow. The way he bites his thumbnail when he's deep in thought, the muscle that ticks in his jaw whenever he's angry, the messiness of his hair when he's stressed, and the way his touch makes me tremble. The quiet authority he exudes without even trying—the kind that makes a person feel like things aren't spinning out of control after all. His humble confidence and his fierce protectiveness and his undivided attentiveness—as though whoever is talking deserves to be listened to. The playful way he jokes with Rosie and the friendly way he used to interact with Leela and the heady way he looks at me, like I'm the only girl who exists.

I fall asleep loving Luka Williams a thousand times over, and when I wake up, I find myself on our beach. It's been so long since I've been here that joy bubbles inside my throat and trickles out like laughter. I want to run out into the waves and spread my arms wide beneath the sun and be here, in this place where time stands still and nothing bad happens and it's just me and this boy I love. But I can't. We have an important mission to accomplish and if I let myself stop now, for even a moment, I'm not sure I'll get going again. I walk along the shore as he stands from his spot in the sand.

He smiles a slow, teasing smile—one that has my stomach doing somersaults. "You found me first."

"The only reason I pick you last is because I'm afraid you're going to talk me out of whatever we're about to do."

"Any chance of that happening now?"

I shake my head.

He lets out a long, resigned breath. And then, without warning, he cups his hand around the back of my neck, pulls me in, and covers my lips with his. His fingers reach up into my hair. His other hand creeps up my ribcage, pulling me closer. Until our bodies touch and I'm clutching the fabric of his shirt and we're kissing like we can't get enough of each other. I know I'll never be able to get enough of him. It's a hungry, desperate kiss, one that leaves my lips bruised and my world rocked and my entire being flushed.

Luka runs his thumb along my jaw and kisses the tip of my nose. "All right, then. Let's do this."

It takes a second—or maybe several—to gain my bearings. To remember where we are and what we're doing and why it matters. When coherency returns, I close my eyes and one-by-one, I find the others. First Cap, then Sticks, Jose, and Claire. Anna, whose dreams turn out to be very slippery things. And then Non and Gabe. Ellen will have to be left behind, seeing as Luka has taken her spot. The nine of us stand on the beach, which lost its cozy, intimate feel the second Claire arrived. I wish, more than anything, that we could do this without her, but we need every Fighter we have.

The nine of us form a lazy circle and clasp hands. Once we're all joined, I think about my grandmother and the joy that will come when she's free. I think and I think and I think. But nothing happens. We're still here, on the beach.

I hold tighter to Luka and Cap's hand and try again.

"What's wrong?" Cap finally asks.

"I'm not sure." Is it because I'm trying to bring too many with me? I close my eyes again and try harder, but every time I should jump, nothing at all happens. I'm still here, on this beach, while everyone watches with an equal mix of curiosity and concern. I look at Luka. As my Keeper, he has many powers. Is one of them the ability to stop me from dream-hopping? "Are you doing something?"

Hurt flickers across his face.

I don't mean to sound so accusatory, but he's tried to stop me before. I'm confused. And slightly panicked, because the entirety of our plan depends upon me jumping to my grand-mother's dream with everyone else. If I can't get us there, then we're done before we even got started.

"Why don't you try Clive?" Cap suggests.

I have no idea why Clive would work when I know so little about him, but since I'm currently out of options, I take Cap's advice. My face scrunches with concentration. There's a shift. A drop. And we're there. Clive stands at attention in a dream space with only the barest traces of fog remaining.

I should be happy. Relieved. But my success only increases my sense of panic. I turn to Cap with my heart in my throat. "Why did that work? Why couldn't I get to my grandmother?"

Luka gives my hand a reassuring squeeze. "Can you get to her now, from here?"

I quickly shut my eyes.

Elaine Eckhart. Elaine Eckhart. Come on, Grandma, where are you?

It's no use. I don't even feel like she's close. It's like she's not sleeping. Maybe that's it. Maybe my grandmother is awake. I exhale. Without all the sedatives being pumped into her system, it would make sense. We take a moment to regroup. We had planned on breaking Elaine out first, since nobody from the other side has been in her room. We'd have time to remove her constraints and safely lead her to a supply closet down the hall from Clive's room, where we figured we'd run into the most trouble. Now however, that won't work. It takes some collective brainpower, but once we have the kinks worked out and a new plan in place, Anna casts her cloak and I pull all nine of us through the doorway.

There are five of them tonight. White-eyed men standing equidistant from each other around the periphery of Clive's room like enemy soldiers. Thankfully, they can't see us. They can't even sense us. Anna's cloak makes us completely invisible to them. Too bad that doesn't make their presence any less unnerving. Cap steps to the edge of Clive's bed and shakes him awake. His eyes open and he sits up. The enemy shifts to attention. Thankfully, Clive is not strapped to his bed, so removing his constraints in front of our malevolent audience isn't something we have to worry about.

Sticks and Non move to the door and peek out. The coast must be clear, because they wave Clive ahead. As soon as he stands, one of the white-eyed men steps toward him, but not fast enough. Gabe throws out a shield so strong, it hurls all five against the wall and they crumple to the floor, unconscious. We hurry out into the hallway. I keep my eyes trained straight in front of me. I don't look left, and I don't look right. This is the third floor. I've been in some of these rooms before. What I saw back then, I don't want to see now. It was disturbing enough the first time.

The lack of doctors and nurses—the utter emptiness of the place sets my heart to racing.

Sometimes, the anticipation of what's to come is almost worse than whatever thing is coming. Like watching a scary movie when you know something is lurking behind a corner, ready to jump out. Once whatever it is has done its jumping, things aren't so scary. I remind myself that it's 12:30 in the morning. Besides the security guards, everybody is sleeping. And thanks to Link and his ability to short-circuit the security cameras, the guards won't see Clive wandering the halls.

We continue toward the stairwell, and as we do, we come across a room with a door that's wide open. I don't mean to look. I really don't. But what's inside, or rather, what's *not* inside, stops me mid-stride. Row upon row of hospital beds. Each one is completely empty. "Where'd they go?"

"Where did who go?" Non asks.

"The patients. When Luka and I came here before, this room was filled with patients in medically induced comas. But now ..." Now they're all gone.

Cap gives me a firm nudge to keep going. Time is of the essence and we aren't here to solve riddles. But now I can't help but look. Into every room's window, I peek. And every room is as empty as the one before it. Cap hurries us along, shuffling us into the stairwell, away from those haunting rooms. We hurry to the fifth floor. Luka is right beside me, radiating so much warmth that the cold impression those vacant hospital beds left behind loses its edge.

He's like my own furnace.

And then the entire stairwell lights up like the sun. An intense blast of heat slams into a dark being one flight above us.

Its body cracks apart, fissuring with light until there's a giant burst—like an exploding star—and the dark thing is no more. It wasn't knocked unconscious. It was completely obliterated.

We all stare, momentarily stunned, at the place that thing once stood.

Cap looks at Luka. "I'm glad you changed your mind about joining us."

By the time we reach the fifth floor landing, I sprint ahead, out from the reach of Anna's cloak. Luka is right beside me, casting a cloak of his own. He's with me as I run and he's with me as I walk inside my grandmother's room.

It's as empty as the rooms two floors below.

"Where is she?" I spin in a circle, as if I somehow missed her the first time. "Why is her room empty?"

Luka takes my hand and pulls me away. "Tess, we have to go."

"No! I can't leave her. We can't leave her." Not again. Not when we're this close. "She's here somewhere. She has to be."

"Get her out of here," Cap says from behind us.

Luka's grip tightens on my elbow. He's dragging me from the room. I'm so confused by all this emptiness, so desperate to figure out a way to find my grandmother, that it takes me half the length of the hall before I feel what has Cap and Luka so on edge. It's as though the entirety of Shady Wood has been plunged into ice. How many from the other side must there be to cause such a dramatic drop in the temperature? And where are they all?

We hurry down the stairs, the coldness growing colder with each flight we descend. Instead of going all the way to the first floor, we step onto the second and run down the hall, toward a back stairwell that leads directly to an exit. As we round a corner, we come face to face with an entire white-eyed army. I've never seen so many of them in my life. They hold out their arms while wisps of black seep from their fingertips. It stretches and curls and creeps closer—a sinister spider web that slinks straight through Anna's cloak and wraps around her wrist.

She shrieks. Her cloak disappears.

And the second floor of Shady Wood breaks into pandemonium.

"Get to the exit!" Cap shouts.

Clive doesn't hesitate. He doesn't question Cap's orders. Like a good soldier, he obeys and runs straight into the heart of danger. Cap, Sticks, Claire, Jose, and I run ahead of him—trying to clear a path by fighting as many as we can, sometimes three at a time, while Non and Gabe and Luka throw out shield after shield. But we are terribly outnumbered and more and more keep arriving, as though stepping through doorways of their own. Two take out Non until she's crumpled on the floor. One jumps on Jose's back, but I spin around with a roundhouse kick that knocks him free. Luka lets fly another intense blast of heat and somewhere in the midst of all the commotion, Clive pushes through the exit door and Cap yells for all of us to startle.

"No!" I shout.

Anna disappears.

Jose disappears.

Sticks grabs his crumpled wife on the floor and they disappear, too.

"No!" I shout again. We can't leave without finding her. We can't leave my grandmother here alone. I've done it once before. I won't do it again. I begin flinging the doors open. Room after room, all unlocked. All empty. "Elaine!"

Gabe throws a shield in front of Cap, who yells again for the rest of us to startle.

I throw another kick and run ahead, for the first time in my life thankful for Claire. Thankful that she's not obeying Cap's orders, but inching closer to me, her face screwed up in concentration as she grabs one of the demons by the wrist, twirls around, and slams it to the ground. I run for another door as Luka blasts five of them back at once, but there are three more at my heel. And just as I'm about to run past Claire, into the final room, she reaches out her foot and trips me.

I sprawl to the ground with a loud *oomph* and in the split second before she disappears, our eyes connect. There's a look of pure vindictiveness in hers. I spin onto my back, but I'm too late. Three of the white-eyed soldiers lunge at me. Luka dives between us, throwing out a shield to protect me.

But they swarm upon him like flies. An entire army of them. Black mist wraps around his hands, binding them together.

"No!" I run to free him, to fight for him, but Gabe grabs one of my arms and Cap grabs the other as I watch Luka being dragged further and further away. I fight against their hold. "Startle, Luka!" I scream. "Startle!"

Only he can't seem to. It's as if the black mist wrapping around his body prevents him from doing anything. My captors, however, do exactly what I'm screaming for Luka to do. They startle. And they take me with them.

Chapter Thirty-Four

Gone

*N*o! No, no, no, no! Please, no! Panic surges through every inch of my body. It crawls across my skin. I kick off the covers with flailing legs and sprint across my room. Tears blind my eyes as I hurl open the door. Lights come on in the hallway. Jillian and Rosie and Ellen all stare out from their rooms—pale and wide-eyed. I sprint through the antechamber, toward Luka's room. I fling open his door at the very end, crashing inside his room.

Please, please, please, no!

He's lying in bed. I see his form through the darkness. But he's not moving. I grab onto his shoulders and shake him. I shake him harder than Link ever shook my grandmother. "Wake up! Wake up, wake up, wake up!" I scream the words over and over and over again, beating his chest with my fists.

Luka does not wake up.

His eyes remain closed.

"No, no, no, no!" I grab him into a hug, unable to comprehend what's happening. Unable to process the fact that he's warm in my arms, yet he's not really there.

Strong hands grab hold of my elbows and pry me away. I can't see who it is, not through my tears. I fight against whoever it is with everything in me. I cling to Luka like he is the last life vest in a tsunami. But this is the physical realm, where I am not strong. Where I am easily dragged away. "We can't leave him! He needs to wake up. Please! I have to go back to sleep! I have to go find him! Please!"

"There's no finding him, Tess. He's gone." The voice belongs to Gabe. He's the one who has a hold of me. He's the one who is dragging me away from Luka's room. It's his flesh my nails are digging into. His legs I am kicking. His arms that are wrapping me into a bear hug.

He forces me out into the bright hallway, where a crowd has gathered. It's the middle of the night, but the hub is wide awake. All but one.

Claire stands among them. I saw it with my own eyes—her foot snaking out to trip me, her vindictive look when I fell. The white-eyed soldiers pouncing and Luka jumping in to save me. Whatever reason I still possess snaps in half. I twist from Gabe's grip and I attack her. I hit and I kick and I claw and I scrape and I scream. "You did this! This is your fault!"

Gabe pries me off Claire, who glares at me from the floor with a bloody lip and a gouge in her neck and a chest that heaves. I kick the air. And I scream bloody murder. But Gabe drags me away, down the hallway. Away from Claire. Away from the watching crowd. Away from Luka, asleep in his bed.

They think I'm asleep. They think I can't hear them murmuring through the walls. But sleep is impossible to find. I am wide awake, scratching the inside of my wrist raw. And I can hear everything.

"Are you sure he's gone?" Link asks.

"Yes."

"But he's still—"

"Breathing?"

There is no reply.

"Give it a few days." Gabe's voice is cold and detached. "The other side will have destroyed his soul by now. It's only a matter of time before his body follows."

Footsteps recede down the hall.

My sanity follows.

I sit in the back corner of my room, knees drawn up to my chest, arms wrapped around my shins, rocking back and forth like the crazy people in Shady Wood. I'm supposed to be numb. This is what shock is supposed to do. This is what I crave. Instead, I am wild. Anguish is the flame and every single cell in my body burns with it. I have to remind myself to breathe.

He's gone.

Gabe's words have opened a fault in my chest. An eruption of emotional lava spews forth, scorching and scarring and burning and melting everything in its path. It can't be true. Luka can't be gone. Not like this. Not ever.

I scratch my wrist, hating the sting, then press my forehead between my knee caps and rock faster. *I* was supposed to be the one in danger. If anyone was going to be taken, it was supposed to be me. That, I was okay with. That, I could handle. But this? Never once, in the midst of all Luka's concerns, in the midst of all his pleas for me not to go, did I consider that I might lose him. Never once did I picture what might happen if I was the one left behind to pick up the pieces.

The lava burns hotter.

He's over there. Across the antechamber and down the hall. His heart is beating. His skin is warm. But Gabe says he's gone.

Gabe says there's no getting to him.

My thoughts race, chasing each other in disjointed circles. I can't pin a single one of them down. The empty rooms in Shady Wood. My missing grandmother. Claire reaching out her foot to trip me. Luka diving in to save me. White-eyed evil binding him up in a black web and dragging him away. Cap and Gabe grabbing my arms and startling me awake when all I wanted was to go with him. To die with him.

I want to blame Claire. I want to blame them. I want to lash out and blame someone. But I keep landing back on myself. Luka didn't want to go. Luka had a bad feeling. He begged me to reconsider. But I insisted on going anyway. I was stubborn. I was unreasonable. And because I went, he had no choice. I shake my head as tears leak onto my kneecaps and spill down my leg. If not for me, Luka never would have been there.

The next morning, I hear them talking through my walls. They murmur in dulcet tones, but I hear them all the same. They don't know what to do about me. They don't know what to do with Luka. They speak of him in the past tense. I plug my ears and resume my rocking.

At some point, Jillian comes into my room. She brings me a tray of food and a glass of water. She tries to get me to eat, to drink. She might as well be asking me to swallow the sun. She sits beside me in bed and tells me things I no longer care about—Dr. Carlyle called. Leela got Clive safely to the Greyhound bus station. The hub's newest Cloak is on his way. Tomorrow, Dr. Carlyle is coming to move Fray to a privately-owned hospital in Northern Michigan. Cap interrogated Claire in her bedroom and she's yet to come out. Apparently, I'm not the only one who witnessed what she did.

The tray of food goes untouched.

Another day comes and goes.

The hub falls asleep.

I wander out of my room, because there's no sleep to be had. I go into the bathroom and stare at my reflection in the mirror. The person who stares back is not me. The person in the mirror looks like a strung out druggie, with deep purple bags beneath blood shot eyes and hair that hangs limply around hollowed-out cheekbones.

I roam the halls aimlessly, my arms wrapped around my waist, until I end up in the common room. I expect to find Gabe by the door, but he's not. Instead, the muted television casts bluish light into the dark room as Non sits on one of the couches, staring at CNN on the screen. I shuffle over and sit beside her. I think the numbness is finally starting to take effect.

The news anchor talks about a possible ceasefire between Egypt and Sudan, then moves on to the continuing decline in our nation's crime rate and several key attributing factors. I don't even try to listen. I just gaze at the screen with glossy eyes—impossibly tired but unwilling to close. The second they do, I will relive it all over again. Luka being dragged away.

A few words spoken by the anchor register in my mind. He's talking about a new initiative by President Cormack to make mental rehabilitation centers available to all citizens, even if they do not have health insurance.

I wrap my arms around my shins. "What happened to all those people, Non?"

She blinks at me through the darkness, the light from the

television casting a ghost-like glow on her face. "You saw the rooms."

Yes, I did. They were empty. Every single one. "What does it mean?"

"You already know the answer." I can practically see her shifting into teacher mode. "You studied the journals. You made the connection."

I blink back at her.

"During the Age of Exploration, there was a high population of The Gifting amongst Native Americans. During the time of Nazi Germany, there was a high population of The Gifting amongst Jews. Right now, at this very moment, can you not think of a people group that contains a high population of The Gifting?"

It clicks. This puzzle piece that's been shifting and wiggling about. But it brings no sense of satisfaction. "The mentally ill."

"Curious, isn't it?"

"You think the government is killing off the mentally ill to get rid of The Gifting?"

She taps her nose, but the gesture falls flat. "We are supposed to keep darkness in check. That's why we exist—to keep it under control. Because uncontained darkness ..." Non shakes her head and sinks back against the cushion. "That is a terror too unimaginable for words."

I should care about this awful terror. I should care that Non is tiptoeing around the prophecy—about a time when The Gifting will face extinction and One will arise with the power to save them and restore the balance between light and dark. I should care that Cap thinks I am that One. But I can do none of those things. Not when my heart is cold and dead inside my chest.

"History has a way of repeating itself," Non mumbles.

I stand from the couch and wander some more, until I'm standing at the threshold of Luka's bedroom. Luka's tomb. I'm not supposed to be here, at night. It's against the rules. I step inside anyway and I crawl into his bed. I lay my head on his chest and listen to the steady thrumming of his heartbeat. Tears leak from the corner of my eyes, soaking through his shirt.

Please Luka ... come back. Please don't really be gone.

The sound of screaming awakens me—a blood-curdling scream that splits the air and raises the hairs on my arms. I bolt upright, heart pounding erratically. Where am I, and who is making that sound? It looks like a cold, dark basement. I rub my eyes and the scream comes again. A cry wrought with pain. A cry that belongs to ...

"Luka!"

It's him. He's here. Straight ahead of me, lying on the cold, cement floor, bound by black tentacles of mist, surrounded by skeletal men with unseeing eyes. He arches up, the contortion reminding me of my mother in her bed when she was being tortured. His body flails as if trying to escape. The black mist lacerates his body and he screams again.

He's alive. His soul is not gone.

I run toward him, this time unencumbered by Gabe or Cap. Nothing is stopping me from helping him, from fighting these men. Until Luka's frantic eyes land on mine and his pain morphs into panic. "No." He shakes his head, beads of sweat pouring down his face. "Startle, Tess! Please, startle."

"Yes, by all means, startle." The cold voice echoes off the walls, bringing me to a halt. It's Scarface. He prowls around

Luka like a lion ready to pounce. "Or are you unwilling to leave your friend behind?"

I look between him and Luka, my mind grappling for a solution. A way to get us both out of this. A way to bring his spirit back to his body.

"We've been waiting for you, Little Rabbit. We've been waiting a long, long time." He smiles a hungry smile and takes a few steps toward me.

There's a blast of white, hot light. It slams him against the wall. It was Luka. Even in chains, even while being tortured, he's still protecting me. The man wipes at a trickle of blood that dribbles down the corner of his mouth. I run toward Luka, determined to break him free. Determined to fight every last one of these monsters with my bare hands. Until Luka is back or I am dead.

My body convulses.

It gives a giant, involuntary shudder. My eyes flutter, and then they open. Gabe stands above me with his hand on my shoulder. My clothes are drenched in sweat. My heart punches violently at my chest. I bolt upright in Luka's bed.

I should be struck through with terror. I should be livid that Gabe shook me awake. But all I can feel is a flood of overwhelming relief. Luka isn't gone. He's still alive, held hostage by the other side. "Gabe, he's alive."

"For now." Grim words from a grim face. He misunderstands.

There's commotion out in the hallway.

Lights come on.

Cap shouts something indecipherable.

Gabe looks toward the noise.

"No, I mean he's really, really alive. I saw him! Just now.

295

He's being held prisoner. They're torturing him." I picture the black mist lacerating his skin, leaving behind angry, red welts. How long before he's damaged beyond repair? How long before he really is gone forever?

Cap rolls into Luka's room with Link close behind. "She's gone."

"Who?" Gabe asks.

"Claire. Non fell asleep during guard duty. When she woke up, something felt off. She checked the door and discovered it was unlocked." Cap drags his hand down his whiskered face, looking weary to the bone. "She's not in her room. She's nowhere."

I crawl out of Luka's bed. "What does that mean?"

"It means she's defected."

"Defected?"

"She crossed over to the other side," Link says. For the first time since knowing him, he looks truly disturbed.

"Can The Gifting do that?" I ask.

"The Gifting can do whatever they want," Cap says. "It's the great blessing and the great curse that is our free will."

I shake away the newest development that is the hub's growing problems. I don't care about Claire. In fact, good riddance. The other side can have her. There is one thing, and one thing alone that deserves my attention. One thing, and one thing alone that matters. One thing, and one thing alone that I will fight for until my last dying breath.

I have a Keeper to save.

About the Author

K.E. Ganshert was born and raised in the exciting state of Iowa, where she currently resides with her family. She likes to write things and consume large quantities of coffee and chocolate while she writes all the things. She's won some awards. For the writing, not the consuming. Although the latter would be fun. You can learn more about K.E. Ganshert and these things she writes at her website at www.katieganshert.com. You can also follow her on Twitter, where she goes by @KatieGanshert.

Want to stay up to date on The Gifting series? Visit K.E. Ganshert's website and subscribe to her mailing list. Read on to enjoy a complimentary excerpt of book 3, *The Gathering*.

Excerpt for *The Gathering*

CHAPTER ONE

NOBODY'S LISTENING

I thought I knew what insanity felt like. When I saw things nobody else could see. When my nightmares started unfolding in real life. When a much-too-popular, achingly handsome boy started watching my every move. When I was locked up in a mental hospital against my will and told everything I knew to be true was a figment of my imagination.

I thought I knew.

But all of that was nothing compared to this.

The hub has erupted into pandemonium. All the lights are on, and since windows do not exist down here—deep in the bowels of a ruined warehouse—it might as well be day instead of the dead of night. Everyone is awake and focused on the defector. The one who betrayed me, the one who betrayed him. Everyone is panicked over what this means—Claire out there, knowing all she knows about our location, our names, who we really are.

How could she do it?

That is the question of the hour. But I don't care about her. I don't care about why she defected or the ramifications of her decision. All I care about is him—the boy across the hall, unable to wake up. But very, very much alive.

Despite what Gabe thinks, Luka's soul has not been destroyed.

I saw him. I heard him. He's being held hostage, tortured by the white-eyed men. His screams echo inside my head. They won't stop. Nor will the way he arched up in agony as black webs of mist lacerated his body. Every second that ticks past is one more second closer to losing him forever. And that is something I cannot let happen. Because if Luka dies, then so will everything else.

I scratch the inside of my wrist and begin to rock like the patients in straitjackets at Shady Wood. Link sits beside me on the couch, mindlessly twisting his Rubik's Cube. Nobody will listen—not Gabe, not Cap, not Sticks or Non. They think I'm in shock. They think I'm in denial. They keep talking about Clive DeVant, who's supposed to arrive with Dr. Carlyle in the afternoon, and Fray, who's supposed to leave with Dr. Carlyle to a hospital in Northern Michigan, but if we stick around until tomorrow, we might all end up in jail.

Jail. My father. He's in the California State Penitentiary for a crime he didn't commit. I let the thought float away. I can't deal with that right now.

"What are we going to do?" someone asks.

"What if Claire's already gone to the authorities?"

"She has all of our names. She knows all of our faces."

"Are we safe?"

Something feral claws up my throat. A wild beast of a thing, but before it can escape, Cap raises his hand. It's a simple gesture, and yet, coming from him—our leader—the hub goes quiet.

"I will figure out what to do about Fray and Clive. In the meantime, everybody needs to return to their room and pack a bag."

The wild beast of a thing claws free. "We can't leave!"

"Claire has left us no choice," Cap says.

"We can't leave Luka here." The hot words scald my throat. I come to my feet. "You-you'd be murdering him!"

Everybody stares.

Nothing can be heard but the steady tick-tick of a clock on a far wall of the common room.

"If you are underage," Cap's silver-eyed gaze does not leave mine, "return to your room immediately and wait for my instruction."

Slowly, the room begins to clear. Ellen and Declan obey first. A tearful Rosie, then Bass, Jose, Ashley and Danielle. Jillian lingers, shooting glances my way, before she, too, obeys orders. Link stays.

"It's time to return to your room," Cap says.

"He's alive."

He paws his face, the palm of his hand scratching against the stubble on his cheeks. I can tell he doesn't know what to do with me anymore.

"We can still save him."

"Luka is gone." The lifeless words belong to Gabe.

"Why?" I practically spit the word. "Because you couldn't get your sister back?"

"Tess." Cap says my name like a warning.

But I don't care. I don't care if I hurt Gabe. I don't care that I'm disobeying orders once again. I don't care about anything but the boy down the hall. Luka isn't gone. At least he wasn't an hour ago. I have no idea how much longer my declaration will hold true. And therein lies the crux of my insanity. I'm standing here trying to convince these people that he's alive while every breath I take draws him closer to death.

Link gently takes my arm. "Come on. Let me take you to your room."

I jerk my elbow away. "I'm not leaving him."

Cap pushes out a terse breath. "We have more pressing matters at hand."

"*More pressing matters?* He's being tortured. Right now, at this very moment. And we're standing here letting it happen." What can be more pressing than that? Yet as soon as the question comes, I know Cap's answer. As captain of this ship, he has to make decisions for the collective whole. It's what he's always doing. He has to think strategically, and if that means sacrificing one for the sake of the rest, then that is what he will do. I absolutely hate him for it.

Link pulls me away.

"He's going to die." I try wrenching my arm free, but his grip is surprisingly strong. "Do you hear me? If we don't get to him right now, he will die!"

Link pulls me further away.

"Gabe!" I turn wild eyes on him—my last hope. If anybody knows this kind of agony, Gabe does. "Please. Help me. Luka is alive. I swear to you, he's alive. We can't leave him here!"

Gabe does nothing but look away from my manic pleas.

And Link drags me out of the room. He circles his arm around my waist and pulls me away while I scream and flail, not strong enough to resist, tears running like scalding heat down my face. Rosie stares out from the crack in her bedroom door, her eyes big and wide in her face. Link murmurs words of comfort I do not hear. He holds me until I've stopped thrashing. Until the wild thing has crawled back inside and curled into a whimpering ball.

"Listen."

All I can do is shake my head. I should have listened a long time ago, but not to Link. I should have listened to Luka, who never wanted to go on our mission in the first place. And yet, I insisted. I ignored his reservations. "It's my fault. He's there because of me. He knew something would go wrong. But I wouldn't listen. I went and because I went, he had to go, too. And now he's being tortured." His scream grows so loud and sharp in my mind that I wince. "You have to believe me. Please believe me."

"Xena, look at me." Link takes hold of my face and tips up my chin so that I have no choice. His caramel eyes are steady and familiar. "Listen to me. If Luka is still alive. If the other side is holding him hostage, it's because they want *you*."

"I know that." And I will gladly trade places.

"So you know what that means."

Another hot tear tumbles down my cheek.

Link catches it on the pad of his thumb. "They aren't going to kill him. If they kill him, they loose their leverage."

"I know that, too. But I also know what I saw. If it continues for much longer, he won't be Luka anymore." My chin trembles. "Please, Link. We can't leave him."

Link's steady resolve solidifies. "We won't."

Those two definitive words do more to calm me than anything else he could have said or done.

"I have an idea. Let me run it by Cap."

CHAPTER TWO

MOLTEN LAVA

"Twenty minutes," Cap says.

I slide onto one of the six dental chairs in the training center and fidget with the hemp bracelet around my wrist. It belonged to Luka. He insisted I wear it in case it offered even a hint of protection. "What if she's not sleeping?

"Then we will have no choice but to leave this place and disband." The look Cap gives me is clear. This is as far as he's willing to take this. If Link and I cannot locate Claire, if we cannot find out whether she truly defected or simply left out of shame, then he will have to make decisions I will not like. "Do you understand?"

I swallow and look away, my head incapable of nodding.

If not for Fray's precarious situation, if not for Clive scheduled to arrive tomorrow, I'm positive Cap never would have agreed to Link's plan. Thankfully, Cap doesn't want to leave. Disbanding in the dead of night without a plan in place is not his style.

"Twenty minutes will be enough to learn what we need to learn." Link attaches a prob to my left temple. Usually, he attaches two. One that sends electrodes to the part of my brain that is most active during sleep. Another that brings me to the dojo—a shared dream space Link created for training purposes. But we're not going to the dojo tonight. We're going to find Claire and we can't wait for sleep to take us in our beds. Time is of the essence.

I rest my head against the chair and squeeze my eyes tight, praying with every ounce of faith I have that Claire will be asleep. Finding her now, figuring out what she's up to, is the first step to saving Luka.

"All right, we're both attached." Link has taken the chair next to me. He grabs my ice-cold hand and gives it a confident squeeze. "You can push the button in ten … nine …"

I squeeze my eyes tight and focus on Claire, the betrayer. I imagine her the first time I saw her, when Luka and I first came to the hub. Her white-blond hair loosely braided down her back. Her regal beauty. The way her nose turned up in the air without trying. The shock of discovering her down here, in the hub, after having studied her file for days.

"Six … five …"

The grating way she flirted with Luka. The victorious feeling of taking her down in the dojo. The hateful look in her eyes when Cap announced he would be training me.

"Three … two …"

Her foot reaching out to trip me as we battled inside the walls of Shady Wood. Her look of triumph when I fell.

"One …"

Wind whips at my hair. I'm no longer laying in the training center; I'm standing beside Link outside a familiar home. I've been here before—with Luka—when we were searching for Claire Bedicelle, one of the patient files Dr. Roth left behind.

And there she is, standing on the front stoop of her childhood home, pounding on the door while trees bend beneath the force of the wind. The blood in my veins turns to molten lava. My hands curl into tight fists.

Link sets his hand on my shoulder. "We'll learn more if she

doesn't know you're here."

He's right, of course. As much as I want to shove my fist in her face, now's not the time. I duck behind a row of emaciated bushes and strain to hear above the wind.

"Please Mom! It's me." Claire glances up at the ominous, swirling sky and pounds harder. "Please open up."

"Claire?"

She whirls around, her icy blue eyes wide with panic, her face streaked with tears. "Link?"

"What are you doing?" he asks.

"I-I'm trying to get to my parents, but they won't let me in." She wipes at her cheeks. "How—how did you get here?"

"How do you think?"

The wind loses some of its strength.

Claire looks up at the clouds. They no longer swirl as threateningly as they did seconds ago. She peels a strand of hair from her lips. "This is a dream. You're spying on me."

"I'm not spying. I'm checking." He holds up his hands, as if to show her he means no harm. "You left without telling anybody. We're all worried."

I grit my teeth. Not one part of me is worried about her. She's been bad news from the beginning. I should have realized the danger I was putting Luka in, the danger I was putting everybody in, by going on such a high-stakes mission with Claire on the team.

Her chin trembles. "I never meant for Luka to get hurt."

"But Tess—you wanted *her* to get hurt?" Link's question is gentle. Unaccusatory. Everything opposite from what I feel.

"I just wanted things to go back to the way they were before she came. I-I wasn't thinking. I made a mistake. I shouldn't have done it. All I want is my mom and dad, but I don't think they want to see me."

Liar. Lies. I don't believe a single note of her remorse.

"Have you told anyone about our location?" Link asks.

"No. I would never do that. But I couldn't stay. Nobody wanted me there. Not even you."

Link shifts his weight. His back is to me, so I can't see his face. I have no idea if he's falling for the act or not.

"I would never put you in danger, Link, never. I just want to go home to my parents. That's all I want." She turns around and beats the door with her fists, begging the wood to let her inside.

"She didn't defect." Link peels off his probe and swings his legs around so his feet hit the floor. "She's not going to give our location away. She just wants to get to her parents."

Cap looks from me to Link, waiting for me to verify.

I don't deny it, even if I don't believe a word of Claire's sob story.

Cap rubs his forehead.

A glance at the clock tells me it's four in the morning. Two hours have passed since I saw Luka, bound and tortured. I'm so desperate to get to him, it feels as though a hole is burning a wide path through my heart.

Cap looks at Non and Sticks, who stand inside the small room. "What do you think?"

"It buys us some time," Sticks says. "At least until Clive arrives and Fray is gone."

"And Luka's back," I add.

Nobody listens.

"Non?" Cap asks.

She slides her hands down her head, flattening her bushy hair to the sides of her face. "Gabe's standing guard above ground. If danger arrives, he'll be able to alert us in time to carry out emergency protocol."

Emergency protocol? I don't know about any emergency protocol. We've certainly never practiced an emergency drill during my time at the hub. But of course there would be something in place. Cap would have thought of that.

He rubs his knuckle along his bottom lip, then pushes out a breath. "You two can return to your rooms," he says to me and Link. "We'll stay for now."

Link's plan worked.

Cap doesn't think Claire will betray us.

He believes we're safe.

I don't.

But I'm willing to risk the safety of everyone at the hub if it means getting Luka back.

Don't forget to subscribe to K.E. Ganshert's mailing list to keep up to date on the latest happenings with The Gifting series. Visit her website: www.katieganshert.com

CPSIA information can be obtained at www.ICGtesting.com
Printed in the USA
LVOW11s2141230916

505968LV00002B/31/P